P9-DHI-615

"Alameddine, entrancing and unflinching, is in easy command of his brico-lage narrative, and he leavens its tragedy with wit."

—*New York Times Book Review*

"*The Angel of History* takes place in a single day, but it reads like an epic . . . [his] writing is so beautiful, so exuberant . . . When Alameddine aims for the heart, he doesn't miss, and he hits hard . . . *The Angel of History* isn't just a brilliant novel, it's a heartfelt cry in the dark, a reminder that we can never forget our past, the friends and family we've loved and lost. It's a raw love letter from those who survived a plague to those who didn't." —NPR.org

"A remarkable novel, a commentary of love and death, creativity and spiri-tuality, memory and survival . . . brilliant . . . [it] hits an emotional nerve."

—*Los Angeles Review of Books*

"Excellent, lissome . . . the novel is a work of social and cultural memori-alization . . . *The Angel of History* suggests that to be alienated—from past love and from the past itself—is to open the door to memory and creation."

—*San Francisco Chronicle*

"An elegy for a lost generation of gay men [and] a structurally inventive bildungsroman . . . *The Angel of History* marks the triumph of memory over oblivion." —*Bookforum*

"Alameddine has beguiled us with his insight and compassion. His stories take the reader into the labyrinth that is the mind . . . presenting the exis-tential drama of a single human life." —*Economist*

"A character study of a brilliant but tormented soul." —*Seattle Times*

"A stylish gem constructed of love and loss. All of it forms a glorious excess of life, death, and haunting memory . . . Alameddine [is] a daring and perceptive storyteller." —*Bay Area Reporter*

"Ingenious . . . a richly textured novel that is a remarkable feat of imagi-nation and a cry to remember a condition that not only still affects much of America but continues to overwhelm countries in Africa, Asia and elsewhere." —*Houston Chronicle*

"Profound, brilliant . . . it offers insight into all the horrors and wonders associated with being that most otherworldly of beings: a human." —*Nylon*

"A poignant act of remembering by one AIDS survivor to a new genera-tion . . . a poetic combination of Mapplethorpean imagery and religious symbolism . . . an unforgettable novel." —*PopMatters*

"Intricately woven . . . powerful . . . The language has a visceral edge to it . . . laden with meaning, symbolism and nostalgia . . . *The Angel of His-tory* effectively tackles myriad themes pertinent to the day and age that we live in." —*New York Journal of Books*

"Provocative, profound, and humorous." —*Lambda Literary*

Also by Rabih Alameddine

An Unnecessary Woman
The Hakawati
I, the Divine
The Perv
Koolaids

The Angel of History

A NOVEL

Rabih Alameddine

Grove Press
New York

Published simultaneously in Canada
Printed in the United States of America

First Grove Atlantic hardcover edition: October 2016
First Grove Atlantic paperback edition: October 2017

ISBN 978-0-8021-2719-8
eISBN 978-0-8021-9011-6

Library of Congress Cataloging-in-Publication Data

Names: Alameddine, Rabih, author.
Title: The angel of history / Rabih Alameddine.
Description: First edition. | New York, NY : Atlantic Monthly Press, [2016]
Identifiers: LCCN 2016018029| ISBN 9780802125767 (hardback) | ISBN
9780802190116 (ebook)
Subjects: | BISAC: FICTION / Literary.
Classification: LCC PS3551.L215 A83 2016 | DDC 813/.54—dc23
LC record available at https://lccn.loc.gov/2016018029

Grove Press
an imprint of Grove Atlantic
154 West 14th Street
New York, NY 10011

Distributed by Publishers Group West

groveatlantic.com

17 18 19 20   10 9 8 7 6 5 4 3 2 1

For Randa,
Rania, Raya, and Nicole

We must forget in order to remain present, forget in order not to die, forget in order to remain faithful.

—Marc Augé, *Oblivion*

The struggle of man against power is the struggle of memory against forgetting.

—Milan Kundera, *The Book of Laughter and Forgetting*

Satan's Interviews

Death

There is a dignity in decay, Satan thought, as he regarded the terra-cotta planter basking on the kitchen windowsill. The sage shrublet growing within was silver-green fresh, yet seemed puerile and fatuous, like an ill-mannered child compared with its cracked, aging container. From the living room, Satan could just see the only window in the dim kitchen, a small rectangle above the always dry dish drainer that had not held more than a single plate in months. Jacob ate his lonely dinners standing next to the counter every night of the week, staring at the blank wall like a waiter in an empty restaurant.

"Are we ready?" Satan asked. "Shall we begin the interview?"

He leaned forward a little in his seat, a black olefin armchair that contrasted with his white suit, and reached for the mini digital recorder on the coffee table, a gesture to emphasize his question; he placed his thumb on the red button but hesitated before he pressed, waiting for some sign from Death that they could begin.

"Wait," Death said. "What interview?"

"You can't have forgotten already," Satan said. "You agreed to do this interview. It's why you're here."

"Sorry, I was thinking of something else." All in black, of course, Death shifted in his chair to a more comfortable position. He had an unmistakable whiff of history about him, and of formaldehyde. "I wish it on record," Death said in a slightly amused voice, a glint returning to his eye, "that you wanted me here. Your asking for my help is highly unusual. It makes me feel so—I don't know exactly—needed, maybe even happy. I want to shout from rooftops, from mountain-tops: you like me, you really like me. You want us to work together, Father. I want that in a memo."

"Fine, most fine," Satan said. "Let's tape your gloating for the record, shall we?"

Satan disliked the machine's unobtrusive silence. Long gone were the days of cassette tapes, or better yet, reel-to-reel players whose fluttery noises might have unsettled his interviewee. He had made sure to place himself between Death and the door, anything to discomfit his nemesis. Almighty Death, Lord of the Underworld, Master of Lethe, imperturbable Death, whose pale angular face and blood-less lips rarely exhibited anything but frosty inviolability, whose usual demeanor was imperiously incurious, looked interested, maybe eager.

"Go ahead," Satan said. "The machine is recording. Tell everyone that I asked you here to negotiate."

"Negotiate?" Death said. His black beret drooped rakishly over one ear. "What's to negotiate? You're losing Jacob and you want my help."

Satan rolled his eyes in an exaggerated manner. He allowed himself a long sigh. "On this evening my first interview with Mr. D dealing with Jacob."

"Wait," Death said, fixing his pert green eyes on Satan. "What do you mean 'first'? Will I be required to meet with you again? I agreed to an interview—just one. You said we must help your protégé. Fine. Though why I should help him or you is beyond me. Work with me, you said. We need you, you said. We haven't even started and you want more. What will I get for all my troubles? Tell me."

"You get my company and so much else," Satan said. "You could have rejected my invitation, but you're here. You may not wish to admit it, but you love him as much as any of us. Look, I can't do this project without you. It's our dance, you and I."

Death sat up in his chair, a grimace flickering briefly across his face. "Do you think this is going to work?" he said, contemplating his finely tapered fingernails, recently manicured and polished in glossy blue-black. "You don't know, do you, Father? A shot in the dark is what this is. Tell me you have a plan at least."

"I do have a plan," Satan said, emphasizing his statement with a grin and a simple eyebrow lift. "Let us begin." He spoke into the microphone. "On this evening, this thing of darkness joins me."

"And you're the prince of light," Death said with a sneer.

Satan dismissed the interruption. "We conduct this interview in Jacob's apartment, which we both know intimately. My partner is unshaven, seems harried and duressed, for in his look defiance lurks. He can't seem to remove his tormented gaze from the photos on the fireplace mantel, all the young men he snatched well before their time. This interviewer believes that guilt nibbles at my friend's usually arid heart, that heinous acts and egregious errors have been committed."

"Oh, come, come," Death said. "Why are you lying? Well, that's a silly question." As he lifted his arm to flick a bony finger, his sleeve dropped and revealed an intricate forearm tattoo: the rape of the Sabine women collaged with various other slayings, Daisy Duck hanging from the gallows, Nietzsche roasting on a spit, Peter Pan drawn and quartered. "Did you bring me here to provoke me? I can play that game. But tormented gaze? Me? Please."

Death stared at the pictures, six of them in silver frames with filigreed roses, Jacob's friends looking young and deathless. He saw everything that had been on the mantelpiece before Jacob's roommate began to spend every night with her lover, before the recent rearrangement: two netsuke Buddhas, one lounging and laughing, the other meditating; a black onyx rosary with twenty-two beads plus one; a small, suffering Jesus with his cross on a short pedestal; and a sand-colored seashell that whispered its longing for home. All were now bunched closer together, a mismatched potpourri, in order to make room for the photographs, each with a small branch of dancing lady in a tiny silver vase before it, yellow oncidiums. The poet mourned anew.

"I'm sorry," Satan said. "I was trying to set the scene. This is for Jacob, not for us. He needs us to help him remember, to harrow the soil and dislodge the silt."

"But you're doing such a magnificent job," Death said. "Too magnificent. You've been back in his life for a year and some, and already your spade-fork has unearthed so much of what he long ago buried. He remembers so often now that he's seeking professional help."

"And thou art most gracious," Satan said. "Yet my role here is not done."

"He will probably check himself into that nuthouse called St. Francis."

"I loathe that narcissistic nincompoop of a saint," Satan said.

"We can agree on that at least," said Death. "Holier-than-thou, PETA-idolizing numbnuts."

"On that convivial note," said Satan, "and without further ado, we begin. How long have you known our boy?"

Death sighed. "Since conception, of course. Where there is congress, I am."

"Why do you remember him?" Satan asked. "What was so special? Of all conceptions, why his?"

"Well, I remember him for many reasons," Death said, "probably the same as yours. He is an Arab, so I would have to attend to his loved ones sooner rather than later. He should have accompanied me early on, such a sickly child he was, but you chose him." He inclined his head against the chair, shut his eyes for a moment, remembering; when he tilted his head back, the beret returned slightly off-kilter, his eyes were brighter, and a rascally grin creased his face. "I tell you, Arabs make my life worth living, such pleasure

6 RABIH ALAMEDDINE

they have given me through the years, just as much as Jews. Arab Jews are the best, of course, their lives full of suffering and dying and no little whining, Yemeni Jews, my, my. But back to Jacob, he is a strange pervert. Obviously, he was wedded to me, so I kept watch, as you have."

"Conception?"

"Oh, that," Death said. "I remember his wondrous conception because of the carpet, what a treasure, what a fucking glorious masterpiece. How could I forget that carpet?"

At the Clinic

Carving Poems

After letting me off, the taxi driver reversed out of the alley at an unholy speed, almost as if he were going to take off into the quilt of lowering clouds now that he was unburdened. I watched with a certain level of dispassion. I had to remind myself that most likely, his risking so much to leave quickly had little to do with me. Perhaps he was in a hurry, hoping to find another fare before returning to his small one-bedroom apartment, or maybe he always drove that way when he did not have a client in the backseat. I had said not a word after I told him where I wished to go. Maybe he wanted to be as far away from the Crisis Psych Clinic as possible.

   I turned around, had to pay attention to where I placed my feet because of the numerous puddles around me. It had just stopped raining, so maybe the driver wished to get home before the storm rebooted. Fresh rain ameliorated some of the noxious odors of the alley, less urine, less decay, less putrid human soup. The aging spherical lamp above the clinic's door graced me with a soft, diffuse light, made a sump on the sidewalk glimmer. I walked into the brick building, wondered if it was earthquake-safe since its sloping floor did not inspire confidence.

An older receptionist with frizzy hair dyed satanic red was manning three windows, two under signs that read TRI-AGE, and the other REGISTRATION. She was Triage at the moment, yet gave the impression that she could slide over to register me before you could say Mephistopheles, or even just Poodle, which was how Satan made his first appearance to Faust, as a black poodle, Here I am! The redhead receptionist smiled awkwardly, kept updating her cheerful demeanor even though I was unable to reciprocate. In reply to whether she could help me, I told her that I needed to see a psychiatrist, I was having hallucinations, hearing Satan's voice again—again after a long absence, and his voice was becoming more insistent. My employers wanted me to seek help, it seemed I made the attorneys uncomfortable even though I had little if any contact with them and preferred it that way. I'd had contact with Greg, also a redhead and a lawyer at the firm, but he'd been dead for a quite a while, almost twenty years now. Her face did not change expression, stuck in smile. Yes, having hallucinations and being in contact with dead redheads qualified me to see someone at the clinic. I passed Triage, praise be. Let me get you to fill out this form, she said, handing me a stack of sheets in small print, which told me that it might be time to update my eyeglass prescription.

A sign on the peeling white wall to my right promised that the clinic would provide quality medical and psychological services with compassion, dignity, and respect for its clients in a collaborative environment. In the spirit of collaboration, the receptionist said she considered my employers wonderful for allowing me to take time off to deal with my little problem, for not firing me, because so few people, and fewer companies, understood that people like me needed to see a doctor to work things out like everybody else. She went on and on while my pen tried to jot the right words on the correct line and check the appropriate boxes. Her voice seemed déjà vu, or rather déjà entendu, but I couldn't place where I had heard it before; it seemed to emanate independently of her, as if she were speaking not out of her mouth but out of the miasma surrounding her, as if the air particles themselves vibrated to carry her voice, which they did, or so science told us.

I was lost, Doc. I would not have come to the clinic had this horrid day not dawned with the news of another drone strike in Yemen, this morning's killings closer to home. Six men, one woman, two boys, and one girl, smithereened with one Hellfire, all al-Qaeda militants according to a Yemeni military official but not according to the CIA, which rarely commented on its killings, in the southern province of Abyan, in the small village of Mahfad, my mother's village, which may or may not have been where I was born, my mother could not remember, because even though she had just returned there, she left or was kicked out as she was unwed. Drone killings were so regular these days that they merited barely a mention in the newspaper or on news programs, but I had yet to grow inured.

Redhead receptionist spoke loudly, so I paid attention and noted that she had black Frida Kahlo eyebrows and a squint nose, she told me I didn't remember her but she did me, she didn't recognize me at first, it had been twenty years maybe, I had grown older, she had grown older and redder, ha-ha, but as soon as she heard my name she recognized me as the one and only Jacob, the clinic's infamous poet. I had no idea what she was talking about. I had arrived at this clinic one night years ago, I remembered that fact but not her, I was in some form of fugue, delivered here by Jim or another worried friend, I was exhausted and strung out, probably from speed, unable to cope with the dying. I remember coming here before being admitted to St. Francis Hospital for three days. That was all I knew before she reminded me. It seemed that while I waited for the doctor I had carved a four-line stanza into the wall of a room and signed my name. I had used an unfurled paper clip, or so everybody decided after the fact, because they had searched me before putting me in the room as protocol required, and I should not have had anything that would cause damage to a wall or to a vein, and they had to change their search procedures because of my fabulous stunt. For months, whenever regulars complained about having to suffer the new indignities, they were told to blame the poet, which I thought was delightful, and the receptionist laughed and laughed, a joyous sound, and earthy. I didn't remember the act or the poem. It was an original, she said, and one of the residents thought it was strangely amusing if not terribly good, he copied it before the patch of wall was spackled and repainted, he handed it out to each visitor to the clinic as he or she was peeled and poked, but then the resident died, and everyone just assumed I was dead like all the rest of us.

What was the poem? She could not remember exactly, it had been so long, but she remembered I was Egyptian, and she had thought of me when millions of my people gathered in Tahrir Square and toppled our dictator. I told her I wasn't Egyptian, which confused her. Wasn't I with my mother Catherine in Mount Lebanon, which was in the Sinai? I did not wish to explain once again that the Middle East was not one country, that Saint Catherine of Alexandria was only a metaphorical mother, I told the receptionist of course everything was in the Sinai, we were all there, the Middle East was one big jumble of odoriferous trash. My father was Lebanese, my mother Yemeni, I spent a few years of my childhood in Cairo, so you could say I was Egyptian, I was all Arabs, look how dark. We laughed and laughed, and I asked whether she was going to search and poke me with the procedure I had inaugurated, whether we should call it autoeroticism, and we laughed and laughed some more, and she said not her, but the big guy was going to, and on cue, the big guy arrived in the waiting room, looking like no one if not Lou Ferrigno, in an ill-fitting white T-shirt that highlighted every steroid-inflated bulge, a teal Lipitor logo emblazoned above his prominent nipple. Would I be able to take him home with me after I was done here, I asked, and all three of us laughed and laughed, and Ferrigno was much bigger than me, his hand could have wrapped twice around my biceps, but only once was needed as he led me into a room.

Together alone Ferrigno's eyes avoided me, I thought he wanted me naked but I felt bare already, as if I were skinless. I, Marsyas, you, hulky hunky Apollo. He would not look at me and that was all right. I closed my eyes, and you know who was there in my head, sitting next to the examining table. Don't worry, Doc, I'm not crazy, I knew Satan wasn't there, I knew I was imagining the indefatigable Iblis as I saw him, I needed company, he was always there. His blazing, insanely blue eyes would not leave me as he said, Let's get out of this goddamn place.

Jacob's Journals

Restless Heart

The beating of your heart kept me awake one night, for months after you died I saw you everywhere, heard you, your voice, sonorous, throaty, reverberating in my ear. I wasn't crazy, I knew you were dead, I buried you after all—I mean, I burned you, cremated you. But I kept seeing you, doing dishes in the kitchen with your back to me, I'd call you as you stacked each plate in our plastic dish rack, but you didn't look back and then you were gone in a flash and I was left with nothing, not even an afterimage. I didn't mistake you for anybody, I never saw you in a crowd, thinking someone else was you, no, it was never like that. I saw you in the hallway, in our hallway, under the Turkish lamp you brought back from Istanbul when you were there so long ago, remember the trouble they gave you at customs for a twenty-dollar lamp, and when you emerged from the swinging doors you were furious, I kept telling you to calm down but you wouldn't, you went on and on because you were angry and you were an American and you could ruffle feathers at airports. While I was alive I loved you while you were alive and I loved you still but I forgot for a while. Forgive me, I couldn't obsess about you all the time, so you disappeared as if I'd bleached my memory, but you came back, you know, like a fungal infection — remember thrush, the white stains that attacked your innocent tongue, looked like the snowy down on old strawberries, we couldn't get rid of it, and you hated it and I hated it and you wanted it over. When, to make you feel better, I joked that the furry fungus matched your white lab coat, you turned apoplectic, wanted to strangle me, I still regret that, I thought it was funny at the time.

You've been gone for decades, you hid deep in my lakes, why now, why infect my dreams now? What flood is this? Once as I was buying groceries in a store where a young third-worlder mopped the floor, back and forth, back and forth, around a yellow sign that announced Piso Mojado, the mephitic aroma of disinfectant assaulted my senses, and you jumped the levee of my memory. Proust had his mnemonic madeleine, but bleach was all ours, Doc, all ours. The tomatoes didn't look too good and I just went home. I'd been a coward, I was scared, do notice I said scared and not frightened, you taught me the difference, you said, Children get scared, men might feel afraid, might even feel terror, but men don't get scared. I'd been so lonely since you died, you left me roofless in a downpour. You gripped the bedrail when you took your final breath and I had to pry open your fingers one by one to free you, it took seventeen minutes because my hands were shaking so much. Even in death you were stronger than I, and more obstinate, the mortician told me it took forever to burn you, thrice he had to put you in the incinerator, you refused to turn to ash. You sincerely believed that the distance between you and me would one day disappear. You told me I was not my mother and you were not my father, but how could we not be, how could we not be, the stones over her cenotaph still felt so very heavy. You held out your arms and said, Join me, but I couldn't, and you said, Let me love you, and I couldn't because you wanted to be so close. You held out the fireman's net and said, Jump, and I couldn't, I felt the fall was much too great, I chose to go back into the fire. You said, I like it when you doze on my chest, but I said, The hair on your chest irritates my cheeks and makes it difficult to sleep. I could hardly bear the beauty of you.

You were gone for so long and I moved along and everyone told me I was alive, but that night, in my bed, each time my ear touched the single pillow I heard your heartbeat once more, once more, once more, once more.

My heart is restless until it rests in thee.

The Congenital Immigrant

I'm the congenital immigrant, Doc, think about it. I left parts of me everywhere. I was born homeless, countryless, raceless, didn't belong to either my father's family or my mother's, no one could claim me, or wanted to. I was a rug-burn baby, a Persian rug burn — my father, all of fourteen at the time, fucked my not-much-older mother right there on the Mahi from Tabriz while sunbeams played hide-and-seek amid the furniture. Both pairs of knees chafed since they stole each other's virginity canine-style and my mother could admire the exquisite deep blue rosettes surrounded by gold lancet leaves repeating all around her, her body on all fours right above the carpet's main medallion, which looked like a fish rising to the surface of a pond at midnight to admire the reflection of the moon. I've never seen the carpet, not once did my eyes fall upon that masterwork, or the penthouse apartment in Beirut's Achrafieh neighborhood, yet my mind's eye rewove the century-old treasure thread by silk thread since my mother never tired of describing it to me when I was a child. In luxury I came to be, she used to tell me, in remarkable beauty I was conceived, deep blue water, gold, cobalt violet toothed leaves that represented the scales of the fish, repeating patterns, ogees and swoops and arabesque arcs, over and over and over. When his parents — I can't call them my grandparents, Doc, I just can't — saw me beginning to form in the belly of their short maid from the deserts of Yemen, they tortured a confession out of my father, they went insane, the wrath of frothy-mouthed Hera boiled in their blood, but they did not bring the shotgun out of the rifle room. They were curious enough to ask how many times the sexual act was consummated — quite a few, it seemed, since my mother's dark blood was insatiable — but didn't think of asking where their son's drone first found its Yemeni target, which was lucky for me because had they discovered that filthy bodily fluid had assuredly soiled their priceless chef d'oeuvre, they would have strung my mother from the balcony and Beirut's bourgeoisie would have applauded in unison and I wouldn't have been born.

You, Doc, wait, I need someone to hear this, listen to me. My mother was kicked out of the palace, which meant I was unceremoniously exiled while still in utero. Think about that, an early immigrant, I learned to travel light, always just a carry-on, never checked my luggage. Do you know the difference between an expat and an immigrant? You're an immigrant in a country you look up to, an expat in one you consider beneath you. I don't know why I tell you all this about me, I need to, I guess, but with this need to tell comes the concomitant desire to forget everything, to bury it once more and forever, to remember my story into some microphone or digital thingamajig and then take the recording to a field in Sonoma or a cemetery in Colma and inter it along with my so-called poems that no one reads and no one should. I would walk to my burial ground, not ride the bus, no matter how long it took, because it would be a ritual of pilgrimage. My memories would blur with my poems, each image would meld with a clod of dirt, each word dissolve into the earth.

I was forced to emigrate while I was still my mother, while I was within someone else's flesh. You never emigrated, Doc, you were born and raised in this town, but I tell you, when you leave, a section of your heart withers on its vine, you start over again, over and over, you mispronounce your name once and once again, Ya'qub becomes Jacob and then, heaven forbid, Jake, you get on with your life, but each time you bid farewell to a place, voracious flesh-eating fish swim up from your depths, vultures circle your skies, and your city's dead quiver with fury in their graves and bang on their coffins, but then your homeland feels too paltry, a canoe tied to a branch by your mother's hair. A caisson of regrets, Doc, a caisson of regrets is all I have left.

For a few years my mother Hagared the desert: from
the Imamate to the Aden Protectorate, Abyan, Hadramawt,
from one corner of the southern peninsula to the other, I in
her arms, or so she told me, from a desiccated village at the
border with Oman to an irriguous one across the strait from
Djibouti, hoping to be taken in by one part of her family
or another. They would feel sorry for her at first, adopt her
for a brief period before someone felt horrifically offended
by being in the presence of an adulteress and her offspring
of sin. North and South Yemen may have waged wars
against each other, roosters who cock-a-doodle-dooed at
dawn from dunghill to dunghill, but the two cocks united
in finding me repulsive. My mother hid behind her veil,
I behind her skirt, and we kept on leaving, which might
have been traumatic at the time, but it was a good thing
because really, can you imagine this faggot growing up
in some obscure hovel with no running water, let alone
air-conditioning, and where would I have found prod-
ucts for this nappy hair? Every night as we wandered the
desert among my mother's tribes, golden jackals howled
about the five million ways she missed my father, jackasses brayed urging her to move to the city, that's what
she used to tell me and I believed her. She told me she
many a time considered discarding me. The moon when
full and camels with gibbous humps whispered in her
ear to offer me, her mark of shame, to the wide womb
of the night, a sacrifice to the Arabian leopard. Without
me she would have stayed, she had a man to take care
of her, a husband, well, many husbands, other women's
husbands, but she kept me and kept me away from the
desert's hunters and carrion scavengers.

On a rainy night as bucketsful of water sluiced the dark and local roses hung their dripping heads in sorrow and brackish runnels muddied the floor of her shack, she wistfully recalled the luxuries of that Beirut apartment, the carpets, the Laliques and Limoges, the white faience chandelier and its Louis XVI sister in crystal luster. The next day she was on the bus out of whichever urine-soaked, dust-plagued village we were in at the time. The first big move for immigrants is usually from the country to the city, and we did the same, except ours wasn't the first move or the second or the third, and I can't tell you how old I was, maybe a toddler, maybe two or three.

You ask what I remember of my mother's country? I remember nights falling so fast you felt as if you were bungee jumping. Stars above, impervious stars and more stars, awe-inspiring, infinite and indifferent, histrionically spectacular, I felt I was a child of the universe. What else? Morning skies that held no secrets, harsh suns you could almost touch, plunging down and exploding, gushing blood and gold in the evening. Browns and beiges and creams, pinks so divine they would convert an atheist, I remember untrammeled nature in its many guises, dales and plains and hills and many a rill that watered hanging gardens, you could wring the sweetness of jasmine out of the soft air. Qat, chewing qat, drinking it, and then more qat, and death, yes, death and funerals, I was so young, but I remember the funerals, so many, and at one for a teenage boy, men took turns carrying the coffin all the way to the grave, and everyone recited the Sura of Yasin over it as always, villagers wailed about a future that would not occur, a marriage that would not happen, grandchildren that wouldn't arrive, and

I turned to my mother's covered face and asked her when her grandchildren would arrive.

I don't have to mention how my mother supported herself without a family, we can both surmise what she resorted to. Yes, Doc, she resorted to that, I'm the lowest of the low, I'm an Arab, I'm the son of a whore.

Satan's Interviews

Death

"Is it true?" Satan asked.

"Which part?" replied Death. "That Jacob's mother was a whore? I'm surprised you ask. I thought she was the reason you became involved in this saga. She was the harlot of all harlots. She was the whore of Babylon, a prostitute with a good heart."

Jacob's cat jumped out of the closet, landed on the hardwood floor with a sizable thump, big boy. His favorite napping place was on the T-shirts on a shelf behind hanging jackets. He glanced at Death for a moment, found him unworthy, ever so dramatically sauntered over to Satan's hand draped over the armrest, and arched his back. Satan scratched beneath the lush black hair with long fingernails. The cat rolled onto his back, paws in the air, and spread himself for belly ministrations. His loud purring included a strange nasal hiccup.

"He calls this boy Behemoth," Satan said, smiling.

"Of course he does," Death said, "and that's why the cat likes you so." His tapered fingers reached toward his newly grown mustache, curled and black and blatantly waxed. With his hand raised, the sleeve dropped once more. Death chuckled, noticing that Satan seemed enraptured with the tattoo. "What were we talking about? Wait, I remember. We were talking about the boy's mother, but you weren't asking about her, were you?"

"No," Satan said, shaking his head, still smiling. "I loved her. She was so good, so adept, she could make Denis blush, and you'd think nothing could embarrass that preening pervert of a saint. I meant the funerals, so many of them, his memories. Wasn't he too young to remember all that?"

"Probably," Death said. "I don't know. There were many funerals, but I can't tell what he remembers. Yemen is one of my favorite places, it's an octopus with each of its tentacles dipped in a different century."

"In one of his poems," Satan said, "he compared Yemen to a poor African nation without Bono or Nicholas Kristof."

"Funny guy, our Jacob," Death said. "One of the reasons he has survived for so long is that his mother took him out of that ill-starred country."

"In Yemen," Satan said, "you could get killed for having a dust mote in your eye and blinking at an inopportune moment. I frequently played with sandstorms just for the hell of it."

"That nation has refreshed and rejuvenated me for centuries," Death said.

He produced a tan leather pouch out of his sleeve. With thumb and forefinger he extracted a pinch of tobacco and began to roll a cigarette. "Yet, that Egyptian hellion Badeea happened to come to Yemen and she took the whore and her son back to Cairo. Things have a habit of working out, as the cliché goes, especially if you had a hand in those things. Badeea was your doing, right?"

From his other sleeve Death produced a match, flicked it lit with his manicured fingernail. The smell of Tartarean sulfur floated in the air between them.

"Are you going to interview the others?" Death asked. "Denis and Pantaleon? Maybe Eustace? You must do Catherine too. She probably knew him best, screwed him up the most—well, after you."

He took a long drag, the tip of his flimsy cigarette growing and glowing, almost afire, yellow flame, red ember, gray ash.

"Jacob doesn't like anyone smoking in his apartment," Satan said.

"Fuck him," Death said.

At the Clinic

White

I shut my eyes, if only for a moment, trying to reduce the vivid whiteness of the walls, I wished for an eye mask of felt that would keep the light at bay, and I wondered how I ended up here in this vesper hour. I was slowly wilting in the waiting room, drooping in a plastic chair that would tax the most robust of backs. Perfect name, the waiting room, waiting, waiting, we were waiting, wait with me, Doc, wait and hope was the motto of Edmond Dantès, the Count of Monte Cristo, and did you know that the Spanish word for waiting and hoping is the same, so why couldn't we call this the hoping room, or would that be too depressing, why introduce our desires into the mix, who wants to be reminded of his longing?

The clinic had a zero-tolerance policy for use of profanity, verbal threats, or any act of violence, or so the white

THE ANGEL OF HISTORY

sign above the door insisted, yet when the man with rickets
and ringworms to my right yelled Fuck, no staff member
made an appearance to admonish him, and the elderly bespectacled lady and the young trans man with the bland
and chinless mug who hiccupped incessantly turned their
heads at the same time, same angle, like sheep in a pen upon
hearing the sharpening of a butcher's knife. The man was
irritated about something, and he seemed to have quite a
few simultaneous tics, his piggish eyes blinked Morse, his
arms jerked constantly, he probably suffered from some
form of chorea.

Ask me, Doc, ask me how I know, well, don't you remember Greg's last days, he was shaking all over and nothing could make him stop and the nurse told me he had a
specific form of chorea, what was sometimes called Saint
Vitus Dance, and I wish I could have shared with you what
I felt the moment I heard that, but every time I mentioned
my saints you turned away, even though everything that
had to do with the plague always referred back to them,
always. Why couldn't you hear me? Because you talk too
much, Satan told me, and I ignored him, and he said, Listen,
mortal, lest ye die, if you like your fourteen saints so much,
why don't you talk to them instead of your dead hubby?
You did hear me at times, Doc, you mocked me but you
listened. The Fourteen Holy Helpers, I told you, my saints,
I grew up with them, I know you heard because whenever
you downed a shot of Jägermeister you said, Down the
hatch with Saint Mustache. You knew that the glowing
cross between the antlers of a stag is the symbol of Saint
Eustace, and you knew about Saint Margaret, who escaped
the belly of the dragon that swallowed her because the cross

she was wearing irritated his stomach, you dressed up as her for one of our parties, not a good look for you, but still, you knew my fourteen.

In the seat next to me, Satan kept smoothing his jacket since these chairs had a tendency to crimp even the sturdiest article of clothing, and his white linen suit with blood-red piping was not sturdy by any means, delicate and diaphanous as gossamer. And Satan said, Anyone who believes a teeny cross can upset a dragon needs to have his head examined.

Repeat after me, Doc, when at night I go to sleep, fourteen angels my watch do keep, two my head are guarding, two my feet are guiding, two upon my right hand, two upon my left hand, two who warmly cover, two who over me hover, two to whom it is given, to guide my steps to Heaven, and Satan said, Now that's one hell of an orgy, hmm, I wonder which two will lead you to Heaven, probably headless Denis and Pantaleon, no, no, Pantaleon always wants to be under the covers, it's Denis and Eustace, who can light the path with his absurd cross.

The irritated man talked to the palm of his hand. He sat in the farthest corner of the room, schizophrenics always do, which meant that I was not one because the other two patiently waiting were a mere three feet across the waiting room, while he was in Siberia.

Look, I said to Satan, I am not like him, yes, I talk to you, but you're only in my head, and once I get rid of you, I'll be back to normal, get thee behind me, Satan.

Walmart sells an oil for that, Satan said, it's called Satan Be Gone, a little dab will do ya.

I was exhausted, in the uncomfortable seat I wondered how long I had to wait, I glanced at my phone for the umpteenth time, no change. The irritated man moaned, informed his hand he needed to pee, and the bespectacled lady discreetly tried to move her chair a bit but realized that it was nailed to the floor, a newbie. We heard careful human steps in the corridor just outside the door, someone was being led out of the clinic, a black man with white face, balancing a towering turban on his head, his strange footwear light on the linoleum in a laggard pace, he waved as he passed by. I had seen the man numerous times before on the downtown streets near where I work, always with theater makeup white on his face, always with a homemade turban, it kept the voices out of his head, he told passersby, it kept the National Security Agency from spying on his thoughts, two for one, good deal, he announced to anyone and everyone. He wore rubber waders, open-toed, obviously hand-cut to show his white nail polish. At the exit, he turned toward Ferrigno, who was showing him the door, and asked, Will you visit me?

Why don't you wear a turban to keep me out, Satan said, and I told him to go home, Hell in his case.

Jacob's Journals

Walter Benjamin

I thought of you. I miss you. Of all things, the catalyst was Didion, our sweetheart. Remember her? How could you not? *Slouching Towards Bethlehem* was how we met. I became mortal when I met you. You stood before one of the shelves of the gay bookstore on Castro Street with her book in your hands, the light from the picture window on the left fragmenting on your face, chiaroscuro meets cubism, Caravaggio cum Picasso. You were squinting to read the back matter. You always took your glasses off while cruising in those days, remember? I was the one who convinced you how sexy smart is. Fuck me with your glasses on. Look at me when you're inside me. Look at me. Cruising in bookstores dates us. They have practically all disappeared now. I stood next to you, as close as I could get, shoulders almost touching, hips almost conjoining, on your face sprang a line of a smile that didn't wish to appear too eager.

It's not a gay book, I said in a voice just above a whisper, wanting to keep my options open in case you rejected me — I wasn't speaking to you, no, truly, I wasn't. Foxlike, your eyes glittered and darted, expressed false surprise — yes, even then I knew you were mocking me. How many fucks did you wait, weeks later you finally admitted that you used Didion's book because you thought I was just the kind of boy who might be a devotee. You joked that the book was about aging Jewish gay lads heading to the old city of Bethlehem, then you mentioned something about an original that I couldn't decipher because my dick was so hard. I wondered whether you were talking about "The Second Coming." Your thin nose twitched, your face lit up. Oh, I'm going to make you come a second and a third and probably a fourth time, you said, and dragged me home. I have to tell you that was a horrid come-hither line, just horrid, but it worked, and now Joan Didion has written memoirs for Oprah. It didn't bother me, I mean, we're all getting old and sentimental, nostalgia overwhelms our defenses, floats over our moats and scales our walls. She's not the writer she was when younger but few are. Don't allow your prose to reach forty should be the motto of every writer, commit Mishima.

A few weeks ago I was going to have dinner with my roommate, Odette, and her girlfriend, Sue, and as was my wont, I arrived early at the crowded restaurant, aggressively trendy of course, one of many that were popping up like noxious mushrooms in what used to be our old haunts. This one was sparkly new but meant to look old — the walls,

everything had an unnatural tinge of gray, which was supposed to be the faded trace of some earlier lost color. I was
on edge, the music was thumping loudly and it wasn't disco,
and the restaurant was pretentious like everything in this
drippy city that brimmed with self-congratulation, and the
waitstaff were obnoxious and the customers more so and
I so hated San Francisco. Oh, I live in the city by the bay,
so I must be cool, I live in a cretinous provincial dump surrounded by pretentious superficially amicable cretins, so
aren't I wonderful?

As the maître d' manqué led me into the bowels of the
establishment, I felt a tug at my hand, a diner held my wrist
trying to slow me down as I passed. I didn't notice at first
and my shoulder was almost dislocated from its customary
socket. I was stopped by two young gay writers—two rude
writers, both remaining seated in the deafening cacophony,
a Tom Something and a Something Bernhard was all I could
remember of their names, two artistes of the nouveau-bland
movement whose manifesto consists of defending the rights
of white gay boys to have dating anxieties and live homo-
happily ever after. Tom Something with his pink, studiedly
pleasant face called me Jake, asked how I was doing, and,
without waiting for a reply, proceeded to inform me that he
had finally fulfilled his lifelong dream of visiting Burning
Man, and no, he wasn't burned at the stake, ha-ha, but he
had problems with ubiquitous sand in his underwear so he
dispensed with bottom clothing altogether on the second
day. I was first confused, then bored, then annoyed, and
he must have noticed since he abruptly segued into the fact
that he had also recently fulfilled his more important lifelong
ambition of being interviewed by Terry Gross. His voice

was coloratura irritating, and I couldn't understand why he was talking to me, let alone regaling me with such trivia. He was gleefully enjoying his rather small turn as one of those writers who accidentally happen to get acknowledged during the short literary cycle.

If all that wasn't upsetting enough, his tablemate, Something Bernhard, had a tickle in his throat that needed clearing every few seconds, a phlegmy warbling frog sound. He relaxed somewhat when he saw my eyes slide across the table toward the book he was unconsciously yet reverently caressing with the palm of his hand. His nostrils flared, his face lit up, his dyed blond hair seemed to turn two shades lighter, sprouting more frosted tips with every ticking moment. He interrupted his pretty friend's Burning Gross monologue and informed me that this was Didion's book, except he called her the goddess, his gay eyes rose toward the ceiling in Pierre-et-Gilles devotion, I could imagine a halo or at least a tiara above his head. He never missed reading any of her books, he said. I admit that I was surprised by both the insipidity of this pair and their assumed intimacy. I wished them gone, I wished me gone, get thee gone, get thee to a nunn'ry, why woulds't thou be a breeder of sinners? Odette and Sue were yet to arrive, and the maître d' had returned to his host station, and I was about to walk away, my habitual leave-taking. Ever since I turned fifty, I have been able to extricate myself easily and painlessly from such situations, for none of these unripe boys care for much beyond their groins or their navels, but I wasn't so lucky this time. The other young one, noticing that they were about to lose their audience, piped up, Can you imagine, she lost her husband and within a year and a half lost her daughter as well, how horrifying is that?

Can you imagine, and alarm bells woke me from a twenty-year nap. It was instantaneous, I promise you, Doc. Zeus launched crackling thunderbolts and Molotov cocktails in Rip van Winkle's head. I began yelling. Her husband died? You think that's horrifying? You feel sorry for her? She's lived a full life. I had six friends die in a six-month period, half a dozen of my close friends including my partner. We were nothing but babies, where was she when we were dying, where were you, you motherfuckers? Adrenaline rushed through my veins, anarchic, atavistic, delicious, a sheen of sweat on my palms, tingles on my forearms, rage in my voice. Even as I was yelling, I realized that the question was silly, I mean, where were they? They were barely in middle school then, probably eight or ten. Same as Yahweh asking Job, Where wast thou when I laid the foundation of the earth? I wasn't even born then, you silly thing, no one was. And these boys, soft-shelled and scared, looked as if they were eight or ten. Frosted Tips reached for his ice-filled glass, probably thinking I was going to spill it on him. Tom Something's knuckles were mottled white as he clutched the sides of the table. I wanted to feel sorry but I couldn't, I just couldn't stop, could not. I was in the midst of an amygdala hijacking. My sanity deserted me, all I had left was rage, long-lost rage. How can you not know your history? I yelled over and over. You with your righteous apathy, how can you allow the world to forget us, to delete our existence, the grand elision of queer history? The music was still blaring but every other noise had faded. I could feel every eye on me, every nervous and baleful glower.

When I was in school, I used to stand outside in the yard during recess wondering if my classmates would jump me once the nuns turned away, same thing in that restaurant. That fear of being jumped seared me inside my own skin, never went away, my love, never did, third-degree burn right under the surface, moonlight easily bruised it. I covered myself with layers and layers, with false fronts and bitchy attitude, but my charred history refused entombment. I felt dirty, congenitally filthy, what could wash me clean as snow, nothing but the blood of Jesus. Give it to me, I'll drink. Fuck me. I can walk into any room and tell you in the blink of an eye where the danger lies, who hates me, who despises me, it's a superpower, I tell you, X-Men have nothing on me.

Frosted Tips looked at me as if I were carrying an AK-47, they all saw me that way, an Arab faggot terrorist. Again I wanted to feel sorry for him but then I yelled, All AIDS books are out of print because of you, because you only read books sanctioned by the petite NPRsie and their indiscreet charm, your fault, your fault, your grievous fault. We refused everything, rejected their heavens and their hells, and you turn around and accept both and you keep saying I do and I do and I do and fuck me more daddy while they shove you in a tiny vestibule and you pretend it's Versailles.

Kitchen doors swung open and a trio of cheerful waiters walked behind me oblivious to my jeremiad, an overpierced juvenile carrying a birthday pot de crème and the other two hovering like moths about the candle. Desserts in restaurants had turned sophisticated, but birthday candles still smelled comfortably familiar. I took a deep breath and practically calmed down. Wherever my eyes traveled, though, patrons avoided my gaze.

I was able to hear you again, to see you, your birthday is March 11. I put it aside for a while, forgive me. I couldn't go on, had to move forward, couldn't bear the burden of remembering and couldn't come to terms with the unbearable. Remember my All Saints birthday? I was always Saint Catherine of Alexandria since she and I had the same birthday, November 25. Saint Catherine of the Wheel, cheese wheels for the day, my spouse was Jesus Christ, to whom I had consecrated my virginity, my constantly rediscovered virginity. Why did you pick Saint Margaret? Did it have anything to do with a dragon or was it because of Ann-Margret? I can't remember. Have to say I loved it when my birthday fell on Thanksgiving and all of us would celebrate with candles on the saintly turkey, Tofurky for me. Better days.

Frosted Tips whispered I'm sorry, insincerely, since all he wanted was for me to calm down and not embarrass him, and his tablemate added that he tried to watch as many AIDS movies as possible. It's a good thing he didn't tell me he watched *Philadelphia* or I would have stabbed him with his butter knife. Quietly they talked, sotto voce, hoping that I would follow suit in spite of the sprightly music. Frosted Tips reached out to touch me and I instinctively jerked back, but I was calming down. Tom Something said that he could understand my upset because he recently watched the movie *Rent*, which was probably not as good as seeing the *Pulitzer Prize–* and *Tony Award*–winning musical, emphasis his, oh how he wished he could have seen the original cast production on Broadway, and did I by any chance see *Angels in America* when it first came out? I almost went for the aforementioned butter knife then, almost, to dab their cherubic faces with room-temperature butter, palette-knife Bob Ross happy trees on their button noses. It was hopeless, though, hopeless, and I realized that even as I showered the ingenues with a fusillade of fuck-yous. My screaming lacked punch, my late fuck-yous lacked the early oomph. I was done. I had aged into a text that could no longer be read. I was drained and unmoored and vanquished, hurled headlong flaming from th' ethereal sky. I could feel discomfort all about me, gentrified diners staring and pretending not to. I'd jettisoned the social ballast, I'd laid down my mask.

Please, sir, we have to ask you to leave, the man or manager was saying to me. He was a big boy with a push-broom mustache and I couldn't see the features of his face but the name on his tag was Walter Benjamin. I am your angel of history, I said, smiling weakly, but then I realized that I'd misread, his name tag read Walter Bartender. Please, sir, he repeated, and his arm approached, but I snapped at him. *Noli me tangere!* You like that, don't you? Walter Bartender must have thought me insane since in this world a symptom of losing one's mind is a readiness to speak it. I walked out of that den of Kens on my own.

I have to tell you that I wasn't able to cry after you died. I'm sorry. I wasn't able to cry for you or any of us. I was terrified of following, desperately clinging to the buoy. How could my heart be reconciled to its feast of losses? For years I thought I was a terrible person for being unable to shed a tear, a disgusting man. Only now do I allow myself a justification or two: my heart was too small, I had to care for you, for all of us, I had to write everything down, I could not deal with loss irreparable, I wanted to speak for the dead, I had to make sure that the living remembered. Well, I forgot the last, didn't I? The weeping willow droops its leaves but it doesn't weep, it never does, it's a fucking tree.

Even with the evening traffic it was more bearable outside, the city's noise unheard from being always heard. The spring sky was the color of unfiltered indigo. Frosted Tips called my name, my butchered name, my country still refused to learn my name, Ya Cube was the first couple of attempts, American Jay Cob after. He held the restaurant door and jabbered cicada-like and had the look of a bird with a broken wing and I held my arm up for him to be quiet and walked away. Get me gone, get me to a nunnery.

I stopped writing for a while after you died, my inkpot dried, not just my tears. When Jim died a month after you, I thought metaphors would never again leave my lips, I'd never rhyme, never sing cantabile, that the prosaic would displace the allegorical. I was wrong, I did write, time passed and I forgot, I wrote because I had nothing else to do in the world, I wrote, my voice as out of tune as I was. I wrote one bad poem every few months, full of splendid adjectives, simply splendid, Mr. Poet, splendid, regurgitating plump, meaty words, sharp verbs, action verbs, not passive, I wrote poems, all of them shit on shit, not a single grain of truth in the entire slop. I knew they were shit but I kept on, fucking hate myself.

I walked home. I needed to sleep.

Behemoth

Ask me, Doc, ask me why I called my cat Behemoth. Because he could have no other name, that's why, he wore his like a watermark.

A rainy winter night two years ago, as I walked home from the overlit subway station, taking my habitual shortcut through the funeral home parking lot, I heard, above the pitter-patter of rain, a tiny peep of a meow coming from the English ivy on the wall, and my heart lurched. I thought I was mistaken at first, there was a wake at the home, not twenty feet away mourners headed toward their cars clumsily to avoid getting wet, traffic noise maybe twenty feet farther, but I heard the tiny meow and stopped in a puddle, gingerly approached the wall, slipped down my hoodie to hear better, felt rain trying to braid the hairs on my head, and there it was again, a gentle plaintive meow. I softly meowed back, and the kitten replied. A man walking by under a loud umbrella said, That's so cute, with the last syllable so elongated as to make Liberace cheer from his grave. I shushed him, forefinger to lips, then dismissed him by flicking my hand in his general direction, and he spat out, Fuck all of you, as he walked away. The kitten and I meowed back and forth until I zeroed in on him, and when I parted the ivy curtain, there he was, my little munchkin, a black soppy mess looking at me with shimmering eyes that said, Help me, I cannot bear such a shitstorm, in luxury I was meant to be, in remarkable beauty I was meant to live, what the hell is this? I put my hand out and he climbed up my arm as fast as light, settled in the crook of my elbow. Take me home now and feed me.

I was inside our apartment in less than a minute, up the stairs without having wiped my shoes on the doormat, which always irritated Odette, and she came out of her room to greet me, but before she could say anything about the muddy prints I had left in my wake, I held up the kitten.

Whenever she was anxious or excited, her tongue worried a dark beauty mole just above the right side of her lip, and as soon as she saw the kitten, the aforementioned tongue went into overdrive, she oohed so sweetly. He was the first pet to enter our apartment, the lease is still in your name, Doc, it had a no-pet policy that we had to adhere to, so we didn't think we were keeping him at first, not till the kitten insisted. Odette had me rush to the pet store two blocks away for food and litter before it closed, and was the kitten grateful? Hell no. Odette had opened a can of tuna and he'd scarfed it down, so when I returned with the cat food, he sniffed at it, raised his black tail, and turned around in utter disdain, a pattern we would repeat over and over, Doc. But he was my baby, mine.

The next day Odette and I took him to the vet, who suggested that the kitten must have been abandoned by its owners, this was no street urchin, we called around, we searched online, no one had lost a black kitten with luminous golden eyes and a barely visible trace of a silver line across his spine, the boy wasn't just cute, he was stunning, a prince of darkness, and you know, Doc, his eyes were spectacular and they were not the same, the insane right eye, more greenish gold, seemed to emit sparkles as if it were sprinkled with tiny emeralds, and his left, a calm yellowish gold, seemed to pull you in, looked like an ancient Egyptian artifact, a pharaoh's jewel, and like all beauties, he double-whammied you with a go-away-a-little-closer look. It was Odette who sweet-talked the landladies, remember them, the older lesbian couple—well, they were old when we moved in and they're astonishingly old now, and they allowed us to keep the kitten.

We tried calling him Othello, but the name wouldn't
stick, he was more Iago in any case, his diva nature was
apparent from the moment his paws walked our hardwood,
but at first we just laughed it off, until the infamous oyster
incident, and then, then we understood, we understood that
he was no mere diva, he was Satan's spawn.

Two weeks after he laid claim to our household and
its belongings—broke one wineglass, chewed one sweater,
made three pairs of crew socks disappear—a miracle occurred: Odette met Sue, whose spike heels and explosively
frizzed hair rang all her bells, Sue, who even in rainy weather
wore halter tops devised from impressively inadequate
swatches of cloth. They met at a bar and Odette decided
to pull out all the stops by cooking a sumptuous dinner for
their first official date, I was to disappear, go to a movie,
read in the library, she didn't care as long as I was out of the
apartment until after midnight, at which time they would
surely be making whoopee in Odette's room, surely, Odette
said, because she was hors-d'oeuvring the guaranteed panties dropper, two dozen fresh aphrodisiac oysters she had
brought back from work. Half an hour before Sue was to
arrive, Odette shucked all twenty-four; on a large salver covered in crushed ice she organized them in three concentric
circles around a small crucible of mignonette, and left all on
the kitchen counter. We were not able to discern whether
Behemoth loved the taste of oysters or not, because he ate
only three of them, but he approved of the brine, having
licked all the shells clean; he disliked the mignonette, which
he simply spilled, but he must have adored the texture of
the mollusks, which he sank his claws into and flung all
over the kitchen, all while Odette ran to her room to change

into her most seductive outfit. The next day, when I heard about it, I decided the kitten needed a devilish name, Iblis was my first thought, of course, but that seemed wrong, the kitten was naughty, but he was no Satan, he had upset Odette's plans but she still scored, and the evening ended up better than she could have hoped, so we couldn't name him Mephistopheles, or Mammon, or Moloch, or Belial, or Woland either.

A few evenings after the oysterpalooza, when I was alone at home, the kitten attacked the remnant of a stick of butter left on the kitchen table, I saw him lift his head, his whiskers gilded yellow, and I knew his name, the most mischievous Behemoth from Bulgakov's *The Master and Margarita*, the greatest cat in literature. Behemoth, I said, and he meowed back, pleased with himself. It was his name.

And sometimes, when you call Satan's cat, his master answers. A single moonbeam seeping through the dusty, perennially unwashed window shone sparsely upon him as he sat at the kitchen table, bright red hair, light blue eyes, different from each other, the right alive and bright, more incubus, a murderous glint in the left that collared you, more succubus, and above those eyes, just beneath the hairline, were barely discolored disks, only a little lighter than the rest of his face, because his horns grew inward, not outward, into his skull, which is why he suffered so often from headaches. He wore an impeccably tailored white summer suit with genuine mother-of-pearl buttons, linen shirt, and an ivory cane topped with the head of a black cat, of course. At first, he just grinned all the time, as if he had something stuck in his teeth, and he snickered when I was lonely. Here I am, he said.

The Whorehouse

High above, in the great altitude of dense Sana'a, you could hardly breathe, but I found it more open than the open spaces of the rest of the country, a city boy I was, like most faggots before me. Even as a child I knew I did not fit in beautiful, bucolic Yemen, its mountains or plains, its desert or beaches. Sana'a, on the other hand, may have been charmingly beautiful with its contiguous historic houses sitting in lambent sienna tiers, but it was a city, a nonpretender, bitter and onerous, oppressive, so of course it felt more natural to me. It was old as well as ancient, the Imamate had kept modernity at bay for generations. We did not stay long, but I believe I would have survived there, could have.

We arrived in a rickety van covered in dust and sand and soot, whose driver, a weather-wrinkled young man sporting a proud mustache dyed with henna, was forced to jam a screwdriver between the glass and its rubber molding to keep the window ajar. We disembarked in the city with few possessions, the clothes on our backs, a most colorful satchel, and my mother's well-functioning vagina. A question here, a whisper there, a lowering of shy eyes, a gasp of surprise, one of delight, a nod in a general direction, a pointed finger, and within minutes of setting our tattered flat-heeled slippers on the city's soil, she was knocking on a pinkish-brown door. I remember every detail of that door, with rows of pomegranates carved into its hardwood, its central jamb studded with tarnished bronze pins that needed a good rub with lemon and coarse sea salt to regain their luster, a knocker through which you could hang a dish towel. I remember every aspect of the house and its eccentric decor: the windows framed by white arches, the indoor fresh fountain, the cupolas above the corridors, all inlaid with small black stones, held together with a cement made from white lime. I don't remember much about its inhabitants, a number of Egyptians, army men, engineers, politicians and advisers, evangelists in their recent beliefs, new converts to socialism, pan-Arabism, and buying sex on the cheap. Of course, what may have been a tiny amount of money to the men was abundance to my mother. She offered her charms earnestly and diligently, and luckily for us, another woman visiting the house took a quick fancy to her, and to me.

Auntie Badeea did not much care for Sanaʿa or anything it had to offer, for a militant Cairene, every other city paled, and the Yemeni capital felt to her like nothing more than an oversize hamlet, she did not wish to spend a second more than she had to outside her beloved Cairo. She had come to work with two other women, and she intended to leave Sanaʿa, the troops, and the two women behind as soon as she made enough money. Three weeks after we arrived, three weeks after my mother had rediscovered her popularity, Auntie Badeea offered her the opportunity of a lifetime, Come with me to Cairo, work in our house, become acclaimed by real gentlemen for a change, and you don't have to veil your face outdoors, you can wear whatever you wish, it is most modern, in Cairo, God wipes the tears off His children's faces. We hardly had time to unpack the one colorful satchel before we were crossing the Red Sea in a rickety boat covered in dust and salt and engine soot, off to the great modern city we went, to Auntie Badeea's house.

Faulkner once said that the best job ever offered to him was in a brothel, that it was the best milieu for an artist to work in, Baudelaire agreed of course, and I learned about poetry in the whorehouse. My mother, with me in tow, was welcomed probably for the first time in her life. Being pretty, kind, generous, she was well liked by both the establishment and its customers; being delusional, slightly unhinged, an indiscreet romantic, she fit right in with the rest of my aunties, she finally found a home. If you ask me, those were the happiest days of my life, hard to believe, I know. We lived in a house with other women who came in all colors and cultures and, like the brothel's furniture, came in all shapes and sizes, my lovely aunties, short and tall aunties, white and black, voluptuous and boyish, Egyptian, Ethiopian, Uzbek, Indian, Yemeni. Most of them, my mother included, sat around in a daze under the hanging lamps, spent half their time in hope and half in waiting, waiting for a miracle that never visited, waiting for something or someone to fly them out of their adopted life. For my mother, that someone was my father, someday her emir would come, and he didn't, of course, and she forever forgave him, or I think she did.

Auntie Badeea, on the other hand, didn't wait for a miracle, she loved her life, and she loved me, older than my mother though not by much, she took me under her wing, more precisely under her skirt, no, not sexual, Doc, I was much too young and she didn't have that much sex in any case, that's why she had the time to look after me. She was dark, darker than me, and overweight, which at one point was popular with clients, primarily Egyptians and other Arabs, but as Russians and Europeans began to frequent the house, she was less desired, she lay beyond their longings. Though she went through the prescribed motions every evening, it was merely gesture, a performance for performance's sake, the motions including painting her face while the men were already in the room, she was the only one who did that. About one hour after evening prayers, she descended the unbanistered stairs into the salon, splayed herself on a duchesse brisée whose bright canary-yellow color clashed with every single thing in the room except for the caged pale-orange canary that rarely sang if there were more than two people around. Once completely comfortable, her heft proportionally distributed about the unusual chaise longue, a Rubenesque odalisque, Auntie Badeea languidly applied her makeup, none of which was store-bought, all natural, organic even, crushed fruits and berries were the lipstick, in a small wooden bowl she mixed galena and other powders for the kohl before her rapt audience, outlined her eyes with a pencil-shaped stick of ivory. European men, Eastern and Western, weren't the only ones dazzled by the theater, Americans soon joined them, and I too stood mouth open, eyes wide, nostrils flaring, enraptured by beauty and ignored by the men.

I mention your countrymen, Doc, not to make you feel terrible, but for whatever reason they visited us in disproportionately large numbers, and truly, pleasing them became the main thrust of our establishment, they always overpaid, and because of their lumpen tastes, they weren't difficult to please. Your people and the Europeans loved watching Auntie Badeea, were mightily entertained, made sure to arrive early whenever they were bringing a newbie so he could witness her great art, but when it came time to withdraw into the private rooms, they redirected their buzzard eyes, they chose to fuck my mother, they sure did. She was younger, prettier, drank Pepsi and 7UP, blushed easily, covered her mouth when giggling, and had just the right touch of nonthreatening exoticness, just a tad. Isn't that also why you liked me, Doc, my tad of exoticness?

Since my mother was busy most of the time, Auntie Badeea took care of me. You would think that at some point a younger model would have replaced her, someone who would have been able to provide the house with a steadier and plumper income, but you'd be wrong. Irreplaceable she was, Auntie Badeea spoke passable pimp in a few languages including English. Idiosyncratic she was, those American men loved being around her, found her amusing if not fuckable. An outstanding cook, whenever she approached a stove, God's stomach would begin to rumble. That was not all, she had a wonderful sense of humor, a lightness of heart, an infectious love of a good joke that I've never seen replicated anywhere in the Western Hemisphere, whenever she told a joke, mountains craned their necks and leaned in not wishing to miss a punch line, when she laughed, men wanted to eat her up, but no one wanted to eat her pussy. You Americans are so fucked up, Doc, so fucked up, you have no clue how cruel you are, clueless cruelty.

Soon after Auntie Badeea finished painting her lady face, she'd joke with the customers, ruckus and raillery and merriment in broken English, goad the undecided into choosing the right girl for his next orgasm, and sit me on her lap, well, on her thigh since she was usually odalisquing. Blow on my face, my sweet Ya'qub, the powder has to dry, sing for me, she'd say, recite Abu Nuwas, I love his poetry but not as much as I love you. When the audience thinned out, she carried me to the kitchen, fed me, made me read aloud to her while I stuffed my mouth with her cooking, poetry, light puerile rhymes first, quite more adult as I grew up, but always rhymes, Arabic poetry always rhymed. She put me in her bed and I slept long before my mother finished satisfying for the night.

Auntie Badeea usually woke to find me inventing the most elaborate games while sitting on the floor outside my mother's door, serving tea to Sultan Ahmad, who entertained King George of Britannica, the latter so enthralled by my tea-serving prowess that he wished to steal me from my master, while I demurred and blushed and covered my mouth and giggled. After my fairly ritualized morning ablutions, brush my teeth, wash my face, under my arms, I was forced to read and write in the kitchen while Auntie Badeea sang and hovered around pots heating atop the woodstove like a mother hen with her chicks. Old Egyptian recipes she cooked, flavored with old Egyptian folk songs, she even sang Yemeni folk songs that she learned during her short stay, lovely songs, not like Ofra Haza, remember her, the Israeli singer you used to like to dance to, whom I couldn't stand, and you insisted she was singing Yemeni songs that she heard while growing up in Tel Aviv, because that's what the album cover said in clear lettering, yet I hadn't heard any of those songs before, and you accused me of being insensitive and racist even, and you made me listen to her over and over and over so I couldn't get the songs out of my head even though I hated them and I hated her, until she died of AIDS, just like all of us, she was just like us, and I felt so guilty for hating her, and I forgave her sins, but I couldn't forgive mine. Ofra's songs did not compare well with those of Auntie Badeea, couldn't measure up, because Auntie's voice was gravelly like sea pebbles on the beach, ideal for those old melodies. Auntie Badeea's singsong melodies bore me across the grooves of childhood.

I sat at the kitchen table with my book or papers, waiting, on the wall an old-fashioned ticking clock, the only visible one since the brothel had Vegas rules, no customer should be able to see the time. I waited, time aged at a chelonian pace when I was a child, I stared at the black hands of the clock, willing them to move, to no avail, I would count to agonizing infinity and back and look up and barely a minute had passed. I remember that clock, round, the size of a salad dish, Arabic numbers on a subdued light gray, an oyster-colored background, I remember the pages in front of me, writing the alphabet slowly, the alef, the standing line, trying to make it fit within the predetermined boundaries, and glancing up at the clock once more and again, understanding that my mother had not woken up. My aunties would stir awake one by one, come down for the late lunch, and my mother would always be the last, always the last. She would be happy to see me, ruffle my most unrufflable hair, but she wasn't a day person and it would take her a few hours to regain full cheerfulness. Her jellabiya was *puce*, I still see it so clearly, Doc, so clearly, *puce* is the French word for flea, it's the color of bloodstains, and was Marie Antoinette's favorite because if you squashed a flea on it, you couldn't see the stain, but even though the whorehouse certainly had its share of fleas, I doubt my mother ever considered the connection. She rarely considered much else than what was directly in front of her, which was where I tried to be. I buzzed around her like a hummingbird around its zinnia, Look at me, look at me, her head was usually down, hair covered her face, she would grunt, hum, ah-huh, and yes to everything I said, until she stabbed my heart with an Enough now, or a Can't you see I'm tired, and I would slouch and begin my second phase of waiting, waiting until she recovered and bloomed.

Slowly she perked up and began to smile, and as soon as she was able to pay me some mind, the muezzin's call would echo from the masjid four streets away, time for evening prayers, the only ones that the entire house observed, the prayer rugs unrolled, Auntie Badeea owned the most intricate and my favorite, fine wool woven to depict a white mosque, its blue minaret topped by a delicate golden crescent, my mother's barely a step up from a straw mat, the women all lined up facing toward Mecca, their foreheads and noses pressed the rugs thrice, while I remained still behind the murmuring hive so as not to distract their humming hearts promising devotion, I waited impatiently for the ritual to finish, hoping for a few seconds of attention, since the end of prayer was the time to get ready for work and the cycle.

The eternal return, the men returned, my aunties preened, evening in full bloom, Auntie Badeea descended the stairs, the laughter, the merriment, my mother left with a man, other couples paired up in rooms, and Auntie Badeea showered me with adoration, What poem shall you recite for me this evening, she would ask, take care of your Auntie Badeea who loves you most of all. She loved me and she showed it, I loved her right back, but not enough, not enough, because even then, when the Austrian or Australian finished fucking my mother, when the Englishman had left a deposit in one illicit container or another, when the Russian returned to the lounge to wait for friends, to settle up his bill or gather his wits, then the American noticed me, I was there with Auntie Badeea. Such a cute boy, the German, the Swede would say, so adorable. The man looked slightly less kempt than when he walked in, more sated, he exuded confidence and I-fucked-your-mother from every pore, he smiled at me, a smile stronger than destiny, such a cute kid, such a sweet boy. I loved Auntie Badeea, I loved my mother, but I worshipped the man, I made him my religion.

Satan's Interviews

Death

"Forgetting is good for the soul," Death said. "Not just good, but necessary. How do you expect them to go on living if they disremember not? We have to forget, we all do. Do you not recall the boy from Fray Bentos, Funes the Memorious? Borges claimed that the boy remembered everything, every minute, boring detail: the shape of mammatus clouds on Tuesday afternoon at two, the rotation of the waterwheel and its circumference, the color of each hair on a mare's mane. It would take the impoverished boy a whole day to reconstruct the previous one since he could forget nothing. In the replete world of Funes there was nothing but detail. He could create nothing, invent naught. The pain of it all, the pain of not forgetting."

He looked around for somewhere to dispose of his shrinking cigarette. His nicotine-stained fingers had been flicking ashes, which formed an arc, a single-hued rainbow on the hardwood before him.

"I dislike nonsmokers," he announced as he stood up and walked toward the kitchen. He stepped solidly, claiming the parquet in the living room as his, the harlequin-patterned linoleum in the kitchen. He opened cabinet doors and slammed them shut. He kicked a folding chair that was leaning against the wall. A startled Behemoth rushed back to the closet. Death returned with a cereal bowl containing the cigarette's remains.

"Did you expect him to stay sane once you dredged up all he had kept interred for years?" Death asked. "You have awakened the bitter memory of what he was, what is, and, worse, what must be. He is hanging by an Atroposean thread, a pair of her scissors will be dangerous enough and you come in swinging an ax."

"Sanity is overrated," Satan said.

And Death said, "It is when a man remembers that he calls on me."

"Of course," Satan said. "But enough about that. Tell me about his childhood, about Cairo."

"You believe the city saved him, don't you?" Death said. "I know how you think. And I disagree. I think it would have been better for him to have remained in one of those asinine Yemeni villages where his greatest excitement would arrive every Friday: to wear a pair of Adeni shoes that went *clack-clack* as he walked and to take them off when he prayed at the mosque. He would be so proud as he lined them up outside with the other men's shoes, his would look so trendy and fabulous, and that would have provided the faggot with all the happiness he could ever have wished for. He'd marry a nine-year-old virgin from the village and spend his time masturbating in the bathroom. That would have been a better life than what you stuck him with."

"And his nine-year-old bride would have had an easier life," Satan said.

"Exactly. She would have remained a virgin, an eternal blossom. We should name her."

"Balqees," Satan said. "A nice Yemeni name."

"Lovely," Death said. "I tell you this: every move this boy has had to make ended up causing him more anguish, and that's just him. If we consider the other people in his life, the suffering these uprootings caused was immeasurable."

"Poor little Balqees."

"You understand nothing," Death said.

"So can you tell me about Cairo?"

"Fuck Cairo."

Eustace

The saint would not sit down. He walked around the two-bedroom apartment, picked up various objects, turned them around in his surprisingly delicate hands before putting them back: a small fruit bowl in the kitchen, a hand mirror in Jacob's room, the imitation Tiffany Mission lamp on the nightstand in Odette's. Brown eyes in a fierce, sad pugilist's face inspected everything. He held every object carefully as if he wished to grasp the heart of the thing; he examined each, hoping to recapture a feeling. An exile's long-anticipated return to his homeland: familiar and foreign, wondrous and disappointing.

"We were taken from here as soon as his lover died," Eustace said, moving from corner to corner. "Uprooted and expunged, our sea lost its shore. Once more we were judged superfluous." He sighed as he riffled through a dresser drawer. "We were with him since he was a stripling cherub, healed him through illness, comforted him during a plague. Yet when we were purged, did he see fit to call us back? No, he condemned himself to the everyday world. And now you, adversary to God and man, see fit to ask me here, to call upon me?"

It was Satan's turn to sigh—a long-drawn-out sigh. "I was banished for a long time as well, but you don't see me still nurturing grievances."

Tall and muscular, almost filling the entire doorway, Eustace faced the living room. He cleared his throat, raised his left eyebrow and an ample brassiere held between thumb and forefinger.

"It belongs to the roommate," Satan said. "I'm surprised it's still here since she isn't anymore."

"He has not seen the light, then?" Eustace said.

"He has seen many a light and you know that," Satan said. "You ran roughshod over his dreams. Was it all fourteen of you so-called Holy Helpers or just you? The stags, the hunt, the quarries, all so well lit. Instead of visions, Jacob is having nightmares."

Satan turned on the mini recorder on the coffee table. A thumbprint bloomed where he had touched the glass top. He gestured toward the seat opposite him. "Come now, let us begin."

"Yes, of course," Eustace said, "commence we must," but he did not move from under the casing, nor did he let go of the brassiere. He held it against his tunic, then strung it on his belt next to the sword.

"I can't believe you'd suggest that Jacob hasn't seen the light," Satan said. "We're here to help the fellow. I need your attention."

"Why me?" Eustace said. "I wish to help, but he's having a psychological crisis. I have little experience in that domain. Should you not begin with one of the others? Maybe Margaret or Catherine? Cyriac?"

"I prefer to think of it as a spiritual crisis," Satan said. "He has forgotten so much. I called you in to remind him. He wants to check into St. Francis, thinks it will be three days of rest and recreation."

"Francis is an idiot, and our boy is not much smarter." Eustace rumbled across the living room, suddenly dithyrambic in his movement, and plopped down on the sagging armchair. "We must rescue him."

"We must," Satan said.

Behemoth poked his head out from behind the closet door to investigate the foot stomping. He seemed engrossed, fixed his eyes on the saint, the Roman helmet and its halo. He prostrated himself, arched his back in a languid stretch before coming into the room proper.

"Why would he think that ending up in the hospital is going to help him?" Eustace said. "Is he blinded by depression?"

"Horribly so."

"What is dark in him we must illumine, what is low, raise and support. How can I help?"

"Tell me about Jacob," Satan said. "What I hear he remembers, what I remember he hears. Remind him of himself."

"Shall I tell you from the beginning?"

"Not necessarily," Satan said. "Linearity can be boring. Why not recall what is best about him, what jumps out at you from your well of memory? Is there something you feel most important?"

"There." Eustace pointed at the floor between them, and Behemoth ambled to the spot. "Jacob prayed on his knees there. He called on me again, asked for my help, and I—no, we all came forth. He needed us."

"Tell me," Satan said. "Tell Jacob."

"There," Eustace said as Behemoth began to lick the old wood where he was pointing. "Jacob broke because of a drop of tainted blood—the shape of the stain was what crushed the poet."

"Sing," Satan said.

"It was the last time his partner the doctor left his bed," Eustace said, "alive, that is. Jacob was exhausted and spent, surviving on fumes of air and methamphetamine. We too were weary. All fourteen of us could see that the doctor did not have much time left in this world. He was in that room there while Jacob tried to nap on the couch that is no longer here. The doctor called out. Even though his voice was weak, barely perceptible to humans, it was a dog whistle for Jacob, who jumped up to walk him to the bathroom. No one understood why Jacob had not put the doctor in diapers. The doctor would have refused, of course, but Jacob could have forced him. It would have saved him so much trouble and so much detergent. As Jacob was leading him back to the bed, he noticed that the doctor had a cut on the sole of his left foot, a minor wound, but blood too craves air, and it surged. Every step of the injured foot stained the hardwood floor. As an experienced caregiver, Jacob didn't panic. Once he had his lover in bed, he cleaned the cut, bandaged it, and filled a pail with soapy water."

"As if he were back in that accursed Catholic school his father sent him to," Satan said.

"Exactly!"

"As it was with the nuns," Satan said, "so will it ever be."

"He had washed floors on his knees before, but he'd never had to remove blood. He began to scrub the stains, sidling from one to the next, feeling more desperate and lonely after each, until he arrived at the seventh."

"There?" Satan pointed to where Behemoth searched for blood wintering in the floor's cracks.

"There," Eustace said. "That stain was shaped unlike the rest, or you might say Jacob saw it differently. To him, it looked like a kerosene lamp, the one in the old rectory in Beirut where with an old, almost depleted click pen he wrote his first poems. He studied the stain for ten minutes, maybe more, as if he were sitting Zen and contemplating its mysteries. Then he broke—he wept, prayed, called us. As it was during the Black Death of the Middle Ages, when a sufferer called upon us, we appeared—we arrived, and he was curled up on the floor, fetal, enveloped in sorrow that should not be borne. We helped bear his grief. Agathius was the first to the floor as usual. Margaret wiped his tears. Vitus and I cleaned. I got on my knees and began to scrub the plague out, but when I tried to clean the lamp, he begged me to allow him some time with it. I must say that I would not have seen anything in that stain, let alone a kerosene lamp. It was a mere blob."

Behemoth's tongue would not slow down, as if the cat intended to uncover layers and layers through licking.

"Jacob saw the light of his childhood," Eustace said. "He wanted to see it. Blessed lamp, an ordinary one with a slippery worm of a wick that kept sliding back into the fuel reservoir at its bottom. He would have to open the lamp and pull the kerosene-soaked wick out with a pair of tweezers. The shapely glass allowed him to see its inner workings — see through to the eternal secret. For the boy, the lamp illumined and mystified. It shed light and flickering shadows, warded off night demons and introduced gnostic ones."

"You appeared," Satan said, "the fourteen saints in all your glory."

"Well, yes, but I was speaking metaphorically," Eustace said. "You see, the boy may have been indoctrinated with more than one religion, but it was at that time, in that space, that he encountered spirit, the most fragile of all, as delicate as dandelion fluff. Accompanied by unreliable light, the boy read and wrote. In the old lamp's cocoon he found a safe space, his secret garden. He left all that when he finally immigrated to America. The lamp was a shining allegory of what he lost, what he abandoned, dishonored."

At the Clinic

Waiting

Ferrigno took the shy young trans man first, the contrast in size was like a Coleridge poem to a Dickinson, and even though Ferrigno carried a clipboard, he didn't have to peruse it or call out a name, he just nodded and was followed out of the waiting room, a strange form of power dynamics that reminded me of how uncomfortable I felt in gay bars because I always thought I was missing the visual cues that the men were exchanging, not that many sent signals my way, yet I wished I had been more adept at reading gay semaphores when I was younger, too late for me now. They're writing songs of love, Satan sang, but not for me, and I tried to shut him up, to no avail, he kept asking me, Are you going to do the poor, poor pitiful me routine, because if you are, I'll just zone out for the next fifteen minutes.

It has been getting worse, Doc, I don't seem to be able to cut him off, I am all wound with adders who with cloven tongues do hiss me into madness, it wasn't always this bad, I went along for years doing rather well, didn't hear his voice, but then one day he reappeared, and he's been getting more demanding, more irksome, hissing, hissing, and I get headaches, I fear the return of the great migraine storms, I need a break, Doc, I need a break.

The man in the corner conspired softly with his hand, whispered of conflicts and intrigues and possible plans of action, though his hand remained tongue-tied as usual, unsure how to reply, and the bespectacled lady observed me while pretending not to. The peal of a church bell shocked all three of us, rang out of my jeans pocket, one round of *titong-tong-titong-tong-titong*. Bespectacled lady, her gray hair tucked behind her ears, glanced up at the NO CELL PHONES sign on the left wall, then back at me with nothing if not deeply chiding eyes, returned to staring intently at her own phone while I hurried to turn the ringer off, and Satan said, Just like you to have a church bell as annunciation, maybe you should wear a garlic necklace to ward me off.

I knew what he was doing, he wanted me to go crazy so he could have full rein, he was afraid that I would get rid of him as I did the last and only time I stayed for three days in St. Francis after you all died, he was out of my life then and I was able to function once more, go to work, hang out with friends, have a life, for crying out loud. Are you sure it was me, Satan asked, it could have been just your run-of-the-mill, garden-variety voice, maybe your fourteen saints, maybe you heard His Mightiness himself, or his son who died for your sins, or maybe the prophet of your true religion, Mo' Ho', or one of the first caliphs, with you it could have been anybody, yet you insist it was the ruler of this world, the tempter, me, I know you know that wasn't the case, but still you choose to believe, I am here now, not going anywhere, get used to it. As smoke is driven away, I told him, so will you be driven, as wax melts before a fire, so will your wickedness perish, and he laughed like a demon.

Odette's text simply asked where I was, but it was in all capital letters, which meant she was furious, happy, or worried, and we can safely assume that it was the last in this case since I had texted her two hours earlier asking if she could mind Behemoth for three days because I was thinking of going on a mini vacation, but she knew me better than anyone else and probably figured I was lying. You never met Odette, Doc, she's my closest friend, my confidante, and my funniest person in the universe, she moved in a couple of years after you left because she needed a place and I thought it would be good to save on rent. She ended up staying because we were ideal roommates. Are you going to explain to him about cell phone technologies next, asked Satan, interrupting me as usual, because you know he isn't listening, he's dead.

Jacob's Journals

Mother Dreaming

I woke to the sound of my mother singing an old Yemeni folk song, one of my favorites, and my heart was uplifted until I began to consider that she rarely woke before me, and once I did, the evanescent song faded into black. Neither my mother nor her song could survive the light of my day, I wak'd, she fled, and day brought back my night. Orange light pressed on my bedroom window.

I know, Doc, I know, my sanity is deserting me. Have you ever wondered about the noun *desert* and the verb? They're derived from the same root, left behind. Since I began to drop the pail in the well of my memories, I've had no rest, no slack for that rope. *Whoosh* fell the bucket and up came salty recollections. Remember the snow globe you kept mocking me for saving, for being so attached to, the one remaining memento of my mother, yet you kept telling me to throw it away, to discard it in some trash heap? I had a sentimental heart, you said, the souvenir was much too ugly, and it was, of all things, a snow globe from Stockholm, of all places. Well, your horrid mother stole it. She did. I don't want to think about that. I do not recall when my mother acquired that snow globe. What I do recall is that sometime after my eighth birthday, my mother began to dream of Stockholm and its long winters.

One evening, a lanky, tall Swede with hair the color of dry hay in high summer, almost as bright as the thin gold necklace he wore, walked across the salon and held out his arm for her. It was a performance, but still, it was the rare client who performed the role of a gentleman, everyone was dazzled. My mother looked around to make sure that he meant her, and only her, she even looked at the wall behind her, at the large carved figurehead of an unknown beast, openmouthed as if caught in mid-scream, with horns and dark brown eyes. No, it wasn't the beast the Swede was after. When she was assured that she was the one he wanted, she stopped being able to see anything but his eyes. She got up off the purple ottoman, hooked her elbow in his, and luckily she was wearing high heels that evening or she would have had to tiptoe. His shirt was unbuttoned down to his belly button, his dangling gold chain reaching just a hair above the shirt's V. He romanced her as everyone watched, then took her into the room and seduced her, and did not leave till the morning cock crowed.

The next day the aunties offered her congratulations over orange blossom water, loudly gossiping and laughing but no ululation because celebrating early would certainly put a hex on the budding relationship. Of course they didn't sleep, my mother, exhilarated and exhausted, told her sisters, he paid for the entire night so they could conjoin, not rest. They made love a number of times and they talked when he needed a little time to recover, it was difficult without a common language, but he was interested in hearing her and she wanted to know him. He told her to apply for asylum in Sweden, and she decided to do just that, but first she had him explain what the word meant. In Stockholm, he told her, God wipes the tears off His children's faces. Apparently, He did not do such a thing in Cairo. She told her sisters that she would live with him in Stockholm and she would cry no more. Asylum, she kept repeating the word over and over, asylum, in the salon she sat, on the jacaranda rocker, asylum, asylum, back and forth, she deserved asylum, had there ever been anyone in the history of mankind who was more persecuted than she, no, of course not.

In the upcoming days, she worked on her application. She donned her coat and trudged to the Swedish embassy fifteen streets and two alleys north, she filled out forms and more forms, she saw a picture of Ingrid Thulin in a magazine and pulled her hair back à la Ingrid. She tried and tried but was unable to get an interview, she was told someone from the embassy would get back to her, no one did. She whined and complained but no one could help her, not at the embassy or at the house. She did not give up, though. She told her sisters that as soon as the Swede returned, she would relate all her problems and he would explain to the embassy that she was special and deserved a visa. Her Swede was important enough to demand respect from the minions at the embassy, she was sure of that, he carried himself as if he was.

As it came to pass, our Swede returned to the whorehouse thirteen days after his first visit, walked into the salon
as if he were in a western, with the shuffling gait of a cowboy.
He acknowledged my mother with a nod before joining the
other men for the pre-fuck amusements. She saw salvation,
saw oodles and oodles of snow in her future and a log in a
fireplace and even a dog, a Saint Bernard with a tiny barrel
of cognac hanging from its collar. This time, though, when
the Swede performed the role of a gentleman, he chose someone other than my mother. She watched him walk with the
same intensity toward another auntie, with the same devotion and desire, she saw the look of momentary shock on
her sister's taut and pale face. To this day I remember my
mother's countenance when the choice was made, Doc, and
that of the other auntie, how the chosen and the betrayed
exchanged stealthy glances, and how my mother unclasped
her hair, locks falling on her fragile shoulders. She couldn't
allow herself much time in shock, within minutes she'd re-
gained her infantile charm. My mother retired to her room
with a different man, an Englishman. That was the day when
my mother gave up.

Home

Auntie Badeea would ask me to come home to Cairo at least
once every couple of months, I would be happier, she'd say.
Why did I have to live so far away? What could be worse
than to dwell here, driven out from bliss, condemned in this
abhorred deep to utter woe? But then, what matter where I
was if I was the same? Every which way I fly is Hell, myself

am Hell. Those lines were assigned to me, Satan said, stop plagiarizing, Milton was writing about me, not you.

Blond God

I know you'll hate me for this, but I went astray after you died, really far afield astray, Pluto-far. Demons hover like moths at the closing doors of life, waiting patiently for the bereaved. He was both my death and my salvation, a brief, intense, motherfucking affair, he almost killed me and I would certainly have killed myself had he not come along to save me, this, this, his full name escapes me, this Viking demigod, but I called him Deke because that's how he introduced himself the first time, I'm Deke, he said, short for Dickhead, and I laughed, of course I fell for him. I was Icarus, he was the sun that couldn't even spell Icarus, of course I fell.

I was feeling deathly depressed and lethargic, spiraling downward, eddies of crappy water whirling down the drain, all of you dead, couldn't force myself out of bed, under the covers I remained, you were no longer there to lift my spirit or the duvet with the pink oleander design, which I once found strikingly beautiful but no more. I found so little beautiful, as each one of you became sick, as you died, one by one, I could see nothing but black. Your physical absence was soul-crushing. I needed to return to work, back to my job, buried daily in the law firm's cloister-like cubicles, needed the money, needed a bump, just a little one, ended up at Kawahi's apartment on Sixth Street, which always frightened me enough that I considered quitting everything

and becoming monastic just so I'd never have to revisit that
den of drugs, but of course I didn't, not then. The middle
of Kawahi's living room was overwhelmed by a coffin-sized
safe, I kid you not, Doc, an airtight steel safe whose every
inch of surface was covered with phosphorous graffiti, its
contents a mystery, sawed cadavers probably, but Kawahi
and his cabal used it as a bench, as a coffee table, to cut the
speed down to salable portions. Three troops sat on the safe
while I was there, one looking like a baby-faced Huggy Bear
from *Starsky and Hutch*, the television series, not the movie,
yes, believe it or not, Doc, they made a movie of that as well,
and I wanted to tell him he was almost two decades too late
but I was nervous and no one would have gotten my bad
joke in any case. Deke stood in well-trod orange high tops
next to the only other white boy in the room, tall he was,
towered over his seated friend, his head almost reached
the low ceiling of the basement room, and above him was
a dropped beam on which Kawahi had written in blood or
red lipstick, WATCH YOUR DUMB, but of course at my height
I didn't have to worry about hitting either my head or my
dumb, whatever that meant. Deke's flat, shaggy blond hair
told me he'd skipped his shower that morning and probably
the day before as well. His hands languidly parked in the
pockets of gray mechanic's overalls without a name on his
left breast, which was why I asked him for it when I shook
his hand, and you know that I don't have a strong grip, you
used to enjoy calling me Limp Wrist, but Deke made sure to
squeeze so hard I almost felt my knuckles pop, and I gasped,
and he knew, he knew right then, he looked straight into me
and said, Buy me a baggie, and I did, of course, anything
he wanted me to do I did without question, I did, I did. He

grabbed the bag when I offered it, glanced at his friend sitting on a filthy fauteuil, fake Italian baroque, and smirked
as if saying, See, this is how you do it, get your own boy.
His friend looked puzzled, not comprehending, a smaller
guy, nondescript, lost in the grandness of the fauteuil, which
you'd think would have looked odd in such a room but
not so, everything about the place was bizarre. The filth
seemed arranged, like the graffiti safe, the red lettering,
the idiosyncratic collection of glue guns on a corner table,
an honest-to-goodness halberd leaning against the wall, no
stench at all except for the vestiges of inexpensive jasmine
deodorizer, and I could imagine that Kawahi's name was
probably Lawrence or Philip, and if there were rats they'd be
bejeweled, that pretend downwardly mobile decor was what
frightened me, the inauthenticity of everything, one committed the most heinous of crimes to defend the make-believe.

Deke, on the other hand, was all authentic. So fine,
this blond god, hair wavy when washed, statuesque, skin
the color of peonies in a Fantin-Latour painting, an ideal
tone if you ignored the purple and yellow bruises that appeared once or twice a week out of the blue, blue eyes with
lashes so long. He was all man, so he said, spermed a baby
and everything, once beat his woman when she got out of
line, she left when she got tired of his bullshit. He was no
Sunday night master done up in black leather drag, he was
no expert in the art of pain manipulation with a box of
toys, he was the real thing, low-class grade-A trade, a little
funky, a little nasty man whose every other word was fuck,
fucking motherfucker, shit, or pussy. I liked the word *pussy*
out of his mouth, I was that pussy, that was me, he didn't
fuck me, though, never, that would prove he wasn't a man,

unlike getting his dick sucked, prison pussy, a mouth is just
a mouth, he said, and he never heard of Freud, or Gertrude
Stein even though he was born and raised in Oakland.

When I left Kawahi's room, he came with me, didn't say
anything, didn't talk, just walked out with me, walked like
a sated big cat surveying the savanna. Outside he seemed
surprised that I didn't have a car, disappointed, but he accompanied me to my apartment. I chatted nervously about
this and that, probably even the San Francisco weather, and
he didn't listen or pretend to care. He followed me into our
home, looked around, asked about your room but decided
not to expropriate it because he didn't appreciate ghosts, said
all phantasms and demons hated him. He claimed my room
instead and my sheets and flowery duvet, and he banished
me to yours. I could suck his dick but being in the same bed
with another man disturbed his sleep. We smoked my rocks,
then the ones I bought for him, then we went to work, he to
whichever garage employed him and I to the bowels of the
law firm, where the slogan JUSTICE MAY BE BLIND BUT SHE
SEES IT OUR WAY 90% OF THE TIME was embossed right above
the entrance to the word-processing room. All infernos have
a sign on their gates. When I returned home he was there,
and he relied on me to feed him and take care of him and
bathe him and massage his tired feet and trim his toenails
and procure his happiness. He made me hungry for a little
affection, so grateful for the little I received, you see, he
was so fine, he was the prettiest man I'd ever been with, he
was preening-peacock vain, how could I help myself, I did
everything he asked. He used to take his two fingers and
walk them through the air, let your fingers do the walking
through the Yellow Pages, I bet you remember that, that

was his signal for me to go get more, and I would, cursing him all the way, traveling in heavy rain or in mother-of-pearl light, peregrinations at dusk, I did what he asked, his laws were not to be questioned, just like those of gravity and the IRS, and the rocks had better not be too small or he'd be pissed off.

Upon my return he barely held out his hand, opened it like a corolla, and kept it steady until he got what he wanted. He lay back on my couch, his gaze, the look of a tiger holding its prey, this epitome of masculine languor, he lit the pipe, and I crawled between his legs, pulled down the zipper with a deep sigh, and as each of the teeth separated, I breathed in the mistral and the sirocco, his flesh recoiled at first, then yielded, and I licked my way down, from the golden hairs of his chest to the treasures of his crotch, and then he would lift my head, let me have my turn at the pipe, and I would fly, float with the winds, he knew just how and when to get me up in the diaphanous air, so high.

I quickly had to learn to hold in the smoke while getting hit, because if I inhaled too much, took in more than what he thought I deserved, and it happened every time, every day, he slapped me so hard my brain rocked in its skull. I would crawl and fly, crawl and fly, cry and fly, until I crashed. He never held me, didn't touch me, even though he knew I wanted him to, just a touch, gently run his hand across my back was all I wanted.

If you saw us in the mornings, you'd think we were lovers. I'd make breakfast and we'd share the Sunday paper over coffee. Except for the bruises we looked normal. I wallowed in all the beating and begging and humiliation and sanguinolent whipping, cared about little, danced with Gog, frolicked with Magog. But he was so fine, this maleficent, pretty white boy, my Charon, he had no compassion but why should he be the only one in the world who did? He'd brought me back home. Then one day he too went out and left me, I don't know why, just disappeared. I thought it was love. I searched the city and all her numbered stars, I looked for him in her bottomless pits and her abhorred deeps, over and over, for days and nights, with fading vigor, I peered into the nooks of Hades and did not find my love. I grieved and cried and keened and mourned, wailed for all the lost possibilities. I wept, howled, then left my kennel and went back to work.

The Bouncing Nun

The pills came in threes, the trinity, Father the Haldol light green pill, Mother the mellow blue Stelazine, and Child the small white aspirin, the last because they were afraid I might drop dead of a heart attack. Put out your tongue, said the big black orderly, blacker than me with hair like gnarled wool, and above his head, on the eggshell-white wall, floated a pinkish cloud-shaped stain that locked my gaze, Look at me, the cloud whispered, look at me. The orderly placed the pills on my tongue and they disappeared like the host during Mass, I transmuted the body of my savior, and you whipped him, stoned and flogged him, and on a cross you hung Christ around your white necks.

When I finally met my father in Beirut he took me to church to cleanse my soul of desert sand and Muslim sin, I was baptized at ten, had water and oil mix with my third eye, and then I had to go on my knees, waiting with my mouth

open for the host, for the priest with his dulcet tongue singing
Aramaic to come at me with his wafer. I was so overwhelmed
being in my father's and His Father's presence that I barely
uttered a word, I didn't tell him that I'd arrived in Beirut
from Cairo, not some desert, no sand there, that I grew up
in a house of sin but it certainly wasn't the Muslim kind, the
only religion going on was men worshipping holy pussy. Oh,
but I worshipped my father, and if that meant I had to let the
Word of Christ dwell in my heart or suck Jesus's cross then
of course I would. Muslim, Christian, I would be what you
wanted me to be, I lived to serve, you know I did.

So, Doc, you're thinking you know how this is going
to end, don't you? You're thinking a priest and me and
only one possible conclusion, but you're wrong, you're an
American, limited imagination. That priest and his coterie of
nuns and priestlets took responsibility for my well-being or
lack thereof; dumped in their reeducation camp, that house
of torture of a boarding school, with no one to ask about
me or inquire after my health, I, the boy with the broken
halo, was never sexually abused by that priest, not that one,
but there was a nun, Sœur Marie-Claire, who offered her
benevolent attention, her gift.

During a Christmas holiday right after I had sprouted
a pubic hair or two, I ended up alone in the room, the other
three boys went home for the break, and Sœur Marie-Claire
woke me up every day of those two and a half weeks. Before
the sun rose, my nun played with my erection, she climbed
on the bed, lifted her tunic, and fell on her sword. She was
fully attired, the whole drag except the underwear, I presume,
I don't believe I ever saw anything past the habit. Always
speaking of herself in the third person, she would say, You

make Sœur Marie-Claire feel good and Sœur Marie-Claire
will make her *petit nègre* feel even better. Though technically I
wasn't, she called me her *petit nègre* because I was the darkest
boy at l'orphelinat de la Nativité by quite a margin, and she
was right because at the end I always felt good. I didn't do
much, I just lay there and she would touch me, her hand going
under my pajama bottoms, and I woke up and she straddled
me, smiling and staring at me with eyes so pale they seemed
to be all alabaster, she bounced up and down, jiggled, must
have been jelly 'cause jam don't shake like that, so yes, she
was the aggressor and I was not consenting, let alone an adult.

When I looked into her eyes, which I always did at orgasm
because I wanted to see, she wouldn't be smiling, or I should
say that the smile would have twisted into a strange grimace,
as if she wasn't happy anymore, and more often than not, saliva would drool down the left flank of her chin, not sure why
that was so, and when I was done, she would just stop. No
more bouncing nun. She wiped the drool off her lips and chin,
looked left toward the door, climbed off my softening erection,
adjusted her habit, Don't be late to breakfast, *mon petit nègre*,
she would say, her back to me, leaving me, leaving me in bed,
and after the New Year she didn't approach me ever again, I
guess I wanted her to, I was the refrigerator abandoned on the
pavement, I was the Haldol spreading within my cranium and
I remembered, I remembered so much.

The Caryatids

I have to say your mother was the evil of evils, Doc, ordained in untempered malice in that dark unbottomed

infinite abyss called California. The best thing I can say
about her is that she left me alone to dispose of your body,
which one might think isn't much, but after what Chris's
family did, what with stealing the corpse and forbidding
us to attend his funeral—well, you were there then, you
hadn't yet died, so you know. I wish your mother had sto-
len your body, cremating you cost so much, they charged
me extra because you didn't burn on the first try, and I
couldn't give you a memorial since there were so few left
to mourn you. She left you because she didn't care about
your death, it was your life she desired, and mine, that
queen of vampires, her heart distended with my loss, her
veins swelled with my blood.

She stayed away while you were dying, you kept telling
me she had a delicate constitution, she couldn't deal with you
wasting away. No mother should have to suffer an offspring's
death, no, she shouldn't have to ache, you said, being around
an unhealthy you would have a deleterious effect on her
health. Damn her and her health. I went behind your back
and called her. I had no one else, you were the fifth, Lou,
Chris, Pinto, Greg had died, and Jim was too sick, followed
you within four weeks. I was an exhausted stretcher-bearer,
I needed help and I told her you were dying, she said she'd
warned me many times never to call, followed by the usual
Jesus was going to send me to Hell for corrupting you, for
taking you away from her, as if I weren't there already—just
one cliché after another, that was your mother, you should
be proud. So many times I asked you to stand up for me,
to tell her that I didn't corrupt you, that no one did. You
should have told her you chose me. This thing of darkness
I acknowledge mine.

She knew when your heart stopped, she must have had a spy, I spy with my little eye something that starts with the letter D, yes, he's dead. Your family waited until the morticians zipped you up in the black bag before descending like a pitchy cloud of locusts—no, that's a Yemeni simile, I should use one of yours—like a herd of buffalo, only less attractive. I'd rushed to Jim's as soon as you were out the door and your mother rushed right in. She convinced one of the landladies downstairs to let her in, she was your mother, she was suffering. Your family arrived with a truck, Doc, with a goddamn truck, she'd been waiting for you to die. She cleaned us out. The landlady described the truck as a moderately sized Dodge, which was probably why Her Maleficence couldn't make off with the beds or the sofas.

The poor landlady felt so guilty. She told me she should have known something was not quite right when your mother went into the apartment with three of your relatives and slammed the door on her, she was wearing a cerise Nike tracksuit, the landlady told me, you don't wear that color when your son has just died.

Your mother took the television, she took all the lamps, the craquelure glass coffee table, she took our music, the albums and compact discs, she stole your shoes, my shoes, your shirts, my scarves, I don't know why she did that. So many little trinkets that meant nothing to anyone but us, all the things that we loved and that belonged with us, your family robbed me of them, except for the tiny porcelain fairy with lavender wings that your mother gave you before she knew you were one, she left that. She stole my notes and journals, figure that one out. She tried to steal the kitchen wall clock, but one of your relatives must have dropped it and left it broken on the floor, I still have it hanging even though it hasn't worked since the day you died. Worst, she walked out with my books and the bookshelf, which was what hurt the most. I tried to understand why, couldn't come up with anything other than unadulterated venom, she judged me unworthy, she wished to extirpate me from your life, to punish me.

The mahogany bookshelf, the only thing in the house worth anything, remember that amazing bookshelf with the caryatids, fourteen delicately carved drag queens holding up the seven shelves. Who knew that wood guy had that kind of delicateness in him, what was his name, Max, wasn't it? We made so much fun of him, Max the I'm-not-gay carpenter, and he wanted nothing to do with us, he'd screw Lou only when he was sure he wouldn't meet any friends. Max wanted to be discreet. Lou had to dress in drag or Max wouldn't go anywhere near him, but Lou loved him even though Max returned to his wife and his kids and his shop every single time. Who knew? Not you—you hated Max, what he stood for, you told Lou that Max didn't love him, that Max wanted a fantasy, your deft knife sliced deep. Why did you think that everyone should hear the truth about love? You were so American. And you were so wrong. When Lou found the virus swimming in his system, he told Max the not-gay carpenter, who turned crazy, wanted to jump off the Golden Gate Bridge, but Max found out he had somehow won the lottery like yours truly, no virus was found anywhere within his vicinity. Max couldn't have sex with Lou anymore, refused to see him again, could not risk exposing his wife and kids to the virus, the truth, or something. Lou was devastated and did not recover, he was obviously never the same after that since he was now both dying and abandoned, not an uncommon pairing in our circles, *sola perduta abbandonata*, he never wore drag again, no wig, no lipstick, no leotard.

For two long years, whenever Max had a spare moment, in secret, without a single person knowing, he worked on the masterpiece, hoping to finish it before Lou died. Foot-long caryatids, each unique, bulging thighs on one, chest hair on another, a Cher impersonator, a passable Asian standing on a low stool, one of the most astounding things I had ever seen, and Max had a shipping company drop it at Lou's apartment. Remember? Lou couldn't keep it because looking at it caused him so much pain, we'd take it, we both yelled, we'd put the mahogany masterwork in the bedroom so it wouldn't hurt him. And your mother stole it and the books within it, I don't know whether she unloaded the books first or just flipped the heavy shelf and all four of your relatives carried it out like pallbearers.

She took my notes and journals, stole the kitten wall calendar with holiday dates circled in red. She wasn't looking for a memento, she drove off with your car and sold it when she arrived in Stockton. I didn't mind that so much, it was your car, and I didn't like to drive, still don't. But the books, she didn't even bother transporting them to the horror from whence she came — I abhor Stockton more than you did — she sold them to the used bookstore down the street, knowing full well that I would come across them sooner rather than later. There's a special place in Hell for people like your mother, she's probably there now, circle four, quadrant B. Quadrant C, Thomas Friedman's, is waiting for him completely empty because no human could possibly do enough evil to have to suffer Friedman's company for eternity, but I digress.

Our landlady insisted that I call the police, I didn't wish to, I wanted to barricade my door so your mother couldn't return, and then go to bed, but the landlady wouldn't drop it. Both police detectives were inconsiderate, kept asking me whether I was sure what was yours and what was mine, as if that mattered. When I told them I was your inheritor, they asked me to bring out the notarized will, and what kind of son would not put his own mother in the will? I didn't even merit a good-cop bad-cop routine, all your faggot earned was two horribles in matching polyester beige sport coats. No, they wouldn't call her to investigate, the poor thing, her son had died that morning. All I wanted back was the bookshelf, the policemen wanted me to prove that it belonged to me, did I have a receipt, a bill of sale, I shouldn't expect them to drive all the way to Stockton to find out if she took the bookshelf.

Amazingly, I saw one of these policemen not too long ago in one of the It Gets Better videos, this one put out by the San Francisco Police Department, he was older now of course like me, white-haired, white face, chubby, still in a beige sport coat—I saw him tell his unseen intended audience, the suicidal gay teens, to buck up and tough it out, they might be getting tortured and beaten up but it would get better, and he should know because he was a heterosexual cop who now had gay cops for friends and they were just like him, and he ended his sappy speech with, You can't control the wind but you can adjust the sail. I bestirred myself, stood up from my couch, my bare feet sinking into the dough of the carpet, I screamed at my laptop still in my hands, You can't control the wind but you can break it, you father of lies, and sat back down on the couch, which I bought after your mother cleaned us out even though she didn't take any of the couches. I replaced the old one, the black microfiber three-seater, after Deke Dickhead the blond god left, because it smelled a bit like him.

The first night after you died I moved that black couch to block the door because the car keys your mother purloined contained a house key and changed all the locks the next day. I couldn't sleep that night. You were out of my life and she was in it, I got the worst of that bargain, let me tell you. The first couple of weeks were not much of a struggle, I'm not sure I was able to feel anything. I returned to work because I had to, took care of Jim in the evenings, but I was separate, living in a glass-bottom satellite that orbited my world. I was walking home on a shivery cold evening under a menacing sky when I noticed the dark cover of *The Collected Poems of Eugenio Montale* in the used bookstore's window, and like a mother goose who can tell her chicks from those of others, I knew it was my copy. The owner bought about forty books from your mother, sold about fifteen, and even though he knew they were my books, my name on my hand-designed bookplates was on each, he wanted me to buy them back. My handsome bookplates made the books worth more. I couldn't buy them back, I just couldn't. Before I'd walked a block, Odette, the owner's young lesbian employee, caught up with me, asked for my address and phone number, and told me she'd get back to me. Four days later, she arrived at my apartment carrying twenty-one of my books—she was small like me, a short wraith of an Ecuadoran, those books probably weighed more than she did. I loved Odette, still do, my everlasting friend. She apologized for not bringing them earlier, she had to wait for her paycheck before she stole the books and quit. She hated that quisling of an owner and wanted to do what was right. She slept over that night, for we both needed company. All we had was each other in those days.

All I wanted was the caryatids, to me they were not inanimate, they were so impeccably rendered they burgeoned with life. Next to your sickbed the bookshelf stood, and one evening more than a year before you died, before any of you left me, I sat beside your insensate form, held your feverish hand. I noticed that though each drag queen, each mahoganette, was different, they were all suffused with an ache of weariness. They'd been given this Atlantean task of keeping a world afloat, a burdensome commission that drained life out of them bit by bit, breath by breath. When I looked closer I noted a translucent haze surrounding each drag queen, a cloud not of dust motes as I'd first assumed, but of molecules of vitality, their life force seeping out of their pores back into the universe, no joie de vivre for my babies. I began to speak to them, to encourage them and ease their burden, and slowly but most surely, the mahoganettes responded with equal measures of kindness and godly gratitude. They also began to help me, to comfort me. They even performed the more difficult tasks: changing Lou's diapers, I hated that but not as much as singing him Liza Minnelli songs while he died. I realized then, when three of my mahoganettes sang *Cabaret* a cappella, that they were the Fourteen Holy Helpers.

Remember when we first met, I brought up the Fourteen Holy Helpers, told you one of the nuns taught me how to pray to them, and you said why not just open the box, why would you want to pray to fourteen Hamburger Helpers? I know you don't believe, Doc, but trust me, I know my saints, I knew the Helpers, people prayed to them during a plague and they came to comfort, they corporealed.

First you have the maidens, the virgins, Saint Catherine with the wheel, Saint Barbara with the tower, and Saint Eustace with the stag and the cross and the Jägermeister — no, wait, Eustace wasn't a maiden, let me start again, alphabetically — Saint Agathius if you had a headache, Saint Barbara if you had a fever, Saint Blaise if you had a sore throat, Saint Catherine if you died suddenly, Saint Christopher if you suffered from plague or fear of flying, Saint Cyriac if you had an eye infection or temptation while dying, Saint Denis if you wished to visit a prostitute in Paris, Saint Erasmus for stomach flu, Saint Eustace for family discord although he certainly didn't help me with your mother, Saint George the vet, Saint Giles if you were a cripple, Saint Margaret if you were pregnant, Saint Pantaleon who was always on call, Saint Vitus if you had epilepsy, and basically all of them if you had bubonic plague or AIDS.

As the mahoganettes sprang out of the bookshelf to help, I began to differentiate one from the other. The short passable Asian was obviously Saint Catherine, who always studied hard, she was easy and first to be figured out. I thought the Cher impersonator was Saint Barbara, but no, Cher could never be a virgin, no, she was Saint Cyriac, Saint Barbara was the one with the crazy hair, which was due to static from the lightning bolt that struck her father. Saint Margaret held you in her gentle arms during your last days, she stroked your face, which looked as if it belonged on one of her painted Romanesque icons, your eyes had grown larger and yellow translucent, she kissed your forehead every so often, kind and so loving, generous with her time always. I loved her. I could see her face as she comforted you even though it was covered with seventy diaphanous veils of the most exquisite black silk, each as thin as mist, as insubstantial as a flimsy flame, seventy veils because she had His face, and she lifted her veils every time she kissed you, and her lipstick left a cerise stigma upon your forehead. She told you that in Heaven God wipes the tears off His children's faces. Did you by any chance hear her? With each of her kisses I felt blessed, even though they obviously had no effect on your health, but I know I wouldn't have been able to carry on without their help. Blaise used to brew a wonderful tea for me when I felt blue, a dark oolong with a slight cherry infusion, whenever I lowered myself slowly onto the couch after a rough patch, there was Saint Blaise with a cup billowing heavenly steam. Pantaleon was the joker among them, some might have thought his jokes were staid or puerile but I found them funny. Does anyone tell worse jokes than physicians, Doc? When I cried, when the high tide of the gulf of sorrow hit my shores, all fourteen dropped whatever they were doing and tried to comfort me, Saint Agathius most of all; one would hold my left hand, another my right, one would hug from behind, usually Erasmus, who is very loving but a bit shy, like a fawn who wants you to stroke him but will not approach until you turn your gaze away, and Agathius would get me to breathe in and out, like a coxswain he set a rhythm for me to inhale hope of a new light and exhale bad worries, in out, in out.

A nun at school, Sœur Salwa, taught us how to pray to the Fourteen Holy Helpers and to remember their feast days, which we, the Arab orphans, must do to keep our traditions alive. She taught us knowing full well she would get into trouble for such lessons, for spreading dangerous dogma and heretical liturgy, according to the French mother superior.

Like her saints, Sœur Salwa believed while knowing what became of true believers. Catherine of the Wheel taught the Word of Christ, Barbara did the same, Sœur Salwa would not let those Western Catholic nuns keep the true Word of Christ at bay, she was true knowing the punishment that truth begot. The pope, blinded by the heretics surrounding him and possibly by Satan himself that day in 1969, had removed the feast days of our Eastern saints from the General Roman Calendar, but just because the Western Catholics stopped believing in our saints didn't mean that we had to.

Sœur Salwa was not a Roman Catholic, not like the French nuns, she was a Melchite, she followed the pope's edicts but not when he was wrong. Had the French nuns known that her lessons included more than the Arabic language, its grammar and literature, they would have replaced her in an instant, decapitated her probably. The wan nuns were there to civilize us, and our only purpose in life was to become civilized. That was what I wanted more than anything else in the world. We were allowed to speak our language only in Sœur Salwa's class, and the nuns spoke none of it. They were unable to fathom what went on in our little world. Heresy, apostasy, place the lentils on wet cotton in a saucer for the feast day of Saint Barbara and watch them grow, light two candles on the third day of February and plead to Saint Blaise the Armenian to free us from all throat afflictions for the year. She showed us icons, out of her front pockets climbed contemporary ones carved and painted in nearby villages, and out of picture books jumped glorious relics haloed in gold leaf. In her windowless classroom, encapsulated in darkness, we sat rapt, infatuated, engrossed in stories of our ancestral heroes, George fighting the dragon, Erasmus surviving one execution after another because of the intercession of angels, hiding in Lebanon, not too far from our school, surviving on what black crows brought him to eat, I offer you a walnut here, I a slice of peach, I give you two Siamese twins of the blackest cherry, and Christ himself interceding on behalf of Dr. Pantaleon to thwart the near-fatal executions, those were stories as good as any by Dumas.

Don't you believe the other nuns, Sœur Salwa used to say, we were Christian long before they even had a country. She taught us our history and our language, we were better than them, she told us, but I did not believe her, and when the French mother superior, with her pale face and refined, masculine features, poured limpid tea into a cup and offered me a Petit Écolier biscuit while I was in her offices, whose windows opened unto a sumptuous garden with a large oak, an olive tree, a bitter orange, and a plethora of butterflies, and asked me what kind of foolishness that Arab sister taught in our classes, I told her, just as any other civilized boy would have, which unfortunately meant that I never saw Sœur Salwa again. I lost her and her Fourteen Helpers, lost Saint Margaret, Saint Catherine, Saint Christopher, and Saint Agathius. Diocletian had nothing on me.

Satan's Interviews

Death

"No," Satan said. "I had nothing to do with his mother-in-law."

"I didn't think so," Death said. "That level of evil is way beyond you, she belonged to Jesus all the way."

"Yes," Satan said. "Even I was surprised at such maleficence."

"No snake is as venomous as wounded privilege," Death said. "That little foreign Muslim darkie stole her fair-haired boy."

Death shifted in his seat, sighed; he considered removing his cape but the apartment still felt a little nippy. "What are you hoping to get out of this?" he asked. "Do you think there's a specific thing he needs to remember, some pearl from within a dank oyster which will lead him to an epiphany? Tell me. If it will bring this interview to a quicker end, I will help."

"Nothing like that, I'm afraid," Satan said. "That happens only in Hollywood movies and bestsellers. It isn't how remembering works. He remembers, he doesn't forget much, but he doesn't think about his memories, he chooses not to contemplate what he left behind."

"Well," Death said, "what did you expect? Wasn't short attention span invented in these united states of amnesia? Multitasking? You want contemplation? In San Francisco, that wharf on Lethe itself? You poor sod. You know that when they remember, they come to me to forget. Come with me, a riparian journey, have a sip from the mighty river, a tiny sip, you'll feel better."

"Tell me about Catherine," Satan said.

"Fuck Catherine," Death said.

Catherine

"Are you sure he said that?" she asked, a bit nonplussed.

Catherine, in a raincloud-gray gown, sat straight-backed in the same chair Death had used, looking glorious. No full halo today, just a barely perceptible ring of gold light floating about her lush black hair, unbound in keeping with the fashion of unwed women of her time. Next to her, leaning against the chair, was the broken wheel, and on her lap lay the executioner's sword, its edge dulled after all these years.

Satan did not reply. He too was slightly disconcerted. Catherine induced nervousness in most on most days, and today she had him brew her tea three times before she declared it satisfactory.

"He actually said, 'Fuck Catherine,' right here?"

Satan finally nodded. She seemed to need his assurance.

"And I assume he didn't mean Catherine of Siena?"

"Please," Satan said.

She was in her usual mood: coolly composed, fractious, and unsociable. She sniffed the teacup; its steam had a distinct, prehistoric aroma that caught Satan's nose as well.

"Of course he didn't, the bastard," Catherine said. "Who other than a few ignorant Italians ever thinks of Siena? Now, what I don't understand is why you involved him in this."

"He was always involved. You know that."

"Don't be daft," she said. "You're better than that. I meant this whole remembering project. Death can ruin everything with a single touch. Oblivion is his trade."

Satan grinned, he couldn't help it, which seemed to irritate his interviewee a bit. She glanced down at the sword on her lap, then back at him.

"You have always underestimated him," she said, "just like all parents. You two have been struggling over our boy forever, and you still think you're winning. I don't think you really know how he works."

And Satan said, "Forgetting is as integral to memory as death is to life."

It took barely a second for her eyes to shift expression. Her wheel lifted slightly off the floor and began to turn at an unholy speed. The blade of her sword sharpened before his very eyes. Saint Catherine, the preeminent intellectual, the divine bride. For the first time since her arrival, she showered him with her beatific smile, and he felt blessed, in spite of himself.

He would have loved to ravish her right there on the poet's cheap Persian carpet.

"Forgive me," she said. "It is I who have underestimated you. You two have always worked together, the angel of remembering and the master of Lethe. You can't forget if you don't remember, and you can't remember without forgetting."

"It's a dance," Satan said, "I'm just trying to lead for a change, without Death or Jacob screwing things up."

"His tune is especially popular these days," Catherine said. "Everyone seems to be dancing to the friendly beat of his drums—not many to yours, not here, not now."

"I'm an acquired taste," Satan said.

"Not everyone's cup of tea," she said, taking a sip.

At the Clinic

Genesis

I have been writing fiction, Doc, you would have liked that, wouldn't you, you kept telling me you never cared much for poetry, so few do these days, few wish to listen to a soul's revelations, and I haven't been able to write verse because Satan is a hungry caterpillar that nibbles at my soul and its insipid revelations, though poetry remains my only love, but I told you once and it remains true, I write to keep ink flowing lest it dry, so prose it is for now. Oh my, Satan interjected, are we discussing your literary oeuvre with a dead person now, do all poets do that, they might as well.

The irritated man unbuttoned swaths of clothing and released astonishing torrents of scents that fractured the air. Shock was first to appear in the bespectacled lady's eyes, followed instantaneously by horror, then terror. She looked toward me, her mouth and eyebrows questioning, surely eager to commiserate, and I wanted to tell her to give herself a second or two and she wouldn't smell anything, that it was the human condition to become inured to even the most intense suffering.

My cell phone vibrated with Odette's text saying she didn't believe me, if I were home, why did I ask her to look after Behemoth for three days, I was a big fat liar, and Satan harrumphed, And you call me the father of lies, you say that all my promises are delusions belched from the bowels of Hell, but whose pants are on fire, huh, whose?

The bespectacled lady stared at me, no longer reproving, but she still didn't seem to have adjusted to the miasmic smell. I told her in a conspiratorial whisper that it could be worse, and when she mouthed a questioning How, I said the clinic could be piping in Kenny G. She snorted, swiveled her head to see if the irritated man was paying attention, and then she smiled, which shifted her beautifully expressive face, every wrinkle could have regaled the world with a story.

Ferrigno returned and nodded at the irritated man, who stood up ever so slowly, the bottom of his sweatshirt did not cover his stomach. His aroma dawdled in the air while Ferrigno seemed utterly unfazed. Before exiting the room, the irritated man told his hand, The carpet crawlers heed their callers, and the bespectacled lady and I looked at each other, delighted, and without missing a beat we sang, We've got to get in to get out, extending the last word to six syllables —*aa-ha-aaaa-ha-ha-out*— as Peter Gabriel did in the original.

The bespectacled lady couldn't be too much older than I if she approved of early Genesis. That was the worst smell ever, I almost suffocated, she said, no longer any need for whispering, and she began to rummage through the boat-sized pink handbag on her lap.

I texted Odette, Don't worry about me, I'm going on a three-day rest-and-recreation off-the-grid vacation, should be fun, come in and feed Behemoth and clean his litter box while I'm gone. Your stupidity defies comprehension, Satan said, do you think you'll be resting and recreating in an insane asylum, if you think waterboarding is torture wait till you try art therapy. That was how I got rid of you the last time, I said, not aloud thankfully.

I saw Genesis, I must show you, the bespectacled lady said as she unpursed all kinds of small papers with surprising earnestness: green, blue, brown, white, white, white, white, yellow, hundreds of them. Ferrigno could not have searched her as he did me, probably no one had, I felt sorry for the big guy for having to be in the same room as the irritated man. I wondered what those pieces of paper were but couldn't see clearly. Ticket stubs, Satan told me, and he was right, for a change. Kiss my butt, he said, I'm always right, you just never listen. She took out a small tube brush, she might need it because her hair had decided to distribute itself strangely during the handbag search, she placed the brush on the chair to her right, my left, took out a sizable wallet, snapped it open for a quick perusal, then shut it, placed it above the stubs on the chair to her left, I can't find anything when I need it, she said. I told her I had the same problem, her assiduousness disturbing me.

She took out a cheap click pen, two colors, blue and red, glanced around but could not decide where it should be deposited. Hold this, please, she said, and handed it to me across the separating space. I held it—held it in my trembling hand, I hadn't seen one of those in years, a relic of a time long past, my heart did a five-over-four beat, take five. Satan beamed, The poet gets his pen, he said, is this your doing, Catherine?

The bespectacled lady leafed through the ticket stubs and papers, stopped at one, adjusted her glasses, sighed, shook her head, announced to the room in an obstreperous tone, Here are the stubs, where are the fucking memories?

Jacob's Journals

How I Learned to Read

I saw a man open a book on the bus, the title was Middle Easterny, maybe *Jihad in the Desert* or *Terrorist in Our Midst*, something exciting, because the cover was the color of what we imagine blood to be, a lush vermilion, which is a lush word that rolls off the tongue exotically, verr-mill-yon. The mass-market paperback had endured many readers, a thumbing too many, it was falling apart just like the first book I was given to learn reading and writing back in Cairo. I was too young, my aunties kept insisting, too young to read, quite a few of them including my mother couldn't even write their names, but I wanted to, I wanted to desperately.

There was a girl in the house, maybe four or five years older, I was supposed to call her sister, but she didn't care for me, not that she abused me like the kids later on, she didn't hate me, just did not care and did not wish to engage.

She faced life, and me, silently. I can't remember her uttering a word, and I can't remember her name now, she was the daughter of an auntie from Morocco's southern city of Agadir, I envied her so much. She attended school, left the house six mornings every week, covered her body with a beige dress, the school uniform. I would have loved to wear that beige dress and become a schoolgirl like my not-sister. She returned through the kitchen door in the afternoon — everyone who lived in the house came and went through the kitchen door, the clients used the front — and placed her book bag on the long table. I would be sitting at the table, enraptured. Yes, Doc, that was the inspiration for my Halloween costume that year I wore a headscarf with two pink pigtails sprouting out of it. As thick as those pink pigtails were, they were nowhere near as lush as hers. Her hair was difficult to tame, though less so than mine, and her tails looked like the arms of a flocculent mohair sweater. I wanted them so much, wanted to wrap myself in them. She would sit at the table and begin her homework. Even then I knew that I could not have what I longed for, her hair or her dress, so I longed to read like her.

The chair I sat on was much too high, my feet had no chance of touching the uneven stone floor, and the long dark oak table stood high as well. I was always short. I could not stand on the chair because each stone below was hand-carved, no two alike, filled with grooves and indentations that were older than Cairo itself. The reading book may have been over-thumbed but it was weighty, bulky, and unwieldy, so I could not bring it toward me off the table. Auntie Badeea and my mother had to improvise, fixing a wooden coffee tray as a bridge between the table and my

seat. In essence, I learned to read and write on a highchair.
I have to say, Doc, that floor lives on for me to this day in
the way each of my feet sometimes lands differently on the
curbs of San Francisco, where a tree and its roots raise the
cement. Years ago, when Lou suffered from peripheral neu-
ropathy and his feet would go numb, he would walk slowly,
always looking down at the ground like a pigeon around
bread crumbs, to make sure he didn't stumble and fall. I used
to walk that kitchen floor always looking down at the stones,
at the atlases of countries and their borders, at the geography
of rivers and steppes and great deserts, at the topography
of hills and valleys, the flesh of my soles wrapped around
each round protrusion, sinking into each shallow crevice.
But most of all, I remember that my feet never landed at
the exact same angle or faced the same way, no one's did
on that floor, as if each foot had sprouted wings and could
travel in any direction it wished.

My right hand covered my ear as I learned to read
because that's what one reciter of the Quran did, he placed
his right hand just below the white turban and rocked
back and forth as he sang each sura. I did the same as a
child, and years and years later, in a smoke-filled café in
San Francisco, at my first reading with a dozen or so young
poets, all as awful as I was, your earnest and naive picka-
ninny faggot approached the microphone, and without my
thinking about it, my right hand covered my ear, I rocked
back and forth, and I blasphemously sang my poem. Both
members of the audience thought it was delightful, as did
the other poets, my performance was so exotic and quaint.
But I was not putting on a show, that was how I learned to
read, and to write too.

One day when I was not feeling well—I was a very sickly child as you'd expect—my mother came to sit on the lower left corner of my bed, my left, wishing to have a serious conversation. I was to begin writing to my father, once or twice or thrice a week, I was to send a postcard to him in Beirut. My father would one day finish high school, graduate from college, make something of himself, and he was my father. I was to tell him of my days, what I was learning, what I loved and cared about, to remind him of me, to make him see that I deserved my dreams, that I was worthy.

The Visit

I know you came to visit me, I know. It wasn't just Behemoth's odd behavior, the instant I walked through the door he rushed down the stairs and jumped into my arms from the fifth step, right smack into me, his claws digging into my chest, drawing three dots of blood that bloomed on my work shirt. I carried him upstairs only to find the front hall light off when I was sure I'd left it on, and the light in your room was on, as was the one in the toilet. At first I was confused because why would you want to use the toilet when you're dead and gone, ghosts don't need to pee, but then I knew it was you because who else would turn your room light on, who else but you? Also, you ignored the faux Tiffany Mission lamp on the dresser that you probably didn't recognize, I put it there long after you left. I felt weird, I was supposed to feel violated, someone was in my house, but no, I didn't, it wasn't someone, it was you, and this was always your house too, in fact it was oddly comfortable, you being there was just right. Was there something you had to tell me?

I sat down, terrifically exhausted, couldn't do anything, not even make dinner, so I went to bed, which was something I never did after work, never that early. I turned off the lights, the lamp next to my bed, another faux Tiffany, and so help me, I felt you lie down beside me. You hugged me, you held me. You thought I didn't know, didn't you? I did, I knew it was you. I slept a Rip van Winkle sleep, dreamt of snow on dark waters and lake baptisms, woke up after ten solid hours. I know you're here. You can come out now. While my mind processed the chaos that passes for thought in the early morning, I had cracked five eggs by the time I realized I was about to make you an omelet as well. Decades may have passed and sometimes it feels like only yesterday that we had our breakfast together. I looked at the one remaining unbroken egg on the counter, a deep brown in its gray carton, I couldn't move, couldn't budge, it hit me how alone I'd been, a blow to the solar plexus that almost doubled me over in pain. I'd had a life since you left, I still worked at the same tedious law firm, I made perfunctory friends, on Wednesdays I had lunch with the other four word processors at the firm, I did yoga on Monday and Thursday nights, meditation on Tuesdays, I went to art openings, I hovered in the back of bookshops at poetry readings, I watched bad television shows with soporific gay characters that were supposed to represent me, I was living, I thought I was content, I was told I was happy. I did a marvelous impression of a man not crushed by dread. Once I felt your warm breath on my neck, I was no longer invisible, you saw me, you always saw me. *Me cogitas, ergo sum.*

You can come out now. You're always welcome. This is your house too.

You left an arc of ashes on the floor, why are you still smoking?

Satan and Me

You never believed in God, Doc, did you? You said if God created man in His image, why couldn't man invent a God that was more anthropomorphic, less gratuitously remote, who, like his enemy, Satan, resembled us? But I believed in God, amidst everything that was happening, I believed in His rachitic existence and I prayed to Him. Was that why I was punished, my heart ground in its mortar to coarse powder, as coarse as your ashes, which had remnants of one or two of your teeth, did you know that? You like many before you endowed the Devil with wickedness and perseverance, you made him fun, witty, intelligent, frisky, lively, ironic, and above all, petty, all too human, like us. The hell he suffered seemed a heav'n to you because spending time with God was like after-school detention. But your European Satan wasn't mine, no, not mine, my Satan was Iblis, a lonely one with mischievous, insanely blue eyes, I knew him, you painted yours with exuberant colors, the life of the party, not mine, my Iblis was there when no one else was, he was my homeboy, always with me, and I believed, I believed in God the absent father and Satan sitting in the corner sulking because he loved God more than anything else and when God told Iblis to bow down before Adam, he refused, To no other but You, Iblis said, I have no way to an other-than-you, I am an abject lover.

After you left, and the apartment finally became empty, became all mine, I used to believe that Satan was outside whenever someone knocked on the door, whenever the ringer ding-donged, I did, I thought he wanted to come in, and worse, that he wouldn't want to leave, that it wasn't just a short, friendly visit, he was looking for a place to live or something, so of course I wouldn't open, who would? When all of you died and the world cared not one whit and church bells in their belfries remained mute, the nice psychiatrist changed my antidepressants and prescribed some other pills to scare my voices away, and they left for a while and when I returned home from the hospital all those years ago I was able to answer when someone knocked. You would think that was a good thing, right, but why, why was opening doors a good thing? If a door closes there's less draft.

Someone knocked this morning, probably couldn't bother with looking for the doorbell, four taps on wood, like the opening bars of Beethoven's Fifth, remember how you thought they were Death knocking and I thought you shouldn't have told me because after you did I couldn't hear the symphony without thinking of Death knocking on my door and I couldn't hear knocking without thinking of the Fifth or the porter scene from *Macbeth*—someone knocked, and drained as I was from the outburst and the jeremiad of the evening before at the restaurant, I descended the stairs clad in my white jellabiya and opened the stupid door. Unfortunately, it wasn't Satan, no, God wasn't that merciful—*knock, knock, knock, knock*, who's there in the name of Beelzebub, here was the epitome of a knock-knock joke, Frosted Tips Something Bernhard, whose eyes were as big and wide as a tarsier's, non-nocturnal of course since it was morning already. He looked so scared that my first thought was to hug him and calm him, you know, mother away his fears, and I felt guilty to have been the cause of such obvious pain, I—I was the one who did this to him. He stood there, trembling a bit, as if he were facing an executioner's unsteady sword. I waited for him to speak and it took a moment for him to utter, I'm sorry about last night. He told me I was one of his heroes, at which point I snorted, a harsh fricative that was uncalled for because, you know, who hasn't idolized the wrong person, who hasn't granted superpowers to cripples, and I could see, and feel, Frosted Tips's soul wilt, as if I had sprinkled salt on an unfortunate slug. He assured me it was true in a simpering low voice, and he couldn't look at me directly, his once-darting blue eyes fixed on my funny dress, my eyes on his neon shoelaces, but that was not what he was disturbing me for, he went on, he wanted me to know that I'd misunderstood his intentions and that he might have said all the wrong things as was his wont, but he couldn't sleep last night for thinking that he'd insulted me, which wasn't his wish and he couldn't forgive himself if that was the case. The only thing I thought of saying, and I did, was to ask how he knew where I lived, and for the first time he glanced up at me, his eyebrows arched questioningly. We all know where you live, he said, anyone who has read your poem, you wrote your address in a stanza from *My New Sana'a* and no one could understand why you'd put your zip code and even your apartment number in a poem, and I told him because it rhymed. There was no intent to harm, he insisted, and he wished not only to apologize but to tell me about himself so I could understand him better. I had to bite my tongue, his puppy-eyed earnestness disarmed me.

I realized that as much as I wanted him gone, I was lonely. I wanted to connect, I wanted something. He had read in a poem that I took a walk every day and wondered if he could join me, we could chat, and it was spring so we could enjoy the blooming trees, to which he had a guide, a book of San Francisco street trees, he held it up so the top of the book covered the bottom of his face including his mouth, and there was a tree trunk on the cover, which made his frosted hair look like its treetop. I asked whether we would stay in the neighborhood or go farther because the length of the walk determined what shoes I wore. He said he'd return in twenty to give me a chance to change out of my housedress.

You hated my jellabiya and never wanted me to wear it even though it gave you unfettered access to my ass, but no, you preferred my brown butt constricted in tight jeans and I was in America and should dress accordingly, and long before you turned ill, when you still had the hots for me, you forced me to wear nothing but tighty-whities around the apartment, calling me your callipygian Caliban and spanking me every time I walked by. I miss you, Doc. I should tell you, though, that I wasn't American, we may have thought I was, but it was not so, it never was.

Frosted Tips looked a bit too pleased with himself when I emerged from my cave, he grinned, his hands behind his back, red strap of his man-purse crossing from left shoulder to right hip, a deeper-red felt Borsalino askew atop his head now covering his blond hair. He pointed to our tree, his book claimed it was a laurel tree, he told me. *Laurus nobilis*, I said, we used to call her Daphne, and he asked why that name. He was young and I unforgiving. How could a poet, even a mediocre one, not know Apollo's Daphne? You used to call her the stupid tree, for Daphne was an imbecile of a virgin who turned down the god in all his glory. Frosted Tips asked if I had names for other trees in the neighborhood, leaning back as he spoke. He had the sort of expressive face that would make it difficult for him to hide his machinations, evil or otherwise. I knew he was going to ask me a question a few seconds before he did, what did I think of the political situation in the Middle East and did I believe there would be peace in our lifetime? I wanted to smack him, slap his face with every step we took, left slap, right slap, I didn't, of course, but I must also have an expressive face because he recoiled a bit without my having to do anything. Still, his earnestness was refreshing. I told him I didn't do Middle East conversations, and furthermore, my remaining life was much shorter than his, so he shouldn't be using the term *our lifetime*. He proceeded to floor me by saying under his breath, though loud enough for me to hear, Grumpy much? I began to laugh, which must have given him permission to let loose. I was the grumpiest person he'd ever met, probably the worst in history, was there anything I liked, where was I when happy gay genes were being handed out, sulking in some corner probably. What could I say, he made me laugh. I remembered how we used to be, all of us, all our interactions, whenever one of us was nervous, meeting someone new, for example, or having to say something that made us vulnerable, we went camp. When Chris asked Jim to be his boyfriend, he couldn't say it outright, so Saint Agatha had to come out, I offer you my love and my breasts, darling, if your ass be mine. Remember? Well, Frosted Tips unleashed his inner queen and she was a jungle cat, not tarsier, and fun — anything but nervous. He went on to say that if I hated gay men so much I should create a new political and sexual identity and call it grumpy. I would want a flag, I told him, it would be gray, he said, I'm thinking gray is too much color, we should go with natural burlap. You need a Grumpy Center, he said, where you can show movies you hate, art exhibits you abhor, and books you can make fun of. He asked if my drag name was Mommie Dearest, and I told him it was Curmudgeka, and he screamed a high C of glee. I had to explain that it wasn't exactly my name, that it belonged to Irish Greg, that we used to call him that, but I told him that since you were all dead now, I'd taken on your drag names. I'd never said that out loud before. I inherited everything including your names. Frosted Tips and I were now joined together at the eyes. We walked slowly, even more slowly than my usual pace, he asked me what Cairo was like, he told me he was from Toledo, Ohio, the town that gave the world Jamie Farr, you know, the Lebanese. I knew who that was, even though my television-watching skills were undeveloped, the actor who Americanized the name Jameel Farah in order to get better jobs, which was a good move because celebrity or not, you don't want to live in this country with an Arabic name, you really don't. You get humiliated at airports, insulted at grocery stores, threatened at gas stations, no, you don't want an Arabic name. He interrupted to inform me that Curmudgeka was out of her cage again. We should talk about trees, I said, that's a safe subject. Our conversation was easy, laughter and silence, this tree is a lemon bottlebrush, levity, seriousness, vulnerability, hilarity, and the southern magnolia is quite proud of its posture.

He asked about my poems, I told him I was having problems so I was trying my hand at prose, some short pieces, even a fabulist story about locking my inner child in the basement, some of my writing was just notes, and along the walk I grew close to him. I have to admit that he began to remind me of you, Doc, don't be offended, I mean the way he walked with high confidence, the way he combed his blond hair, which I could see only when he removed his silly Borsalino, the way light took delight in his face so bright, no obtrusive nose to darken it with shadows, white like yours. The next day I received a postcard with a picture of tombstones in the Père Lachaise Cemetery, and in tightly controlled script Frosted Tips thanked me for the walk and called me enchanting and challenging. He sent a second, a picture of Half Dome at Yosemite, and asked how I felt about the latest drone strikes in Yemen because he objected to them, and if I would have another walk with him on Friday, he'd bring his book of arbors.

The second walk was just as charming, we identified no fewer than seventeen trees, he much more active than I, more jittery, running ahead of me every few minutes and then waiting for me to catch up, so much we laughed, so much. When he dropped me back at my door, I suggested that if he was free sometime, we might take in a movie or something. He was smiling when some realization hit him, a look of horror scarred his face, his eyes bulged out far like a snail's, his mouth fell open, I felt my heart drop to the ground leaving a trail of snail slime in its wake. My, what had I done? I didn't mean we should have sex, but it was too late. He had already been bitten by his regrets. A rose, a sprig of jasmine in the glass vase with water, and Caravaggio's boy, bare shoulder exposed, was reaching out toward a sumptuous bunch of red cherries when a lizard bit his finger. Pain and horror and shock registered on his milk-fed face. He was busy the entire week, Frosted Tips said, not sure whether he had any time, his husband was so demanding, rarely allowed him to do anything by himself. He in the prime of his life, bitten by a vile, venomous old queen, a hateful methuselah, a detestable homo, a black lizard. I have been so lonely, Doc, so lonely, hurled headlong flaming from th' ethereal sky.

Jacob's Stories

The Boy in the Basement

Latched, lethargic mind this morning, I could not concentrate on much. Slow thoughts, as if I were counting the seconds between lightning strikes. One, two, three clouds and half a dozen shoots of the bamboo grove reflected themselves in the toaster on my counter. I poured myself a cup of coffee. I was lassitude, inanition incarnate. More clouds, rosy gray, tried to obscure the March sky. The grove outside hid a singing bird, its trilling floated into my home, the original coloratura. As hard as I tried, I could not discern the camouflaged bird through the canes and their lees and plethora of leaves. I wasn't sure whether it was a robin or a song sparrow, a confident triller. A well-paced melody it was, interrupted, disconnected, a bit melancholic.

Sheets of last Sunday's *Times* covered parts of the kitchen table where I had been working. I covered the face of some happy writer with my coffee mug. In my bathrobe and cloud of morning musk, I began to put the finishing touches on the papier-mâché horse, pushing and squeezing distended muscles on the forehead and neck. It may not have been great art but it did look like a horse — a horse with a hind leg that dried a tad shorter than the others. I was pleased with the fact that I chose not to paint it, picking the correct color would have been too cumbersome. Anything but bright pink would disappoint the boy.

The table displayed hardly a scratch, testifying to the miraculous permanence of Formica and sixties plastics. I considered pouring myself another cup of coffee, delaying the weekend ritual, but chose not to. It would be better to get it over with and be done.

Cold drafts wintered in the long, dark corridor leading out of the kitchen; gelid air almost froze my toes. I should have worn socks with my slippers. I should have worn my eyeglasses. With the horse under one arm, I braille-punched the alarm code, the six numbers of my birthday. After which, I needed three tries to fit the key into the lock. Always had to watch my step descending the stairs to the basement, been procrastinating on changing the ceiling bulb for a couple of years. Turned left at the bottom and unlocked the second door. Blinding lights, the boy loved bright.

He turned around from watching the television as soon as I opened the door. "Hello," he sang out.

I smiled in spite of myself. His greeting has had a seraphic effect on me for as long as I can remember, yet it seemed to surprise me each time I entered his domain. I asked him to turn the television down. He was earnestly addicted to an idiotic children's series about a young nanny and her charges. He must have watched each episode about thirty times.

"Is that for me?" he asked, standing on the couch and pointing toward the gift in my arms. He teetered a bit, then steadied himself by leaning one hand on the sofa's back, the berm to the cushion's river. Equilibrium was not his forte, nor was equanimity; most excitable he was. Fashioned by no metronome, his movements were sudden and unpredictable, ever herky-jerky, as if he wore roller skates.

With a sweep of my elbow, I moved aside all the toys on the coffee table, creating space for the horse. Even though it seemed that he could not contain his excitement, he sat down and picked up a doll that fell off, a Girl Scout with a high chignon. His eyes looked at me, then gleefully at the horse, then back at me, but his fingers, operating independently, fixed the doll's hair, an updo, a sweep back, a fingernail tease, a beehive.

"That's a beautiful horse," he said. His eyes gleamed wide and bright. "May I touch it?"

"Yes, of course," I said. "I made it just for you. I know you wanted a unicorn, but I ran out of material."

"I would love a unicorn," he said, placing the doll by his side, and his hands under his behind. "Can we make this into one with more paper?"

"Probably not," I said.

He noticed me looking at his tricolor barrette, quickly dragged it from his hair without unsnapping it, and pocketed it.

"That's okay," he said. "I like horses too." He leaned forward and stroked the horse's back, once, gently, twice, three times. "It's so beautiful. Thank you."

I wanted him to know that I thought of him, little things impress him so. Carefully, as if it were made of gossamer and silk, he lifted the horse off the table and hugged it tight to his bosom.

"It's the best gift ever," he said.

I did not sit down, not wishing to give him the impression that I was staying. At least a dozen Barbies sat on both sides of the television, serried left to right according to outfit color, red to violet.

"Best ever," he said, and kissed the top of the horse's head.

He looked up, showered me with one of his rapturous smiles guaranteed to halt lightning in mid-strike. I felt my testicles twist in their sac.

"Can I come out today?" he asked.

I shook my head.

"I can change," he said, pointing to his short skirt and beaded slippers. "I can wear something better."

"We can't," I said. "I'm going out for brunch." I tried to look away from his eyes, but that always proved difficult. "There will probably be alcohol."

"That's all right," he said, still petting the horse. "Maybe tomorrow. Can you stay for a little while?"

I shook my head. "I need to shower and get dressed."

"Will you come back tomorrow?" he asked.

I looked back only when I reached the door. Still smiling, the boy stood by the sofa, pointed at the little horse beside him, wobbling, trying to find its legs. The horse took a couple of steps, then teetered—always would because of the shorter leg. The boy bent down to steady his new foal friend, who nuzzled him, rubbed against him, and nickered softly, grateful for the early help.

I locked the door, climbed back up the stairs, locked the basement door as well, set the alarm, and returned to bed.

Satan's Interviews

Catherine

"Cairo?" she said. "No, I wasn't there. I don't particularly care for that truculent city, never did: too crowded, too dirty, too new. I'm sure it has some redeeming virtues, but I have yet to discover them. I hail from Alexandria, after all. If you wish to talk about Cairo and the whorehouse, try Agathius, or even Pantaleon, who showed up quite early. I didn't appear till Beirut."

Catherine noticed Behemoth coming into the room. She extended her hand, hoping the cat would approach, but Behemoth hissed as if face-to-face with a mortal enemy.

"It is the sword," Catherine said, "which frightens some animals."

Behemoth sauntered over to Satan and jumped onto his lap. His sharp claws dug into Satan's thighs as he kneaded before lying down. Satan winced but did not interrupt, even as a small dot of blood stained his white linen pants.

"I'm sure it's the sword," he said. "Now, why did I think you were the first?"

"I was the first to appear to Jacob, not the first in his life," she said. "In later years, Jacob would revise his stories, remembering a certain light during a thunderstorm, erroneously thinking it must have been Saint Elmo's fire. So of course he thought Erasmus appeared to him, but he didn't know who that was as a child. Erasmus may have been there in Cairo. I don't know. The boy was so sickly then, he was seen by many doctors, even an Italian living in Cairo at the time. So he may have misremembered seeing Pantaleon, who was indeed in the Egyptian capital with the boy, but it was by no means for healing. He loved to watch fools fornicating. It's one of his many vices, charming as they may be. No, the healing was left to Agathius. He arrived because the boy grew up with intermittent migraines, and when you prayed while in the excruciating grip of one, Agathius was there. He watched over the boy in his early years probably more than any of us. It should have been Denis because of the boy's latent sexual proclivities, but Denis dealt mostly with ordinary headaches, hence his nickname, Saint Aspirin. Agathius should be called Saint Triptan. He has always been the kindest of us in any case."

She lifted the teacup off its saucer, held it with her pinky pointing out. As she bent her head to take a sip of the still-steaming tea, the circle of gold intensified momentarily before settling back into a mild buzz.

"Do you believe the migraines could have been psychosomatic," Satan asked, "or were they genuine?"

"Genuine, of course. He was in pain, that much was certain. Did he receive the attention he so desperately craved because of the migraines? Of that there could be no doubt. Even though Badeea was his primary caretaker, his mother looked in on him when he was suffering, and for that I can tell you he would have endured any pain. We all knew that. Even Agathius mentioned a number of times that whenever his mother entered the room, or simply acknowledged him while passing in the dimly lit hallway, the boy's heart released its anchor no matter the suffering. But I doubt he ever induced a migraine to get attention. With the nuns, every time he had one, he ended up sleeping alone in the infirmary, which had a much better mattress than the one in his room. No one disturbed him, he was left alone with his thoughts. He treasured those times and their priceless solitude. And then, you know, the migraines brought us to the fore, not just Agathius. In that tenebrous infirmary, when darksome night through the window blued his world, I introduced him to the rest of us. I told him, and I can't recall the exact words now—I told him it was time to meet his salvation."

"And then the migraines stopped," Satan said.

He petted Behemoth, who purred in his sleep, his fur emitting tiny sparkles of static each time Satan's hand passed through.

"That they did, for a while. Denis would tell you that he cured him, his aspirin better than any of the triptans, and you know, he is right in some ways, but it was by no means his healing that did so. For generations, sufferers prayed to Denis for help with their headaches, but I never understood the logic. Having one's head chopped off does not make one a head healer. A number of our order were beheaded—Barbara was by her father, but no one assumes she can manage headaches. Now, Agathius has a talent for it. During the plague, the entire population prayed and begged for help. Agathius did all the work and Denis's reputation grew. How these things work remains obscure to me. People were never my forte. Denis ended up helping the boy accidentally when he led him down that deliciously aberrant path."

"Getting whipped cures migraines?" Satan said. "Whoever markets that will become a zillionaire."

"Don't be obtuse," Catherine said. "It is unbecoming. Who knows how these mechanisms operate? All we know is that as soon as the boy understood his needs, the moment ecstasy revealed herself, pain vanished. I do not know why. However, it seems that migraines, like desires, are recrudescent. Once Death purloined the souls of his friends and he decided to be a proper citizen of this scurvy world, the migraines returned, maybe not as frequently, but he still suffered."

"Could it be that migraines are caused by boredom?" Satan asked.

"Once the boy gave us up, he confined himself to a life of inanition."

Agathius

"Well, I for one loved Cairo," Agathius said, running his fingers through his palm leaf, which still appeared as if it had been broken off a tree only a few moments earlier. "Still do."

He had a large head with more scalp than hair. The centurion's chest guard reflected the golden light of his halo, and its ringlet engravings looked like fish scales. Agathius looked like a giant goldfish—a five-foot-three goldfish, he was a short Greek, after all. Worse, with the layered steel shoulder protectors, he could have easily walked on for a part in a number of television shows from the eighties.

"Why would you show up for the boy?" Satan asked. "He was a Muslim at the time."

"He asked for help," Agathius said.

"But you hate Muslims," Satan said.

"I do?"

When he was confused, Agathius's eyes grew large and more transparent, making him look like his painted icons.

"You were the patron saint of the Greeks and Slovenes fighting against the Ottoman Empire," Satan said.

"Yes, I was," Agathius said. "The Greeks called on me, as did the Slovenes, and even the Croats."

"The Ottomans were Muslim," Satan said.

"They were?"

"I'm getting a headache," Satan said.

"I can help with that."

At the Clinic

Morpheus

It was darkening outside and inside had not adjusted, the hour of the lamps, the ceiling lights felt dim and antiquated, the bespectacled lady's skin was turning a shade of citrine, the cream wastebasket in the corner a vitamin-enriched urine yellow, my dark skin unaffected. The bespectacled lady had given up the search, with quite a bit more care she returned all the stubs and knickknacks to the handbag. Concentrating and earnest, her mouth seemed weighted at the corners. I was about to give her pen back, but Satan chided me for being stupid, Such a silly boy you are, he said, so ungrateful, and I slid it into my jeans pocket, my hand remained there, caressing it, and I began to click the red, counterclockwise from the clip, then the clockwise blue, red, click, blue, but she did not seem to notice, didn't remember that I had her pen. Hopeless you are, Satan said, and I told him he was using Yoda grammar, I'm poetic, he replied.

The bespectacled lady told me she saw Genesis at a concert in 1974, or around that time, she couldn't recall the exact year, she said, I am too old in memory.

Ask her to repeat that in Yoda grammar, Satan said. Well, she wasn't going to remember a silly click pen, I told him, and I hadn't seen one in ages, but I felt guilty about keeping it, not that I haven't swiped pens before, but never had I taken one from someone so helpless. She won't even remember she ever had a pen, Satan said, treasure it, you ungrateful buffoon, write. Here's what I'll do, I told Satan, I will spin the pen in my pocket and then click one of the buttons, if it turns out to be the blue one, I return it, red button and I keep it. Hey Catherine, Satan yelled at the ceiling, see what I have to deal with here, he's going Matrix Morpheus on me.

I didn't have the chance to do anything, *thud, thud*, went the sound of heavy footsteps on the linoleum, and Ferrigno came for me.

Jacob's Journals

Caterwauling

I was sad, Doc, reading about another drone strike in Yemen, once more in Hadramawt, not too far from the provincial capital Al Mukalla, a city that consisted of two broken-down houses and three jackasses when I was a young boy. Three men were traveling in a truck when a missile hijacked them to their maker. Suspected al-Qaeda militants, terrorists, al-Qaeda, terrorists, terrorists, Yemenis were always that, four men and a boy in a truck full of concrete blocks on their way to build a house, dead terrorists, a party of seventeen, two men, ten women, four children, and a young bride trying to get to a wedding, al-Qaeda, al-Qaeda, al-Qaeda. My head hurt, and I shut my eyes, hoping to keep the world at bay, hoping to avoid a headache.

I hadn't been able to find my reading glasses for two days, I had a number of inexpensive ones strewn around my apartment but I kept my favorite pair next to my bed, and they had magically disappeared, I'd looked for them everywhere. Your mother has been dead for a while, Doc, so maybe it's her ghost, ha-ha, tell her to stop it. I must have dozed off, because I opened my eyes upon hearing an ambulance siren caterwauling one or two streets away, and came face-to-face with a big-ass raccoon whose eyes were darker than night itself. The size of a pit bull terrier, he was climbing the fire escape, only the cold, divisive glass separated us. I screamed, Behemoth jumped off my lap, I held my breath, but the raccoon did nothing, kept staring at me through the window, admonishing me for being such a scaredy-cat, such a frightened soul. I was insulted. I banged on the window, and the raccoon, deciding that I was too powerful an enemy, gingerly descended the flimsy ladder. Yes, I was the king of my realm, I was unable to do anything about drones, but I crushed raccoons, I stomped, I triumphed; I, Saint George, would defeat the dragon. I should have scared it more because I began to worry that if it could climb the fire escape ladder, it would be able to come into my apartment through the deck, whose door I leave open for Behemoth. Lo and behold, half an hour later while reading in bed wearing a pair of the cheap glasses, I looked up and saw the same big-ass raccoon walking down my hallway. This time when I shouted, the monster did not look as blasé, there was nothing but blackness where its eyes would be. I jumped out of bed naked, followed it as it rushed onto the deck and descended the ladder, not so lackadaisically this time. I banged on the metal fire escape trying to frighten it, but the raccoon slowed down upon reaching the ground, knowing there was little danger left, it sauntered off into the neighbor's boxwood hedge. The raccoon had eaten all of Behemoth's dry food on the kitchen floor.

In another kitchen on the other side of the world, fifty years ago in Cairo, I encountered a little monster who ate whatever scraps of food he could get his paws on. The mouse was no intruder, though, he lived in the walls of the kitchen. I assume there were others, but only one, my Shemshem, made his appearance while people were around. Shemshem, a brown mouse no bigger than a child's finger, would poke his little pink nose out of any number of cracks in the wall every time I sat down at the long table for dinner, his head swiveling one way, then the other, testing the terrain with experienced eyes. He watched me knowingly, because I always dropped food, the first few times accidentally, but after watching the little bugger scamper across the uneven floor and stuff his pygmy cheeks before rushing back to safety, I began to do it intentionally. Absolute appetite he was, and I loved his boldness, the way he scurried, his stride quick and jerky, yet also supple. I stalked him for a while, tried to catch him, tried to make him mine, was never able to. He was training me. Auntie Badeea suggested that I should think this out, a man without a plan, she said, is like a gun without gunpowder, lay some crumbs for him, but don't frighten him. I sat before one of the small holes in the wall, my legs spread, the soles of my bare feet on either side of the hole, and crumbled some white goat cheese between my thighs. Shemshem exited his home, trusted me enough to go for a piece of cheese, but as soon as I moved to trap him, he darted back to his safe hovel. Patience, Auntie Badeea said, patience extracts sweet out of a lemon, so I waited and waited, Shemshem would come out to eat his cheese, and I didn't move or breathe, and I allowed him to return home when done. We did this a number of times, at least once a day, and it was only much later that I realized I had not caught him nor did I want to anymore. I felt Shemshem understood my loneliness. He sat on his haunches and I on mine, he ate and I watched, his eyes conversed with mine, friend to friend.

One day, Shemshem stopped appearing, and even at such a young age, I did not need anyone to tell me that he had died, Death is no stranger to an Arab. It is one of the reasons a Yemeni wears a janbiya on his side at all times, Death should always accompany a man, my mother told me, the knife its symbol. Shemshem might have been tiny but his disappearance weighted my heart, crushing heft, devastating gloom, I sat on the floor gazing at the holes, hoping to change what I knew I could not. Trying to help, my mother, fully dressed and made up, ready for a night of labor, knelt next to me, stroked my cheek with her perfumed thumb, told me, Don't become attached to animals, my dearest young one, for they all die, and the hurt never goes away, the pain returns over and over, again and again, and eats at your heart until what you have left cannot hold even a grain of love. I wish I'd known how to listen, Doc.

My next attachment was to a goat, a kid really, all white with blue eyes, I was bigger than he was, if barely. He belonged to one of the neighbors, who had a pen that faced our house, six or seven goats and a donkey that brayed at night, whose tail never ever stopped sweeping side to side, all of them wore brass bells around their necks to warn the neighborhood children of their movement. The children teased and mocked the animals when they were in the pen but left them alone if they were out, the animals seemed mostly serene, and the adult neighbors tolerated the goats because they quickly dispensed with any weed that dared make an appearance in the narrow alley between houses. As long as I did not wander into the maze of streets at each end of ours, I was given freedom to roam the alley at the back of the whorehouse. A vast world, full of wonders and children and a baby goat.

He was an awkward kid, could not walk straight, which was not completely his fault since both sides of the alley angled down toward a middle aqueduct no wider than a hand that was supposed to direct rainwater away from the houses but was rarely effective if what dropped from the sky was more than drizzle. I called him Afkah, and I loved him. He was funny-looking, with curvy, droopy ears so long I could wrap them around his head. Unlike the other children, I did not tease him when he was penned, but since I was smaller than all of them, Afkah came after me at first, wanting to regain some dignity after being mocked for so long. He had only short nubs for horns and he ran at me and I turned to get away and he headed my butt, a head butt, ha-ha, and I fell down, the yellowish dust talcuming my short pants. Afkah was allowed out of his minuscule pen only during the day, at times with one or two billy goats, mostly by himself.

One afternoon, around three o'clock or so, he and I were alone in the alley, a rare occurrence, and the unthinkable happened, two city dogs, growling, hunger-driven, seeking new haunts, marched down from the east entrance, they risked appearing in daylight for the chance of catching unwary prey. Afkah was too paralyzed to run away, as was I, he started crying out like a child, and I did as well, we sounded like twins as we sidled closer to each other. Afkah shook so much the brass bell around his neck jingled. Auntie Badeea came out of the kitchen, yelling and cursing, brandishing a long wooden spoon, the dogs ran away. Afkah cried like me, and then when his owner carried him away in his muscular arms to be slaughtered, Afkah wailed like a baby and I wailed back, I remember the man's broad shoulders, his dark jacket over his jellabiya, Afkah's tiny legs dangling from both sides of the man's waist, Afkah's head, drooping and frightened and howling. I remember Auntie Badeea holding me, I in front of her, cocooned in her red paisley jellabiya, nestled between her thighs, her hand on my chest as I sobbed.

I don't know what possessed the owner to send me a dish with a small piece of roasted Afkah over rice, maybe he thought I would find it so delicious that I'd understand the need to eat friends, maybe he was asking for forgiveness, maybe he was inherently evil, I don't know, but I refused to eat, of course, have not eaten any kind of meat since, ever, no goat, no lamb, no cow, no turkey.

The howl, Doc, not the silence of the lambs, the howl stays with me, I hear it, I scream, I raise my arms to the sky, I try, Doc, I try to defend myself, to protect my soul. Auntie Badeea used to say that jackals have howled at the innocent moon for aeons because they mourn the fact that they are not eternal, that when Death with his pale eyes comes for them they will be no more, unlike us who climb up Jacob's ladder to Heaven in God's embrace or fall to Satan's fiery Hell. I don't think so, Doc, I disagree. Jackals howl because we don't. The howl has been traveling for thousands of years, from the beginning of time, when Adam and Eve tasted the fruit and Satan triumphed and his son, Death, was born, when loss became our intimate, across deserts and seas the howl moves, loaded with dust and grime and brine, searching for souls to remind them to grieve, but we pay little attention, always avoiding, always moving forward, our souls filled with termite holes that the howl passes through, only whistling. Lost we are, so the jackals and coyotes, the wolves red and gray, howl for us, howl at the baby-faced moon.

When I was ten and my mother wanted to send me to my father, she gave me what turns a boy into a man, the object of every Yemeni's desire, a janbiya. Even though I did not mind attaching a curved knife to my belt, I could not fathom that a rhinoceros had been killed for its horn to make a handle, and Auntie Badeea and my mother kept assuring me that no one in the house could afford a rhino-horn hilt, that my janbiya was nothing but good old plastic, tastefully finished and well polished and trim and right for my slight hand, yet I howled. I shamed my mother and aunties. I'm good at that, Doc, I was just not good at being a man.

And Doc, when the raccoon ran away and I went to the kitchen to drink a glass of orange juice because the fear had left a sour coppery taste in my mouth, I found my preferred eyeglasses in the fridge. I have to ask you, Doc, did you put them there?

Bloom

Our world was young, verdant, and dewy-eyed, but it was already a prison. We were hothouse flowers, we bloomed and perished, wild, exuberantly colorful, attention-grabbing, out of season, out of place, out of context. Well, you were. I made it through, did not perish. Greetings me, O favored one, the Lord is with me, hail me, chosen one, blessed am I before all other faggots. I was left alive so I could be lonely. Who would have thought that I, the foreigner among you, the most frail, would be the one who survived? Not you, Doc, that's for sure. You thought I would die long before you, and I should have. In you I shall die, you once said, and all the time you used to tell me to go to hell, maybe you were right on both counts. Go to hell was your favorite curse.

Remember Mandeep, I'm sure you do, the Indian boy you salivated over, the one who was so flustered when you made your bad joke about being the man to go deep in him that he stuttered for a few minutes like a stuck gramophone, the one who wanted me. At one of Greg's infamous bacchanalia, you kept staring seductively at Mandeep and he paid you no mind, yet he followed me onto the deck, handed me a joint, and once we looked at each other, he saw in an instant what you never could, he knew he could not offer what I needed that night or any night, he said he hoped I would find what I was looking for, but then you came along and put your arms around me possessively for the first time in so long. If he wanted me, you would get him. You liked us short and dark, didn't you? I took you aside, told you I did not want to do it, you stood hunched and baleful, you said it was our chance to recapture what magic we had in the beginning, only in the beginning, that if I did not bring him to your room I might as well go to hell. Magic? You were naked, I was naked, Mandeep was naked, three on your queen bed with its luscious linens, but instead of the sizzle and sparkle of James Brown funk, we were dull New Age music.

I excused myself for a minute, left your room for mine, got dressed, then left my room for hell. Come on get happy, get ready for the Judgment Day, shout O Mohammad, we're going to the Promised Land. It was ten on a cold night, I was shivering and sweating, the fog draped itself over the city and its lights like a luminous shroud, dampened noise, all things became unmoving, unchanging, uncaring. Denuded of time, the fog made the numened gray city eternal, like Death. I walked looking for him, the man who knew what I needed, I walked to the place where I was most likely to find him, paid my four dollars, signed my name as Judy Garland, and descended into the obscurity of that opprobrious den. Darkness outside, more inside, and the smells of bodies that needed a shower, of damp clothing, most of all the foul, intoxicating aroma of male secretions. Where was he? Through lightless tunnels I searched, into black rooms I peeked, dark labyrinths, dark was our world. Heard the unmistakable sounds of assignations but he was not there, a smack echoed in a chamber, a crack. An exit sign in dim red illumined but was the more dark, darkness visible, served only to shape sights of lust, to outline immortal desire.

There, in a room of more shadows, leaning a left shoulder on the wall, I found him, covered in black leather, fitted jacket zipped all the way, collar up, gloves, tight pants and studded codpiece, high boots, skull mask, only the white of his eyes showing, wore his niqab as naturally as my mother did back in Yemen. Come here, boy, he said, show me your ass, I turned around, dropped my pants, bent over, hoping to pass inspection, I felt the leathered hand touch, grope, maul my ass. He ordered me to look at the wall across from us, really look, but I could not see much at first, it was dark and my glasses were too weak, but slowly, as my squinting eyes adjusted, the penumbra shrank, and the tools of his trade emerged, the instruments of my pain took shape one by one, his pleasure, my hunger, my unrelenting erection. No doubt he could offer what I needed that night, he was he. The hunt was over, the prey had trapped the predator.

Fourteen lashes is what we start with, he said, nothing less, then you can leave if you want to, but if you don't then you get shackled and twenty-one more, and when you've had enough, another seven, and then we rest, maybe, but I don't think you have what it takes to become a good boy, I should kick you out of the room now and save myself the trouble. Every word reverberated in my mind, every word recalled another.

A coiled rope on the wall recalled the one used as a belt by the ascetic Sœur Emmanuelle who taught us French history back at l'orphelinat de la Nativité, she was ancient and smelled of decay when I arrived at the school and died the second year I was there, but I remember the rope as it dangled from her habit, and the never-too-clean wimple around her cracking face, ascetics always needed a good hot shower. Can I, no, may I smoke a joint, sir, I asked. Most leather masters are grammarians, Doc, or grammar fanatics at least, I kid you not, language Nazis, that's what they are, they can't abide slack usage. Above the rope, the veins of a cat-o'-nine-tails, riverine with its black tributaries. He shut the door gently before I felt the sting of the riding crop, only the tip, once, a quick twice. I barely flinched. He suggested that the boy must like it, but those taps didn't count as they

were only a warm-up, I should take off my clothes and lie
butt up on the sheetless mattress where other dogs had
lain with lice and ticks and fleas and parasites. I, worthless
mongrel, was to count lashes, sets of seven, to ask for them,
and to thank him for each. Would that he begin with the
riding crop, he paced around the bed, watching and being
watched by his pitiable pet, but blindness quickly descended
upon my eyes, a blindfold, and the age-old ritual began, a
rush of blood in my veins, the scratch of a match, the smell
of tobacco embers and their smoke, a deep inhalation, and
the lush excitement of anticipation.

And *thwack*, the blistering pain of inextinguishable fire
shot through my entire body, my mind flooded, it was no
riding crop, One, thank you, sir. I was to ask for the next
one, his voice both mellifluous and malevolent, I could hear
his boot-stomping pacing. Two, sir, *thwack*, it felt like the
paddle, I was sure it was the paddle, Thank you, sir. You
guys should have called me Pinto, he might have been the
most ardent bottom among us, but I was the one who exploded every time my ass was banged, boom goes the Pinto
into a cluster of fire, staphyloflames. Three, sir, and my body
became a separate entity, it reached back to the paddle, it
was both mine and not, I was my body and not, touch me, I
kept wondering whether you were in the process of fucking
Mandeep, Thank you, sir, four, I saw the Indian boy beneath
you, in pain and pleasure, discomfited and discontent, but he
was already there, why shouldn't he go through with it, five
was the harshest yet, I almost howled, Thank you, sir, six,
please, I was the lowest of the low, I was in heaven. Seven,
my clammy hands tried to clutch the nonexistent sheet, my
nails dragged on the skin of the mattress, until Saint Denis

came down from Montmartre, the highest hill of the city of light, to hold my hand, which stopped twitching upon his touch. Even behind the well-worn blindfold, I knew it was he, since he carried his haloed head in his other hand, nestled in the crook of his elbow, and the halo's light could always penetrate any blindness, Come, my boy, he said, let the pain become your ecstasy, and it was so. Denis, like me, was a cephalophore, a head-carrier, the only one of the fourteen, which of course he would be because his name comes from Dionysus, when Denis's head was forcibly detached from his body, he became the patron saint of the city of Paris and his boulevard was where all the working girls and boys plied their trade, made so much sense, the head and body separate but equal. One, ouch, thank you, sir.

I returned to the dungeon over and over, I kept coming back, could not stay away even had I wanted to, I felt guilty being there while you were at home, Doc, and Saint Denis was understanding, offering comfort by reminding me that Saint Margaret was taking care of you and Curmudgeka Greg was there as well and even though you had a low-grade fever, you were not so much sick as cranky, and you would recover many more times before you died nine months later, but still the look your droopy eyes gave me when I left, with the thermometer erect in your mouth, were you the drama queen or what, covering yourself up to your unshaved chin with two fleecy wool blankets, Where are you going, you mumbled, with the red top of the thermometer moving up and down and sideways, and I said that I needed a break, and Greg told you not to worry because he was there and he was a sober Irishman for the night, but you told him that he was sicker than you were, and he replied, Not tonight, I'm not.

Ready for more, faggot boy, the master said, you're too dark for me to admire my handiwork, I should bleach your ass next time. Only when he stopped, between sets, did I begin to doubt a bit, like during the break after odd games in tennis, I had time to wonder whether I should be in this match, but it was fleeting, the need overcame all, hit me. Call it, God the demon demanded. One, please, and the riding crop was so painful, filled with utter woe, I rose on my knees, howled across time, even Saint Denis flinched. Please what, asshole? Please, sir. He pushed me back onto the mattress, wetter because of my sweat, my chest squished against it, my belly slid. I concentrated on him, his voice, his movements, his touch. Uh-oh, the head of Saint Denis said. I felt rope tighten around my wrists, then my ankles, criss-crossing across my back and legs. I felt free, Doc, free, you never understood that, probably still don't, you privileged jerk. I could see myself in the mirror, helpless, my body sub-jugated, tense with anticipation, I could see his reflection in the mirror, only his front, his earnest steel-blue eyes tracing my body up and down admiring his handiwork, slapping a paddle against his gloved hand. You don't get to count anymore, he said, sneering and smirking, and the blindfold returned me to my natural state of blindness. Much better, said Saint Denis. You will feel my wrath, the white man said, you dare not sit still when I whip you, sand nigger, and my mind detonated.

Sand nigger wherever I went, my mother's ancient blood coursed in my veins, sand nigger because I was an Arab, nigger because I was black, nigger because I was queer, nigger because I was an exile, nigger because my dick got hard when you whipped me.

The man assaulted me with switches, the whistle and swish of each before immeasurable shooting pain, fast and furious, I struggled against the rope and he laughed and Saint Denis berated me for not being able to handle a good whupping. Poor Cyriac had his limbs torn out of their sockets, Saint Denis said, and was clubbed to submission and then beheaded because he refused to give up on our Savior, who was I to complain about a bit of flogging. And of course, as expected, though I seemed always to forget right before the revelation, as the agony peaked, ecstasy descended unto me like an annunciation, I drooled all over my face, rubbed my face on the soggy mattress, growls in my stomach, howls in my throat, my entire being shook, Praise be, said Saint Denis, Good boy, said the man. All flesh was born to suffer, Sœur Emmanuelle used to say before she died, in French, of course. My Father hath chastised you with whips, but I will chastise you with scorpions. A beast with stinging claws slammed into my ass, the fire stoked once more, each swing of the cat with studs was a blacksmith's bellows before the ever-ascending flames, tears mixed with snot mixed with drool mixed with sweat, I turned human. You earned back the right to thank me, the man said, hitting me with the delicious cane, Thank you, sir, I thought he must be swinging it with both hands, Thank you, sir, I screamed, and I felt real. There was hope for me, he said as he untied my bonds, I hear bells, Saint Denis said, divine joy in his voice, beatification, here we come. One more set, he said, and don't you dare move. Praise be. You're going to remember this one, boy, when you're alone at night, you'll pull out your little penis and jerk off thinking about me. I heard the whorl of a whip behind me, this one had metal of some sort, probably another cat, but I waited and waited, and it arrived and arrived. You know, Doc, Verlaine always felt religious after orgasm, but why wait is what I say.

All fourteen helpers had to come help for the final round, they held me down as my body shivered and jerked, they cooed soft nothings in my ears to keep me in this world, infinite synapses fired orgasmic transmitters, electric currents coursed at will. First dibs on his hagiography, yelled Saint Catherine, this one is mine.

The master stopped, I heard his boots walking, then the snap of his codpiece, the unmistakable slapping sound of masturbation, then he sprayed his semen all over me. I lay vanquished, in triumphant glory. He told me I could move now if I wished, but I could not, I did not wish to, I did not know how to, and he took off his glove, poured alcohol into his hand, the liquid soothed me briefly but then it smarted, its smell reminding me of younger days when Auntie Badeea cleaned my scraped knee and bandaged it. You were a good boy, he said, massaging some aloe soothing salve into my burning skin, a very good boy. The fourteen could do nothing but chorus. Glory, glory. He lay next to me, hugged me, his bare fingers wiped the slick wetness off my brow. He asked if I wished him to remove the blindfold.

I kept thinking about you lying on your queen bed, under double blankets in your lovely room, in our clean, well-lighted place, so now I can ask you what I could not then, did you love me, or did you love a lesser version of me?

Satan's Interviews

Death

"Have you considered, Father, that maybe you're the one who needs to forget?" Death asked, his tone dulcet, his voice mellifluous. "I understand your work, I do. I'm not suggesting a change in vocation or attitude, only that you're looking a bit haggard today." With an open palm, Death arced his arm, a gesture meant to include his father's white suit. "You should send this to a good French cleaner, recapture its creases. Maybe you need to disremember this poet, or poets in general. Poets should be forgotten, if you ask me. Stick to activists and Noam Chomsky."

Satan grinned. Behemoth woke from his nap on the small rug under Satan's feet and meowed questioningly. Satan held out his arms and the cat jumped into them. Both purred.

"Oh my," Death said. "You look more lively already. Maybe you need to remember your cats more often. Blofeld can't hold a candle to you."

"Well, I do have more hair." On cue, Behemoth pawed Satan's red bangs, licked the Devil's cheek. "And Behemoth here is more delightful than any Bond cat." Satan cradled Behemoth in his left arm, scratched the vulnerable belly. "Do you really think I should abandon Jacob?"

"Abandon?" Death said. "That's an interesting choice of words. He's trying to abandon us, specifically you, to extirpate you from his consciousness. That's the one thing we're certain of."

"It's just a phase," Satan said.

Death and Satan looked at each other; conspiring smiles turned to chortles, then laughter.

"Jacob is tired," Death said. "Maybe he wishes to rest."

"Poppycock," Satan said. "He's been resting so long he's almost a full-fledged Yemeni."

"The heart weary of its grief desires forgetfulness, Father," Death said, playing with a ring on his bony finger, rotating the inlaid, split-flint jewel around and around and around. "You don't seem to have much compassion for my work. A fatigued heart will always call my name, will always long for my cup."

"He has been partaking from your chalice for so long it has glued itself to his lips," Satan said.

"He's a special case. Death of an intimate is akin to slipping a coat over the one you're wearing, and another, and another, a heavy load. Jacob wears many coats."

"The sartorial metaphor is lovely," Satan said, "but those coats have become ratty and rancid. Let's get him to shrug them off. It's time."

"Why now?" Death said. "Why did you come back after all these years?"

"Because he has been sleepwalking through life since his friends died, because he has been so lonely without me, because his poems were getting more and more boring, his dreams more banal, and, worst of all, he began to write stories."

"That's insufferable," Death said.

"Help me," Satan said.

"It might be too late," Death said, "and would that be too bad? Let me play your advocate. It's not as if his life is that awful now. He's employed, he has a friend or two, a funny cat, and cable. And he does yoga. Would a further descent into oblivion be so terrible for our poet?"

"He could write a novel," Satan said.

"Gag me."

At the Clinic

Ferrigno

He not only called my name, he looked me in the eye and pronounced the name I was born to, Ya'qub, with the 'ain and the qaaf, so he was probably not Lebanese, maybe Syrian, I thought, and he grinned, obviously amused at my confusion, I wasn't standing up, I wasn't following him, I must have been gawking, and only his lifting eyebrows nudged me into a standing position. He didn't speak as we walked the corridor, and those who follow his guidance need have no fear, and neither shall they grieve, but I stumbled, just a bit, almost crashed into his ample ass, he didn't look back, I thought it would have been somewhat convenient had I been rolled in a wheelchair like an invalid, Dead man rolling, Satan yelled, and the light was a weakened yellow or an ochered white with a scumbled pink reflecting off the red line on the linoleum that led somewhere, into the labyrinth to some unknown grail.

Where are you from, I wanted to ask his stacked ass, O gluteus maximus mounds of Olympus, but the words would not roll off my liquid tongue, I gnawed dissatisfaction, the strain returned of my desire to own the elusive one, or at least to bury my face in it for a while. Alive, Satan said, it's alive, it's aliiiiiiiiiive, do we have an erection yet, has the sleeper been awakened? Oh, shut up, I told Satan, and I wondered whether Ferrigno knew how seductively his body moved as he led me into the examining room, his stride a spark, the flexor twist of his forearm as he turned the knob a kindling, the hairs, the hairs strolling up the elbow, those hillocks of biceps. This hulk is not your doing, Catherine, is it, Satan said, must be Pantaleon, I know you guys are good, but this is outstanding.

In the room, I sat on the pressed wood chair, didn't have to be told which one, to the side of the small desk, not in front of it, minimal furniture in a small room, no photo or print or painting on the wall, no picture hooks, no nails, a small high window to let arbitrary light in during the day. The counselor will be right with you, said Ferrigno, and yes, he had a noticeable accent when he spoke English, he wasn't Syrian, he didn't look North African, I kept staring, I longed for the days when nurses and orderlies wore uniforms with names, but all his too-small T-shirt said above his prominent nipple was LIPITOR. You can call him Lip, Satan said, and Ferrigno grinned and said, Iraq, in case you're wondering, a small village along the Euphrates, not too far from the Syrian border, and I know all about you. He did? The receptionist had told him about my poetic misadventures, and I didn't ask about patient privacy, but I did notice the Leather Queen tattoo peeking from under the sleeve of his

white shirt, black blue black blue white, only the bottom
of the red heart showed. He would probably love to whip
your scrawny ass all the way to Yemen, Satan said, just give
him that simpering puppy look as if you're willing to lick
his boots every day of the week and Sundays, you used to
be so good at that.

No paper clips to write on the walls, Ferrigno said, if
you must, use a Sharpie, he took out a brown one from his
pocket and handed it to me, I can clean this off easily, he said,
no need to worry. I held it before me, stunned and stultified.
With an I'll be back when you're done, he walked out of the
room looking pleased with himself, and I could register little
but the sleek brown Sharpie between my fingers. Come on,
Satan said, this must be Margaret, am I right, deluging him
with pens, I'm in awe. Please be quiet, I told Satan, but my
phone buzzed and it was Odette again, asking me to tell her
where I was and to stop bullshitting her.

I was desperate for quiet—so desperate that I looked
forward to wearing the hospital gown for three days, having
my droopy old ass uncovered for seventy-two hours, nothing
that required my attention, Paradise, I attend thee, Satan,
begone. Fat chance, he said, now look at all the empty wall
space, be a bad boy and start writing, why don't you? Are
you crazy, I said to Satan, why would I want to write on the
wall, it doesn't work that way, and my two thumbs begged
Odette to look after Behemoth, I swore that I would tell her
everything as soon as I could. She texted right back asking
a most direct question, should she be worried? I hesitated
but only for a moment, decided to tell the truth, No, I typed.

Of course she should be worried, Satan said, if you
check yourself into the hospital you become even more

boring than you have been, that's worrisome, I can't believe
you, can't believe that my protégé, my boy, whom I have
nurtured and suckled since he was a mere zygote, still thinks
that Paradise is some desired destination, why would you
wish for an eternity without life, beauty without ugliness is
nothing if not bland, Paradise is the most tedious place ever,
in comparison Disneyland is a Wagner opera.

Trust me, I texted Odette, I will explain everything in
time, you need not worry. I am here, she said, you're not
alone, and I understood what she was referring to because
six months before she met her fiancée—they're getting married, Doc, they are—Odette was horrifically depressed, she
felt she would remain single for the rest of her life, and one
night she sat on my bed crying into a ball of tissues salted
with tears, she did not want to die alone, and like many a
lesbian and gay man before us, we made a pact: we would
always be there for each other, we would not allow the other
to feel alone in this world, which was basically a renegotia-
tion of a much earlier pact that we'd broken, that we would
get married if we were still single when both of us turned
forty-five, but we forgot about that one, senility of middle
age or maybe she was dating someone at the time, I can't
remember. She wished to remind me of the new promise,
and I was glad, I was not alone.

And Satan said, But ya are, Blanche, ya are in that
chair.

Jacob's Journals

Sage

While I was in the whorehouse, what I knew of Lebanon came from two sources: my mother's stories about the plush apartment of my father's parents, and a weekly Lebanese television series that the entire house watched, a breathtakingly irritating and compulsively watchable show about the simple life of a married couple in the mountains, a show that celebrated tradition, family, and unfortunate hairstyles. We gathered in front of the television before the show began, all of us having bathed or cleaned up, as if we were going to prayers, the serial required its own ablutions. When the last commercial ended and the black-and-white screen flickered and the show's opening music emerged from the speakers, the energy of the room palpably shifted, a new presence entered our world, we all felt it, just as Faust did when Mephistopheles appeared at his side.

Each episode always began with a shot of husband and wife in their home, she wore dark skirts, lighter tops, and always a cardigan, sometimes long translucent white scarves covered her head but we could still see how much hair spray she used, he wore the odd outfit of the Lebanese mountains, fez and black drop-crotch pants, you can't touch this. As soon as either the husband or the wife spoke the first word, my aunties would begin to talk back to the Lebanese couple on the screen, Good morning, Abou Saleem, Good morning to you, Umm Saleem, Good to see you again, Hope you had an uneventful week. This might sound strange to you, Doc, but believe me, every single woman in that house talked to the television, when my mother needed to go to the bathroom, she would excuse herself from whoever was on the screen, women driving in car commercials, men lighting up Kent cigarettes, Pardon me, she would say, I will return momentarily.

The show itself was overstuffed with homilies and platitudes, every episode had a moral lesson to impart, Yes, it's true, blood is thicker than water, Everything happens because God has a master plan, and the episode always ended with the lecture, the wife distilling the episode's story, telling the men about life, love, happiness, the value of cooperation, the wisdom of the village elders, at which point my mother and every auntie would nod her head, Uh-huh, Yes, You say the wisest things, Jewels tumble from your mouth, I wish I had someone like you telling me this when I was younger.

Just when I thought I knew all there was to know about that silly little country, a third source began to arrive by mail, my father's postcards. When I wrote him my first postcard, he replied the same day, but it took a while for his card to arrive, during which time my mother had insisted I write him one a day, so when she rushed into the kitchen waving the postcard, I was ecstatic, not just because of that card, but for all the dozens I expected to course like a waterfall through the opened floodgates. The arrival of each card, like the Lebanese television serial, brought the entire whorehold together, all turned still while my aunties examined the picture, Look, so much snow on the mountains, Amazing cars on the streets of Beirut, Is this a damascene dagger I see before me, What kind of forest is this, Behold God's miraculous colors in this sunset. I had to read the descriptor of each picture aloud, sunrise on Mount Sannine, the city of Tripoli, sunset on the rock at Raouché, before passing the card around, and then I had to read my father's prose when it returned. What my father wrote sounded similar to the television platitudes, Stay in school, my son, Honesty is the best policy, Obey your mother for this is right, Do not forsake your mother's teachings. At the time, I found his words uplifting and loving, and his claiming me, his bastard, calling me his son, was as great a gift as I could ever have hoped for. In his eyes, I was human.

During the rest of my time in Cairo, those postcards were what I lived for, I waited for them, the house waited, my desultory life had found a purpose. Auntie Badeea transcribed my mother's letters to him and he replied, and though I never knew what was in them, I presume she lauded me, hoping he would be proud, hoping he would want me in his life and get her in the bargain, she must have implored him to help me. She insisted that I use the biggest words I could think of, that I ensure the perfection of my spelling and grammar, that I stress the paucity of available opportunities for a boy like me who was far, far ahead of children my age. Her ploy half worked, because at some point, I'm

not sure when, my father told her that I should fly to Lebanon without her, that he would be in charge of raising me
to become a productive member of society, that I needed a
good education, which meant that she would have to give
me up, she and Auntie Badeea and the house itself would
no longer have a claim on me, for my own benefit, of course.
My mother might have taken a few years to mull over the
offer, or a few seconds, I don't know when it was made, but
Auntie Badeea broke the news to me when I was ten, my
mother and the rest of the aunties with us in the kitchen.
I was going to Beirut, a great city, a wonderful city, I was
going to be with an amazing man, this father of mine, and I
would be taken in by his exceptionally rich family, who could
buy me everything I ever wished for and things I didn't yet
know existed, happy days to look forward to.

     A decision was made, coffee stains and tea leaves were
consulted, and a date for my departure was chosen. The days
after the decision bred moroseness in my mother and aunties and unbridled elation in me, where they saw parting, I
saw meeting my father, my desideratum. Every auntie in the
house chipped in to buy me fancy clothes and even a suit,
they did not wish me to feel inadequate upon meeting my
prosperous family, did not wish to embarrass themselves,
they had had a long discussion as to what would be the ideal
outfits, decided that I would wear western clothing since I
was going to modern Beirut. I have a picture of myself all
dressed up, your mother didn't filch that, Doc, a cotton suit as
white as goose down and a shirt to match, shorts that barely
reached my thighs, shoes and socks also white, even the belt,
my darkness a contrast, I'm smiling, mouth open, all teeth,
as fresh as dew I was. My mother knotted the tiny black tie

that dropped below my belt, her cologne, a scent of violets, reassured me. I was the young bride being sent to a new family, never to be seen again. You're my young man now, my mother said, trying to instill courage in my veins, but none was needed. I had no idea that the ritual was a final farewell, everyone expected me to break down in tears, all the room was bawling except for confused me until my mother brought out the janbiya, light and fake, and I began to howl and the whore chorus stopped crying, This is not good, one auntie said, how is he to become a man, that one, I never thought he would, may God watch over him, and Auntie Badeea put the knife in her belt and my mother shut her eyes until I calmed.

When the day came for me to leave, I carried a small potted plant in a paper bag, a sage for my tummy aches, its green leaves with goose bumps peeking above the top of the bag, an old Arab tradition, travel with earth, with home mud, stay rooted to your land. Palestinian refugees kept keys to their houses for generations, hidden in boxes, in kerchiefs, their adult children's children not knowing what the houses looked like or where they were, yet they cherished the keys, and in a poem Bertolt Brecht compared himself to a man who carried a brick to show how beautiful his house once was, and the nice Lebanese stewardess who watched over me took the sage away when I boarded and forgot to return it when she delivered me to my father.

Soil

I thought we were all fighting the fight on the same side, not so, Doc, what you wanted was to become respectable, ignoring history, not knowing that once you climb the ranks of the upright someone has to replace you down below, but you did not want to know that. I look around me, Doc, and try to imagine where you would fit now, where you would want to, would it be with the khaki-pants crowd, gay-married with picket-fenced children, or with the freaks that come out at night, because unfortunately, the two mingle no more, the first are terrified of being soiled.

Me, Doc?

Me, through and through, from skin to soul, I am sullied and soiled.

My Muse

The great Czesław Miłosz fervently believed that he was only a vessel for his muse. Now I thought the same, believe me, and I waited patiently for my muse's deliveries, as I always have, but unlike Miłosz's, my muse was a bitch. She inundated me with endless chatter, from the beginning she entered our contract with mala fide intentions, Doc. My muse needs an enema. I want a replacement, a trade-in. The infidels in the Holy Quran declaimed, Shall we abandon our gods for a crazy poet? Well, I abandoned my gods for a crazy muse who had trouble with rhythm, who mocked my use of a rhyming dictionary, the one Greg bought for my twenty-fourth birthday, and you admonished him, Don't encourage the boy, you said.

English was my third language, Arabic my mother tongue, the romantic Rimbaud's French my bridge and my crutch, I began to write at an early age, in Arabic at

first, of course, in the whorehouse, encouraged by Auntie
Badeea, who believed that poetry would correct whatever
was wrong. It was easy in the beginning, words flowed, my
muse was gentle and seductive, the poems were lousy, of
course, I was a child, but I loved them, felt they were in-
spired, but perhaps that was because my poems were heard
and appreciated, I could write no wrong, my aunties lauded
anything I recited, in their eyes I could see my face. I had
little audience after that, and what I had was indifferent.
At l'orphelinat de la Nativité I wrote my poems in French,
two or three I submitted as class assignments, thankfully
all lost to your mother now. I wrote those poems in the
library, which was once the rectory, hunched over a notebook, consoled by a dozen open books on the table, aging
poems with lines devoured by silverfish. While the other
boys rough-and-tumbled their way through their years of
school, I composed mediocre verse, where they wanted to be
the next Pelé or Charles Bronson, I idolized Baudelaire and
Rimbaud, he who ended up in Yemen, I too wanted to recite
the unutterable, to turn silences and nights into words, to
make the whirling world stand still while hormones whirled
within me. While insane slathery rain battered the rectory
window and pinecones fell off their tree, I churned out implausible lines, mixing the arcane with argot, pretentious
they were, silly lucubration.

But when I began to write in English that was when my
poetry matured, no longer a mélange of the great and awful,
it distilled, decocted into pure mediocrity. Some of my lines
were published, so I wasn't bad, I wish I were, mediocre
poetry is worse than terrible, it's a sin. Let me try, Doc, you
always used to accuse me of swimming against the current,

THE ANGEL OF HISTORY

said I always managed to do the opposite of whatever was in vogue that season, and I did, eternal rebellion, that was me, but whether I flowed with or swam against the current, the work remained stuck in that river, my poems that I considered idiosyncratic were anything but, they wore the same drenched clothing, soaked in the same water, a great poet has nothing to do with currents, Doc, she is the eye of a storm, neither its thunder nor its lightning.

I loathed the poetry of nostalgia, so I chopped down the olive trees of my ancestors, if I hear one more stanza eulogizing the scent of orange blossoms in Palestine, I will buy a gun, I swear. In response to much-lauded poems dealing with implausible angst, the mild suffering of the fortunate, mine soared on magic carpets offering a bird's-eye view of the world. I despised false domestic poems most, my reaction to those was the elegy "Jeffrey Dahmer Was My Lover." Perhaps I thought I was fighting the dishonesty of contemporary poetry, but mine was fraudulent as well.

My failures were my fault, my cowardice, my muse kept offering Socrates's cup, Drink, she would say, and I hesitated. Maybe it was Satan, I disliked them both. That was why I tried prose, a story here, free verse there, anything to get me out of my dull quagmire. I miss so many things, Doc, I should have saved one small, warm, true thing from the Flood so I might go on living, maybe from the rectory days the two-color click pen, or maybe the yellow pencil, upon its body the pensive marks of my teeth, keeping me company through dozens of bad poems until it was no more than a nib that I disposed of, I should have kept it, for gratitude if nothing else, I am nothing if not a betrayer.

Sarin

I keep looking at online videos of home, a missile, a bulldozer, a bomb smacking a wall, the house genuflecting, the home kneeling, the roof diving, dust rising, the women howling, drone strikes in Yemen, car bombs in Lebanon, shots of the entire Middle East, beatings and non-coups in Egypt, chemical weapons in Syria. Images of children dying of sarin gas flicker on the screen, mouths trying to capture air for lungs used to breathing, noses dripping with an uninterrupted flow of mucus, there was a time when I could watch similar scenes and be no more affected than any American watching horror unfold on the safe screen of television, Oh, that's sad, can I have another beer? Something had shifted within, the wall that defended my heart had crumbled. I was pulled into the drama, I was in Douma, I was in Damascus's suburb Moadamiyeh, I stood above the suffocating child, the dying mother as she wiped her child's face, the father holding both, I was there, I was there with my attendant. Look at that, Satan said, happy times for Mr. D, you can't negotiate with him now, sarin turns him on so, how gleeful he is, so many souls to take, Death doesn't mind the overtime, look how quickly he moves from one to the next, waiting, shivering with anticipation.

I told Satan that Mr. D looked a little different here in the Middle East, and he replied that Death grew younger with each life. Marvel at Death, he said, look how childish he is prancing around in such excitement, by the time this so-called Arab Spring is over, he will be back in his pram shaking his rattle.

I could not keep at it, I had to leave the apartment, to take a walk, Behemoth jumped when I entered the bedroom,

I realized that I was rushing, moving erratically, my cat was my metronome, I slowed down, I was shivering, took a long calming breath, I gathered my sneakers, a baseball cap that made the sides of my hair look like oversize earmuffs, Hell hath no fur like my hair. Around the corner from my apartment, fifty-seven steps to be exact, was an intersection with heavy foot traffic and few cars, on the northwest corner a Palestinian called Faisal ran an idiosyncratic smoke shop that specialized in drug paraphernalia, sixties tchotchkes, his biggest sellers were hookahs painted to look as if they were tie-dyed, he had a sign on his window that announced, WE CHEAT POTHEADS. On the southwest corner a Syrian called Pete, Boutrus Americanized, ran a grocery store with his wife, Sofia, and their three children.

Both Pete and Faisal were smoking outside their stores, the first pretended not to notice me as I passed by, his head went down, I allowed him his privacy, did not call out or acknowledge him. At the beginning of the Syrian uprising, he would not stop talking, so proud he was, We're marching peacefully, he used to say, and they shoot at us, massacres, but we show up knowing that we might die, and then they dare to tell us we're not ready for democracy. No longer proud, like the phoenix, Arab shame raised itself eternally out of its ashes. Faisal, on the other hand, acknowledged my passing with a nod, He's having a rough time, he said, meaning Pete, he hasn't been able to sleep for a while, he had such high hopes, it's humiliating. But not you, I said. No, not me, he replied, and not you either, we're used to humiliation.

You know, Doc, I have a different definition of the walk of shame from everyone else, we should call returning home with unkempt hair and wearing the same clothes after a night getting fucked the walk of mild embarrassment. When I meet another Arab is the true walk of shame, every day it's one thing or another. Wait, you might not know Faisal, I think you would like him, but you do know Pete, of course, he's a lot older now, but he's still the same grocer, his eldest was about six when you died and he's married now, do you remember, you used to try to embarrass me every time we walked into the store together, you'd hold my hand or grab my ass in front of Pete, you knew it made both him and me uncomfortable so you always went for it, for a while I had to walk the two extra blocks to the Korean grocery in order not to face the Syrian, it was only after you died that Pete and I began to see each other for what we were. And now he is too ashamed to look at me.

Anger

My mother was angry once, I don't remember the cause, just the manifestation, it was just one time, her madness was the quiet kind, usually she was the easiest person to get along with, swayed with the prevailing winds, built sand castles after a sandstorm, but that time she raged, took a kitchen knife to the cloth on every piece of furniture in her room, not the drapes, the throw blanket, or the carpet, but the earth-tone seats of three chairs, the headboard, the pillows, the sheets, the wool blanket, the bed skirt, and the mattress itself. In wild gestures, she swung the blade, slashing and stabbing and screaming incoherently, frantic demons possessed her being, and none of the household dared enter her room, we stood outside the door, my aunties and I, all of us quivering and quailing, all of us trying to talk her out of the insane destruction, until finally Auntie Badeea was able to pierce her fury, We'll have to repair or replace all this before evening, Auntie Badeea said, let's not add any more work. My mother halted the massacre, her delicately embroidered jellabiya had a diagonal tear from her left side to just above the belly button, no blood, though. Torn pieces of bedspread studded with shards of mirror lay on the floor.

She turned and faced us, I am still young, she said, her eyes confused at first, then guilty, her knife at her side, clutched fiercely, her hair Medusa, her demeanor Medea, my mother.

Jacob's Stories

The Drone

If you looked at Mohammad's village from a bird's-eye view, as I usually did, you wouldn't have been impressed with the boy's crumbling house, or with the village architecture either. Heck, you would probably have mocked it with no little disdain, just as my guys back in Florida did on a daily basis. ("I can bring this house down with four slingshots, George." "Well, Dick, I can bring this house down with one Hellfire missile." "Bring this house down, George.") The houses had a kind of style, but it wasn't ours. They fit in their surroundings architecturally, but we weren't that fond of the surroundings to begin with, were we? I mean, how could you be, it was arid and poor, all browns and beiges and creams and off-whites. ("Diarrhea colors are all I see, George, all I see, and it's worse in night vision.") Not a sprig of real green. Which was why our boy had to go quite a distance from his house to fetch firewood, and that is where our story begins, that was how he and I met that fateful day, a day that would live on in Rooseveltian infamy or glory, depending on which side of the fence you preferred to dangle your legs from.

Up high I was flying that day, above the incomprehensible land beneath—beneath me both literally and figuratively—poking my upturned nose into everyone's business as usual: who was walking home, who was making lunch, who was making bombs, who was pissing in the outhouse, who in the wind, who was having sex. ("They're fucking doggie-style, Dick. It's not missionary. Look at 'em go at it!") Above the Tappi area, about ten miles from Miramshah, a group of girls stopped playing and hid behind outlying rocks upon hearing my approach. Can you blame them? I'd killed two of their friends only two months ago, and it seemed I'd sprayed three of the girls below with shrapnel. It was unintentional, I didn't intend to kill the girls, Nabeela and Naeema, both blue-eyed and under ten. I'd aimed for the sorry shack where their militant father slept, and it was unfortunate that the girls shared the same address. My Hellfire sucked the air out of their home, *whoosh*. ("You brought the house down, George!") That was me, not the other prowler of these skies, my partner Kurt Z. Full disclosure.

And since I'm disclosing here, let me add that I enjoyed watching my Hellfire hit its target; the sensation electrified my circuits. The colors—reds, oranges, yellows, blues, browns, ochers, purples, every imaginable color burst before your eyes with each explosion. The smell of napalm in the morning did not compare; it was overpowering, like garlic in a meal, you smelled only napalm. With my hits, I smelled fire and cordite and nuanced residues of human roasts. The feeling of firing a rifle? A machine gun? Pshaw. All other sensations were as the tinkling of a doorbell to the throbbing of Big Ben, which, incidentally, was how Lord Wolseley described shooting and killing Negroes in Africa. Can you imagine what it would have been like had the British had us at the turn of the twentieth century? Wowza!

The landscape stretched before me like an interminable tumbling sea of sand and rock. The light was expansive, the sun hammered down relentlessly, its beams cut like sabers, stabbed at your eyes like rapiers. The air against my face was like thin ice crackling, except it was nowhere near cold enough for ice even at the heights where I was cruising. I missed the feel of fresh rain, missed its fragrance, missed the soughing of leafy treetops. A tree, a tree, my kingdom for a tree. In the offing, the white sky and white earth were welded together without a joint. Suddenly, as if someone had slapped me and jolted me into a deep sense of recognition, I felt a frisson of something ominous in the atmosphere, a smell of some sort, a different air density, a thickness, a spark, something I couldn't identify. I warned Dick and George, but neither could decipher the feeling, or what I was saying, for that matter.

"George, Dick, something weird is going down," I said into my telecom.

"What's that damn hum?" George asked.

"I see dead people," Dick said.

"Where?" George asked.

"Target six seven three just entered his demesne."

"Dead in two minutes and thirteen seconds," George said.

I put all my senses and missiles on full alert. I assure you that never before had this land, this sand, these rocks, the very arch of this blazing sky, appeared to me so hopeless, so stark, so impenetrable, so pitiless, so invulnerable, so foreign. I saw a haze in the distance, a bright mist, and then my nose turned downward. My right wing had lost its way, my mind heard a voice, George, "I'm losing him, Dick. What the hell is happening? Did a terrorist shoot him? Damn, damn, damn. They can't blame me for this. If they dock my pay this time, I'm going to sue."

The desert loomed as a frightening declivity that I was bound to visit, its floor rushed to greet me. I was lucky enough to crash-land in a valley with few rocks, my bottom sliding on dry sand for only a few feet. The excessive friction saved my life, but it erased the paint off my underbelly. For years while flying above this godforsaken land I'd been exposed to the powerful forces of erosion, suffocating sun and wind, bubbling heat, and I'd still remained presentable. My first encounter with the actual culture on the ground and it was a Kelly Moore holocaust.

Need I tell you that I was terrified? I tried talking courage into my senses. I could barely move and I certainly could not take off.

What could I do?

I had no idea.

I surveyed my surroundings, but every grain of sand looked like every other grain of sand, they all looked alike in this country. I knew where I was. I'd scouted this valley before, there wasn't an inch of earth for hundreds of miles that I hadn't spied on. I knew the lay of the land better than anyone else. I sprawled broken-winged and helpless two hills away from the village, in a valley rarely visited.

I gauged my situation and realized that I was done for. With Herculean effort I could move a few inches at a time, I could maybe shuffle a wheel here and there. My right wing had betrayed me. Since the air held little or no moisture, I would not rust to death, but I couldn't tell you which of the two possible fates awaiting me was worse: that I would spend the rest of eternity by my lonesome, undiscovered, sand blanketing me inch by inch until I was buried alive, or that I would be discovered by the villagers, who would slow-kill me with their shepherds' staffs and rakes and hoes and rocks, but not before I Cheneyed a couple of their faces. The rest of my life wasn't going to be pretty and neither was I.

Then Mohammad appeared, and what a vision he was. A vague shape rose behind the hill, transformed into a silhouette haloed by the sun's mucous disk, a paper puppet like Karagöz, their infamous passionate fool of the Ramadan shadow theaters. I was taken aback by the sight at first, but once he took one step down the mountain and the sun no longer obscured as many details, I saw him for what he was, a possible terrorist. His swarthy complexion gave him away, as did the ascetic aspect of his billowy clothing: no color, no denim, no Gap Kids, no Diesel.

I tried to contact Dick and George, to no avail. I was on my own. I cocked my missiles. I scanned him for weapons and found nothing other than a bundle of five emaciated branches cradled in his arms like a newborn babe. I calculated that a branch could sting but not kill me. He'd have to come close enough to swing the flimsy weapon, which I wouldn't allow because I'd shock and awe him into oblivion, or at least the Middle Ages. Still, I didn't appreciate that look of maleficent curiosity upon his face. Mohammad descended the mountain with no fear. These people, without exception, couldn't wait to ascend to their imaginary heaven with seventy-two pom-pom-wielding houris with whom they could perform delightfully imagined debaucheries — imagine, a Heaven with virgins instead of the Virgin. This approaching boy showed a surprising lack of awareness of his approaching death. I wished to show him a Schwartz-kopfian graph detailing what one of my Hellfires would do to his body. I was just about to blast him to kingdom come, not his nymphet-infested one, when he fell on his butt and slid down the rest of the hill giggling like a schoolgirl. Mohammad spanked his behind to rid it of sand and dust, and without bothering to pick up the branches, his weapons of mass destruction, came at me still laughing.

"Doobly goobly gook McCain?" he asked. His teeth coruscated in the dazzling sunlight, such white teeth in a dark face.

It is said that General Horatio Herbert Kitchener, who in 1898 saved Sudan by killing tens of thousands of Sudanese, once had a Negro boy flogged to death with a whip made out of hippo hide (ancestor of the chicote of Congo, the sjambok of South Africa, and many others) for not being able to communicate in English. You might erroneously think this was a harsh sentence since the boy had never met a white man before Kitchener's army stomped his village, nor had he heard of, let alone heard, the English language, but you see, the death was accidental. Kitchener, beloved of the British and Queen Victoria, wished only to teach and civilize, to educate the boy and his people.

As enchanting as Mohammad was at that moment, I
too wanted to teach and civilize the damn boy. He should
know better than to talk to me, obviously not from his village, in his local language.

Once more I cocked my missiles, when he suddenly
said, in the queen's tongue if heavily accented, "Hello. My
name is Mohammad. What's yours?"

"Ezekiel," I said, still a bit leery, until the boy reached
over and hugged my nose. The disarming Mohammad and
his discreet charm persuaded me to uncock my missiles.
You had to give these people credit, their innocent nature
allowed them to be genuine and loving. As an example, I'll
bring up another flogging story, not that I'm obsessed with
the subject, but it's not easy to find stories of these people
that don't include a good whupping. A Swede working for a
Belgian company in the Congo, Lieutenant Gleerup, related
how his bearers' bad behavior would force him to flog them
until one time he whipped one Negro so hard that Gleerup,
not the Negro, fainted. The Swede (and it's important to emphasize his nationality—think Stockholm and its delightful
syndrome, think Nobel Peace Prize) wrote of how tenderly
the flogged man treated him, covering him in his own white
cloth to keep away the sun, caring for him, laying his head
on his lap while another Negro ran down to the river to
fetch water for him, so that soon Gleerup recovered and
was able to wield the chicote once more. Nice people. I
tell you, black people back in Florida have lost that earthy
genuineness, their simple nature. Our noble savages have
misplaced their nobility.

The boy spoke once more. "Hello. My name is Mohammad. What's yours? Would you like some tea and crumpets?"

THE ANGEL OF HISTORY

That was confusing, and I began to wonder whether I was misunderstanding his heavily accented tongue.

"I like marmalade on my toast in the morning," he said, "and in the evening, I like brussels sprouts. How about you?"

"Is this some form of code?" I asked. "I'm not sure what you mean by brussels sprouts. Is marmalade a metaphor?"

"English, yes." The boy clapped his hands once in joy. "It always rains in London, but we make cotton in Yorkshire, and these kippers were swimming in the Channel yesterday."

I understood then that open communication wasn't going to be an integral part of our relationship, but he hugged me again and released all my inhibitions.

The first time he circled me, I felt like a cow at the market being examined, the second time, when he whistled appreciatively with every step, I felt I was the only girl at a fraternity party, which elicited discomforting and confusing feelings, enough so that without my even realizing it my missiles cocked on their own accord. But then the boy rattled off a few gook phrases, pointed at the five dry branches, and with waving arms gesticulating to indicate an explosion, he added, "*Whoosh*," which I figured meant that he had to return home and build a fire. I thought that was terribly sweet until I realized that he was leaving me for the night.

As I watched him climb back up the hill, maneuvering through the slippery scree, his feet finding an ideal landing every time, I knew it was going to be a difficult night. At the top of the hill, he turned and waved at me before disappearing. For the first time in my life, I was alone. Without Dick and George, without NPR or Sirius, here at the quiet limit of the world, abandoned to the indifferent stars above, near no accustomed hand, I felt lonely, so lonely.

I felt sorry for myself, spent the first few hours thinking about my fall. Adam and Eve had nothing on me. I was once king of these skies, a silver shadow like a dream roaming the air and high spaces of this middling east. I surveyed all and knew everything and more. That evening I was lonelier than Bonaparte strutting on the volcanic beach of Elba, reviewing his triumphs while desperately trying to contain any incidental eruption of thoughts about Waterloo. I was bereft until I noticed that Mohammad had picked up only three of the branches. It might have been unintentional but it certainly was propitious; the remaining two bits of wood formed a cross on the desert floor.

A cross of firewood before my eyes, a sign for me to see. Blessed be divine interventions.

My mood soared again, my wings might not have been able to fly, but I was uplifted. My fall was divinely ordained, obviously. This was my burden, I, the best of my breed, was placed here to veil the threat of terror, to continue this war of peace. I would lift these people, teach and enlighten them. I had a mission and I finally knew what it was. I would open this village to the civilizing influences of commercial enterprise—oh, and democracy, of course.

The rising sun woke me up to a glorious cloudless morning; its rays fell on the ground like white ashes and warmed my face. This severe land was warthog ugly, but I could hardly bear the stark beauty of my American intention. My heroism almost embarrassed me. I wanted to thank myself, slap my own back. If only I could see a bald eagle floating in the sky above, I would be complete. My heart brimmed with joy and the morning peaked and Mohammad came down the mountain once more. Oh, what a meeting it was. He was happy, I was happy. He could spend the whole day with me. Oh, what a time we were going to have.

Even though I couldn't move around much, we were still able to play. We began with hide-and-seek, though I always had to be the seeker since I couldn't hide. I might be slim and sleek in the air, but I stick out at ground level. Mohammad hid behind rocks, and each time I'd shoot a round or two at the rock behind which I thought he was hiding and we'd laugh and laugh. He tried to teach me a song in his phlegmy language, but that didn't work since the villagers' primitive tongue meant nothing to me. I taught him a number of songs—well, just the hooks. We spent one delightful hour on "Bootylicious."

Such fun.

He warned me, though. He told me that if the villagers found out about me, they would come out in force to kill me. To make his point, since his language skills were so incredibly primitive—why anyone would choose to speak that fricative language instead of the elegantly simple English is beyond the understanding of my firmware—his dramatic gestures included an exaggerated drop of a guillotine. Like Anne Boleyn, Marie Antoinette, and John the Baptist, I would be beheaded—roll, roll, my pilotless cockpit.

It almost happened. The next day, when Mohammad came back to play, we were discovered by his father. He was looking for his son, who had ignored his chores for two days running. Once he crested the hill, I heard his shrill gasp all the way across the valley, as did Mohammad. We separated instantly. I should have been more frightened, or more courageous. I could have shot the man right there and then and saved myself a lot of trouble, but I wasn't thinking. We were having such a good time. Even when he called for his son and I looked up at him circled in sunlight, all I thought was why couldn't these people add a touch of color to their wardrobe? What's wrong with denim? Back to Bonaparte for a moment, the little corporal whose reputation has been unfairly maligned; shouldn't it be time for a Napoleon Revival? You know, when he invaded Egypt—well, when he befriended Egypt, delivering its people from their despotic masters—he made it mandatory for all Egyptians to wear the tricolor cockade, the knotted ribbon preferred by French Republicans. He tried. Who wouldn't want to pin a cockade on these villagers? The English attempted to civilize, but Gandhi kept all the Asians in diapers. Hopeless.

I didn't worry much about Mohammad's father seeing me because I believed in the righteousness of my cause. I assumed he understood that I was there to save him and his cohort from a life of terrorism and dogma. When Mohammad rushed up the hill, I realized that I got ever so lonely when he left me. I had never felt like this toward anyone before. I had never felt this, never experienced anything like these inchoate feelings, sweet and frightening. If my face could have moved or shown any expression whatsoever, I'd probably have blushed.

The joy morphed into fear when the entire village came at me, roaring menacingly, men with shepherd staffs, women with spatulas, children with sticks. I screeched, "Terrorists, terrorists. You're all damned for eternity if you don't stop this campaign of terror against your betters. Stop being jealous of my freedom. Stop or I'll shoot."

They didn't stop. I pondered the fact, if ever so briefly, that after all these years, these villagers, not just Mohammad, couldn't understand the tongue of enlightened people everywhere. There must be someone who did, but I wasn't about to let them squash me before I found out. I released the safety on all weaponry. Mohammad walked backward, desperately trying to stop the indecent mob, and forcing me to hesitate for a moment. I couldn't see his pleasing face but I heard the pleading of his voice. He kept repeating, "Doobly goobly gook McCain."

Could I risk hurting my beloved?

Yes, of course. Collateral damage. We were trained to deal with that.

The ratio of innocent per terrorist varies from one primitive nation to another—innocent Iraqis were worth more than Afghanis who were worth more than Pakistanis (there are so many of them) who were worth more than Yemenis who were basically worthless because we had to kill them a few times. As an example, a colleague killed the leader of al-Qaeda's affiliate in Yemen. It was the third time the former Guantánamo detainee Said al-Shihri had been reported dead in a drone strike, so whatever collateral damage had to be incurred to rekill him was acceptable, of course. Every strike killed an al-Qaeda leader, and sometimes we killed them over and over, and since no civilized person could possibly tell the difference between one Muslim name and another, everything worked out.

The accidental death of Mohammad the innocent, if it did happen, should not stop me from shooting so many terrorists.

Baby terrorists glared menacingly at me from behind makeshift BabyBjörns as their minatory mothers hurtled toward me. Muslim rage. These people were always raging and fulminating and boiling and frothing. They looked like a zombie cheerleader squad. Every day was a bad skin day for the members of this tribe, who should have used more moisturizer to weather the sun and heat.

The village cleric, who was just about to trample Mohammad, was in my gun sight. I had to admit that he was a disappointment since we'd assumed at least this one Muslim had been rehabilitated. Two years ago, we convinced our Saudi allies that their reeducation camps shouldn't be only for failed suicide bombers, that for the good of the universe, they should expand and take in some of the freaks of their religion, and the village cleric qualified as a freak by any standard. We sent him to jihadi rehab, where he allegedly traded bombs for crayons, where he put his finger paints and pastels to paper in order to regain his freedom. You would think that art therapy wouldn't work for Islamofascists, but you'd be wrong. Most patients were so terrified that other terrorists would find out about their artwork that they retired from suiciding.

I wouldn't be able to kill every single one of the terrorists because there were more of them than I had bullets, but at least those I hit wouldn't be able to keep coming at me. I loved my bullets. At the end of the 1890s, Europeans with their modern rifles were saving Africa with almost total success — almost, because an African terrorist usually continued his charge even after being hit by four or five bullets, sometimes injuring his savior. Imagine that. The Europeans solved that problem by inventing the dumdum bullet, named after the factory in Dum Dum outside Calcutta, with a lead core that exploded its casing, causing large, horrifically painful wounds that would not heal. The use of dumdum bullets between civilized states was prohibited, of course. Europeans used them only for big game hunting and killing terrorists in undeveloped countries.

I was ready. Just as I was about to make the village cleric's run his last, I heard the sound of Kurt Z above me. My partner might be a pain in the aft, but he certainly had impeccable timing. I had seen the panic that vanquished these people when they heard us flying low, but I had never witnessed it at eye level. The terror was awesome. They never knew when, where, or who we were going to hit. Female terrorists screeching, trying to find their terrorist offspring who stood quailing in the middle of the melee, terrorists bouncing off each other like bumper cars. Shock and awe, baby, shock and awe. The terrorists climbed the hill and ran away, dispersed to their respective scorpion-infested hovels. I couldn't help gloating. I repeated to no one but myself, "Yeah, baby, yeah, baby," and it turned into a mantra that sent shivers of energy and Kundalini ecstasy up my spinal algorithms. I was yelling, "We're number one, we're number one," when the Navy SEALs manifested out of thin air. Of course, I knew that the six of them dropped into the valley by parachute, but they were so professional, so efficient, so cool, that they just seemed like macho magical beings. If you asked me to choose between a unicorn and a Navy SEAL, I'd pick the latter every single time.

All of a sudden, I felt the great men wrap hemp and cotton around me and my wings. I would allow them to do anything. The ropes around my belly felt ticklish. The chafing of the rough landing made me extra sensitive down there.

One of the godlike guys said, "I can't believe they make us go to all this trouble for this heap," which was when I heard George for the first time in over twenty-four hours, but he wasn't in my wires, he was coming out of the SEAL's headset, and George said, "Hey, numbnuts, one of Ezekiel's wing nuts costs more than you'll make in a lifetime, so shut up and bring him back."

I should have realized that the guys in Florida would be able to resurrect me. If they could make a mushroom cloud out of nothing, if they could mine the moon for its minerals, surely they could raise me up. Up, they lifted me up where I belonged, and I expelled all the sand from my orifices, probably the same way Deborah Kerr did after her famous scene in *From Here to Eternity*. Up into the sky I was lifted, my wings spread, vertical, nose heading toward the clouds. I felt — I don't know, maybe like both a god and a human. The ecstasy was so intense, I was blinded by the beauty surrounding me, and God, the real one, appeared before me, luminous and golden. "Listen, my son," I thought he declaimed, but I couldn't be sure because I blacked out. All light, the golden and the luminous and the ordinary, departed.

I woke up unable to remember anything. It seemed I had retrograde amnesia. Someone had pressed the refresh button. I did feel refreshed and rejuvenated; I was born again, praise be. Baptized with a new name, I wasn't told how long I'd been asleep. Dick and George had to reintroduce themselves.

"Come on, Azrael," said George. "Let's go kick some new Muslim ass."

"And some old ones too," said Dick.

"Okay," I said, because I was laid back and easygoing.

I was a happy camper, but something was missing. Sure, I enjoyed bombing Jeeps and camels in Yemen, jerry-built shacks in Afghanistan, holes-in-the-walls in Pakistan, mud huts in Somalia (the best if you, like me, have a pyro-mania tendency), loved watching terrorists and collateral damage explode and disintegrate, I even enjoyed going to confession after each flight, but my life seemed incomplete, and because of my amnesia, I couldn't put my viewfinder on what exactly was lacking. I prayed for guidance with my Bible study group, searched for inspiration, but nothing seemed to work.

One day I was flying reconnaissance for my partner, Kurt Z, who was supposed to Hellfire an al-Qaeda opera-tive, and something caught my eye. In a village that seemed hazily familiar, I noticed a beating. In the public square, or the sandy unsanitary shape that passed for one, an old man was caning the exposed buttocks of a young boy. I was shaken. I couldn't see the face of Mohammad, but the cheeky image fired all kinds of electrons in my capacitors.

Oh, Mohammad, there was no boy but you.

Those buttocks were to me like the madeleine to Proust. Memories flooded my cockpit. I remembered everything, and joy filled my heart once more. I couldn't bear to wit-ness Mohammad's suffering. I intervened. I swooped down, buzzing the proceedings. The ensuing alarm reminded me of the last time I saw these same villagers panicking, and this time I forgave them their past trespasses. Everyone ran around directionless except Mohammad, who looked up and recognized me. He waved and my heart skipped a beat or two.

I heard George scream, "He's freaking out again, Dick. He's doing his own thing."

"I told you we should have put him to sleep," Dick said. "I warned you. These Muslims are insidious, once they put their claws in you, you're a goner."

I didn't care.

Events, however, conspired to turn both Mohammad and me into heroes. Kurt Z, who was following the terrorist Jeep, had planned to vaporize it as soon as it entered the village. The chaos of my interference forced the vehicle to change course. Kurt Z had to hurry up and Hellfire the Jeep into smithereens. The fact that Kurt Z ended up not blasting the entire village was noted by its inhabitants, who realized that I was not only a champion but their savior.

Oh, what happy times. I was feted and lauded and garlanded with desiccated flowers—lest we forget, their land is a desert suckhole. Since Mohammad had saved me and I had saved the village, he was declared the village hero. Such love, such joy, who deserved this much happiness? Everyone lived happily ever after, but more important, everyone was able to drink a Starbucks once the franchise opened in the village. My dream came true, my vision. McDonald's, Wendy's, Appleby's—everybody came, everybody profited. Capitalism rocks. I wanted them to have better shoes, but the villagers couldn't afford those, so they got the next best thing: a factory that made shoes for Nike where all the villagers could work and join the global commercial enterprise. The factory offered Mohammad a pair of black rubber moccasins with white piping and had them stamped with the Nike swoosh, which made the boy happy, so happy.

THE ANGEL OF HISTORY

We brought democracy too. You should have seen how proud the villagers were when they showed me their thumbs ink-stained violet, like children showing their parents a report card with gold stars. They elected Mohammad's mother as the mayor. We improved the lot of women in the area. You're welcome, oppressed women everywhere.

All of us back in Florida were so proud of our babies, so proud that we could offer them the benefit of our wisdom and our joy.

At ten fifteen every morning, the shoe factory allowed the first-shift employees a four-minute-thirty-seven-second break, and Mohammad, industrious worker that he was, would use that opportunity to rush to the top of our hill and wave both arms frantically as I timed my flight to be there for him each day. He looked so sweet in his uniform of red, white, and blue, even though it was still a thobe or a kaftan or whatever they called it, because, you know, we respected everyone's tradition and all that.

Satan's Interviews

Pantaleon

"Let's face it, I wouldn't recommend that he return to his home countries," Pantaleon said, his tone rushed, his words racing one another to the finish line. "Though I don't know if remaining in this one is good for him. He should have gone to Germany from the beginning."

Braced on Death's couch, cross-legged, both heels ensconced under his butt, Pantaleon still gave the impression of mad hyperactivity: spastic hand gestures, bobbing brown curly hair that veiled and revealed his eyes many times per second, the Picasso harlequin top, and the blindingly fuchsia ballet tights that highlighted every vein and sinew. Pantaleon was the gayest of the fourteen, and the happiest. Satan loved him best.

"Please," Satan said, "do elaborate."

"Depravity, darling, depravity. Let's face it, like all true poets, ours is a depraved fuck, bless his loins. I mean, really,

he has done things that made me blush. Can you imagine?
Many homosexual men of his generation were delightfully
wanton, shamelessly lewd, but few sank to his level —
self-tempted, self-depraved."

"Praise be," said Satan.

"Glory, glory," said Pantaleon. When he grinned, the
gold in his halo took on a pinkish hue. The space around
him seemed sentient. "In its heyday these United States of
America could have competed with the best of them: the
bathhouses of the seventies, the dark rooms, every single rest
stop in Alabama. That golden age has faded now, tarnished.
America is now Cerberus with all three heads licking its
balls. What happened to all those leading men of the great
bacchanalia? They either died of AIDS or accepted roles as
supporting actors in the middlebrow drama series of hetero
culture — you know, if they're to kiss, we must have sunsets
in the background. Once they were proud to explore every
crevice of life in the margins, now their ambition is just to
get along. Color me unimpressed."

A delighted Behemoth wanted to burrow under Pantaleon's shirt, kept trying to lift the hem with the top of his
head. The saint pulled his shirt out; Behemoth vanished
under it, nuzzled against his skin, purred in a fetal position.

"And Germany?" Satan asked.

"Not just Germany. I'd recommend any place that's still
weird. Germans remain creepy, thankfully. At least once
a month someone puts up a cannibalistic ad wishing to be
eaten. Jeffrey Dahmer would have had an orgiastic feast.
Our poet would have walked the land sporting bleeding
buttocks and a never-softening erection. Such poems he
could have written."

"Do you remember his Dahmer poem?"

"Of course," said Pantaleon. "He was obsessed with what happened to the poor Laotian boy. Konerak his name was, yet no one remembers the fourteen-year-old. He escaped Dahmer's apartment, the police found the boy on the street. Dahmer told them that Konerak was his drunk lover and the police returned Konerak to be strangled, chewed, and swallowed. I think that was his best poem, the boy immigrant trying to explain to the cops that he was being eaten, once, twice, again and again, and no one listening, no one understanding."

"So what happened to his poems, what happened to Jacob?"

"He matured into a poet with the soul of a priest."

"Yes," Satan said. "Remind him."

"Is it a coincidence that our poet became chaste when gay men were being told to put their dicks back in their pants? They wanted us to wear khakis, for crying out loud."

"Us?"

"Well," said Pantaleon, his halo changing to a lush rose gold. "I partook a little, darling, only a little. How can one not? But our boy no longer did. He was spiraling down, down, down, into the dark unbottomed infinite abyss. Then the guy in the garage was the final margarita straw. I understand why he had to pull back."

"What guy in the garage?" Satan said. "He thinks Deke Dickhead was his final perdition."

"Does he, now?" said Pantaleon. "I beg to differ."

"Sing now," Satan said. "Give us the voice that tells the shifting story."

"Well, now." Pantaleon pulled his knee up to his chest, origamied himself into a pose from a Schiele drawing, and Behemoth under his shirt did not seem to mind. "At the time, Jacob's need was as punctual as a cricket, and one night, not too long after Dickhead left, it chirped. He used one of those Internet sites that help you find an erect penis in a flash, and he found one that was connected to a married man who wanted Jacob to give him a blow job in his garage while the wife was asleep in the house. Of course, Jacob rushed over. The man would not speak to him, shoved him to his knees, and began to fuck his throat violently, which made Jacob regurgitate all over himself, nothing on the married man, who kept face-fucking him until he ejaculated, mixing liquids in a gullet. Once done, the man threw Jacob out on the street without a paper towel or even a tissue. Covered in vomit, Jacob could not get on a bus, had to walk all the way home."

"Poor Jacob," Satan said.

"Poor Jacob? He loved it. Humiliation was the blood that nourished his erections, shame his sustenance. That was probably what scared him. That walk home, the disgrace, the dishonor, the indignity, his desire, his longing, he couldn't deal with it then."

"So he killed a part of himself," Satan said.

"Killed?" said Pantaleon. "Don't be such a drama queen, darling. You can't kill desire. You can suppress it for a while, sometimes a long, long while, but one's longings are eternal. Trust me."

At the Clinic

The Counselor

As the world turned to darkness, I waited in the room all
by myself, through the page-sized window I saw dark gray
blackening from the top of one building to the top of another.
Then the door opened and smacked into the wall. Sorry, she
said, embarrassed, almost giggling, as she strolled amiably
into the room. She casually introduced herself as Jeannie,
I'm one of the counselors here, she said, bubbly voice, It
says here, gesturing to the form in her hand, that you wish
to see a psychiatrist because you're having problems, let's
see if I can help first. She lowered herself onto the opposite
chair, the office was so small that I could practically smell her
mouthwashed breath and the hand lotion she used. Everything about her screamed high school, her chestnut pigtails,
the three-tiered gingham skirt, the blue leggings, the black
ankle-high boots, she was all reined-in energy, a cheerleader

anxiously waiting to cheer a touchdown. Don't be fooled, Satan with the insanely blue eyes said in my head, look at the tightness around her eyes, no makeup can cover pain if you know how to look. Her eyes were blue as well, watery blue, like a baby's.

What brings you to our happy home, she asked, her voice, her tone changing, she might have looked young, but in an instant she seemed less so, she had an ease and effortlessness about her that I envied, I wanted to tell her everything, everything from the beginning, not just mine, but the beginnings of this very world of ours. I can't afford to fall apart, I said, I just can't. Just then, a light outside the window went on and the room felt fresher. We work with metaphor, Satan said, a translucent slick of sweat lay on his Adam's apple, tell her you're afraid of remembering, terrified of this bubbling well of memory, tell her.

How can I help, she asked, opened her notebook, un- capped her ballpoint, and leaned forward. I told her I talked to imaginary people, mostly you, Doc, my partner who had been dead for almost twenty years. She waited, as if what I had just said was not enough to certify me insane, but just in case, I emphasized that I was not insane in that I knew you and all the rest resided only in me. A seam in my mind had come undone, but the dress still held its shape.

She smiled and scooted back in the chair, the streetlamp threw faint light upon her, if I moved my head just slightly, I could see the high stanchion the lamp dangled from outside. Do they talk back, she asked. Sometimes, I said, yes, some- times the imaginary people talk to me, but not you, Doc, you're just there, silent, shunning me, I live while you died. Tell me about him, she said, and I wanted to know what she meant. What could I tell her about you? I don't know, she said, anything, maybe start with his name so we don't have to just call him your boyfriend. What an odd way of putting it: name you and lose you, the banality of demystification. What was your name? His name was John, but he went by Doc, we always called him Doc, he was in med school when we met, became a pediatrician because he liked children except he didn't like the work that much, he hated how awful the parents turned out to be, he didn't consider that when he was in school and when he began to work he thought adults with ill offspring behaved awfully, he received the hurricane brunt of their anxiety, but then, you know, he didn't get the chance to practice much because he became quite a bit sicker than the children he ministered to and died. How did he die, she asked, and Satan replied before I could, Heartbreak, he said, AIDS, I said, AIDS killed all of us.

She hesitated, looked down at her chart, then her well-worn notebook, When did he die, she asked. A long time ago, middle plague, I've always thought I handled it well, all the deaths, but then this denial thing is amazing, I mean, I was hospitalized, I had a breakdown, I had to get cleaned up, get all the drugs out of my system, I replaced them with prescribed ones, I'm clean now, of both kinds, no Haldol, no Stelazine, no weed, no meth, are you going to put me back on antipsychotics, I'm sure you have new ones now, Stelazine used to drive me crazy, and the Haldol, oh my, Haldol turned the whole universe into elevator music, twenty-four hours a day, seven days a week, Barry Manilow and Yanni got gay-married.

We do have new drugs, she said, I would probably recommend that you start a new regimen, but let's see how this goes and what the psychiatrist says, no drugs at all, she asked, you didn't write down any antivirals in your chart. I was never infected, I said, I deserved the disease most, but the virus never visited me, or maybe it did, and then the Fourteen Holy Helpers cured me, kicked the virus and its malicious affiliates out. What was that? Oh, nothing, I said, in those days I had saints as imaginary friends but then Doc's mother stole them.

She scribbled in her notebook, at least a paragraph or two, when she concentrated, she was the one who looked insane, And how did John die, she asked again. Badly, I said. Very badly, Satan said, snickering, funny you should credit the silly saints with healing you, and not me, Death came for you and I intervened, busy man he was those days, I sat him down, told him your soul was mine, a long time ago I claimed you, you child of pestilence, you squashable worm, after all I have done for you, you ungrateful Arab, I sat Death down in the corner, told him he'd accompany you to Sheol over my dead body, we negotiated your survival, I offered much.

I told Jeannie the counselor that you died over a period of eighteen months, and I felt so helpless, you were the fifth, in order, Lou the lovelorn was first, I'm not sure who voted me primary caretaker, maybe you guys thought of me as the natural servant, every nonwork moment was devoted to loving Lou into the next world, changing his diapers, besmeared with shit and shame, I so hated that, and then Chris, then Pinto, bless him, and then Greg, that was so awful, I loved my redhead Curmudgeka, work gave me a three-month leave, he was the attorney who hired me after all, and then it was you, not two weeks later, and then Jim after that, which was unfortunate because poor Jim always got lost in my mind since your death made everything else seem minor, although, God knows, your death was anything but minor, you couldn't go quietly into the night, could you, you want this, you want that, I'm hurting you, you think I'm happy you're dying, I'm poisoning you slowly, you think I think you're not dying soon enough, Doc, I wish you could just shut the hell up.

Finally, Satan exclaimed.

Why now, she asked, the two words announced with a long breath in between, almost a sigh. I can't afford to lose my job, I said, I wouldn't know what to do, I have nowhere else to go. She wrote in the notebook. I understand, she said, but what I meant was why has your boyfriend returned after all these years. I have been feeling more alone lately, I said. She remained quiet, observing me, waiting for me. Triggers, Doc, she was looking for triggers, maybe she was hoping for just one, but they were numerous, so many, where would I start. This morning, I said, when I walked into the office, I usually arrive early, long before anyone else, I wake up at four in the morning so I can put in my eight hours without being disturbed too much and I wake up early anyway so it's not much of an inconvenience, I walked in at five thirty, which is an hour and a half before Joanna comes in, the other two word processors at nine, and today she was there earlier, like me, because she had a lot of briefs to work with, but what surprised me was not her presence as much as what she looked like, what she wore, an old-fashioned dress, a French one, I presume, from the sixties, maybe even the fifties, she's much younger than I so she must have bought it used or inherited it from some relative, it was gorgeous, white dotted with cerise fleurs-de-lis, tight only at the belt, and the way she pinned her hair back, bunched up with lots of unhidden bobby pins, she looked so young, yet matronly, from a time long past, she looked like a number of my aunties, and I stood there rooted, gobsmacked, she looked like my mother. Joanna asked me if anything was wrong, and I replied that the dress was lovely, she twirled coquettishly but I had already sat down at my monitor.

I was tired for some reason, and at noon, when all four of us were there, I must have slept while sitting, which had happened before, certainly not often, maybe twice, and while sleeping I dreamt I was in front of the monitor watching a YouTube nature video of an unnaturally large snake slithering along asphalt, I could see only part of its trunk, and then there was a little bunny eating out of a small bowl and the snake swallowed the bunny and the bowl in one bite and kept on slithering, except I noticed that the body was viscous, mucusy gray, and it was not a snake but a snail with its proportionally large gastropod shell, spirally coiled, of course. I was frightened, it seemed so unnatural, I might have screamed, and this voice in my head, this Satan with insanely blue eyes began to laugh, and I told him to shut up and that was when my officemates called the office manager with her high nasal Oklahoma accent and it was decided that I should take the rest of the day off, which was basically a little more than an hour, and maybe seek psychiatric help, so here I am.

Jacob's Journals

Why Hast Thou Forsaken Me?

I wanted to run to my father, my short legs began to, but I hesitated, halted in mid-run, an indescribable crowd, waiting, coming, going, who were all these people interrupting the reverie, between him and me were bouquets of balloons, of flowers, so many faces disappointed that those of us coming out of customs were not their loved ones, accusing looks, knots of people gathered behind the barriers, my father among them but separate. The accompanying stewardess asked if I knew which one he was, I nodded, of course I did, I had memorized every feature of his beautiful face, the handsomest man in the universe, I pointed to him, while he looked at the Polaroid in his hand to make sure before bathing me with a gracious smile. He wore white like me, a fine linen suit and a pale lavender shirt, a movie star to my eyes, and a crocodile belt of the same color as the shirt, not only was he the most dashing man in the entire airport hall, he had the lightest skin of all, the stewardess offered him my paltriness and her most seductive smile, Take him, she wished to say, though I am more worthy.

My father shook my hand. Next to him stood an older man whose purpose in life seemed to be to provide a contrast to my father's youth and health, I assumed at first he was my grandfather but he was introduced as Monsieur Lateef, it took me a few years to understand that he was the family attorney, there to make sure that the transaction flowed smoothly. The car trip from the airport to Monsieur Lateef's house, me in the back with my father, the driver and the lawyer up front, turned out to be the longest stretch of time I would ever spend with my father, forty-five holy minutes. I would see him a few more times, and he would talk to me on the phone every now and then, but he was busy, of course, he had just graduated with a master's in business and was embarking on a nepotistic career, so you could excuse him, he did his job, fulfilled his sacred obligation, he extracted me from the whorehouse.

I was lost in the grandness of the fancy car's backseat, he asked all the ritual questions, repeating those he had asked in his postcards, how was I, what did I enjoy, was I looking forward to my new life, I did not have time to ask him anything, thinking I would have other opportunities. He entered Monsieur Lateef's house with me, showed me the guest room, where I was to stay for only two nights until Monday, when I would move into my new home, but he had to leave now, he would see me the following day, wished me a good night's sleep. It was not, the bed was too soft, too luxurious, I tossed and turned all night, sank into the mattress, drowned, thought I was going to disappear inside it, swallowed whole by this leviathan. All my life, Doc, I never got used to soft comforts and box springs for slumber, you wanted us to sleep in different beds, then in different rooms, my asceticism troubled you, you said, harshed your mellow.

Next on my father's list was the extirpation of all my sins, the killing of my prophets, on Sunday, the Lord's day of rest, the priests' day of labor, he and Monsieur Lateef led me by the hand to church, For my greatest good, my father said, I was to be civilized, to be taught the manners and customs of the sophisticates. What a place to annihilate my upbringing, to cede my being and its vast lands, my first church, saffron in its stones, bright red tiles, crowned with a tragic and nondescript cross, from where I stood its verdigris looked like moss. Framed by the brilliant sky, Heaven's azure, another cross, this one of Lebanese stone, smaller and more intricate, reigned atop an outdoor arch that I had to pass under as the bell pealed, my father's palm on my back guiding, nudging, prodding me forward, through archaic doors I entered, in the nave of the church I lost my balance, I stumbled but caught myself, my heart lurched in my chest, my father clutched the back of my shirt, he grinned, Monsieur Lateef remained stoic, had not changed his expression since I met him. Long pews filled with parishioners who all glanced back to mark my entrance, indiscreetly examining this convert in ill-fitting attire, I was led up the middle aisle, the church's runway, to be judged by the fashionable, to the front pew, to face the altar.

Once the service began, the heavily decorated priest rambled on and on in Aramaic, Jesus's language that I assumed few worshippers understood, the thudding of my heart was louder than his voice. I watched only a dark-haired boy, not much older than me, sitting back within the apse, clutching an openmouthed dormant censer, around his neck, like a scarf, fell a beautiful saffron-yellow stole with tile-red crosses, my eyes would not leave him, but his jaded eyes remained on the painting of his Savior upon the wall, He whose thorn-wrapped heart burned with an intense flame, whose wondrous eyes watched us all. It was in that church that I took my first Communion, that I fell to my knees and stuck out my receptacle of a tongue, waiting, waiting for the host. Take this, all of you, and eat of it, for this is my body which will be given up for you, take this, all of you, and drink from it, for this is the chalice of my blood, the blood of the new and eternal covenant, which will be poured out for you and for many for the forgiveness of sins, do this in memory of me. God, I miss quaaludes.

It was in that church that I was baptized into a new life in the constant company of low-grade terror and Christ, my savior, it was in that church that I became civilized, almost human in their eyes, the congregation congratulated Monsieur Lateef and my father for their great charity, both were happy to receive the plaudits for they knew they had done a most magnanimous deed, a mighty service for the Lord, reviving my soul, saving me from condemnation, whoever believed and was baptized would be saved. That night after my father had bidden me farewell, he was bound to leave me, always, I slept with the Holy Spirit for the first time, slept in that sinfully luxurious bed for the last time, and the next morning, Monsieur Lateef, whom I never saw again,

delivered me to the disapproving French mother superior
and l'orphelinat de la Nativité, his hand on the low hollow
of my back shoved me into my naked new life.

River

AIDS was a river with no bed that ran soundlessly and in-
exorably through my life, flooded everything, drowned all I
knew, soaked my soul, but then a soaking, a drenching, was
not dying, and I swam, floated when I could, and I thought
I had triumphed, only to discover years later that the river's
persistence, its restlessness, trickled into tiny rivulets that
reached every remote corner of my being. But you know,
Doc, rats always survive floods — both floods and sinkings.

Ibsen

When Ibsen was writing *Brand*, he kept a scorpion caged
in an empty beer glass, and if the scorpion grew listless and
lethargic, the playwright dropped in a piece of fruit, upon
which the creature would cast itself in a rage and inject it
with all its pent-up venom, after which the arthropod was
rejuvenated, whistling happily. Homos, homos, homos, kill,
kill, kill, fags, dykes, sting 'em, smite 'em, there, there, we feel
much better, but now we're gay-married in the armed forces,
so al-Qaeda, al-Qaeda, al-Qaeda, kill, kill, kill, Hamas, Aya-
tollah, bomb 'em, drone 'em, I'm so tired of all this, Doc.

   Don't lose it now, my Iblis said, you're still mildly sane,
bid adieu to this forsaken place.

Anklet

At some point in the middle of the night, I woke and didn't
know where I was, dread, wide awake, who was I, where
was I, I twisted about in panic like a cat in a bag, like Behemoth when he thought I was about to bathe him, but I
calmed when I heard the sound of the tiny tinkling bells of
my mother's anklet in a far room, distant, the distance from
Cairo to San Francisco, what I heard was not the gentle,
comforting sound of her sensuous gliding from one corner
of the kitchen to another, carrying her plate to serve herself
another helping, seconds, but the jarring, parlous jingling
of rough intercourse, my mother wishboned, her ankles
way up, lifted in the night air, soles facing ceiling, which
was when I realized that it was all imagined, the work of a
sickening mind, a joke of Satan's, for I had never heard or
seen my mother's assignations, she was always careful to lock
the heavy door to her room, she was discreet in that, at least.

Dear Mother

One trigger led to another, Doc, I used to think that a depression was built brick by brick into a great wall, but no longer,
my depression was a large pile of stones thrown haphazardly
by God, Satan, fate, while I added the choice pieces. In a
rucksack, I carried bricks down a spiral to Hades. I arrived
home drunk, I had not had a drink in years, not even a glass
of wine, but after work, I got out of the subway station,
was attacked by fuzzy city lights, assaulted by a frenzy of
anxious people spreading in all directions, and there was a

bar and it was happy hour and I was unhappy, I was siren-called, When was the last time you had a martini, a desert-dry one, come in, come in, so I did. Two gin martinis only, no more mostly because I could not bear to be in that bar where young preppy gay boys with pastel sweaters tried too hard to be delightful and delighted, all of them mushroom stumps of the same fungus, two martinis and I swayed all three hundred and some paces to my door, not the man I used to be, soused, my mind insensate, my body walked me home by rote, a beast of burden without its Sherpa, I could not fit the key into its hole for at least a few minutes. One of the landladies downstairs opened her door to check on me, you might remember her, Kim, the kind lesbian, she held my hand, steadied it, key into its slot, she hugged me before letting me stumble into my apartment, I did not weep.

I lay down on my bed, stared at the oscillating yellow ceiling, layered with a few more coats of paint since you left, I shut my blurry eyes, purple spots rimmed with fiery green floated between my eyeballs and eyelids, thoughts spun in a spiral like a sandstorm, whorls of memories, while the world kept marching forward, I continued to sink inward. Satan lay beside me in a white dishdasha and headdress in Saudi fashion, his bulk shifted the mattress and canceled my indentation, his massiveness pressed heavily upon my heart, I could feel his smile, his glee, without my having to open my eyes, Come to Papa, he whispered, his breath moistened the skin below the first ridge of my earlobe.

Dear Mother, I wrote in my head for the millionth time, Though a million times I should ask your pardon, it would not be enough to cover my sins which cause me in-tolerable shame, nowhere near enough, I should never have

left, I should not have wanted to leave so much, I wished for
something different, for something better, every night cats
meowed about the five million ways I missed you, I blun-
dered on but I was not living, in Beirut, God did not wipe
the tears off His children's faces, He did not wipe them in
Stockholm, San Francisco, or anywhere else, I was wrong,
we both were, forgive me.

I wrote to my mother on the day I landed in that impenetrable country, Lebanon, and once every three days
thereafter. I still heard her, Don't write to me every day,
she told me while I was leaving, that would be too much,
but every other day, no, you must write to me every three
days, I can't last more than that without hearing your voice.
Of course, she would not hear my voice, she could not even
read my words. One day I had this brilliant idea of sending
her my voice, I had seen another boy recording on a cassette tape, I copied him and made and mailed a tape to my
mother, I poured all my love and longing into it. I did not
know whether she received it, she never mentioned it, and
I did not ask, did not want to embarrass her just in case
she could not afford a cassette player. I regret not asking.
Her letters back were always perfunctory and precise, like
a well-considered levy: how was I, she missed me, what
the weather was like, what astounding things I was learning, whether I had enough food, warm clothes to deal with
the inhumanly freezing cold of Beirut, she wanted to know
everything about my daily, even hourly life, yet she rarely
shared hers. She sent some pictures, none of which remain.

I worry so much now, Doc, I worry that I have forgotten what she looked like, every day I make sure to paint her
face in my memory in order not to forget, but the moths of

elision eat at the final canvas, her eyes so black and how she looked at me, her smooth skin was what she was most proud of, as smooth as warm marble in a mausoleum, her smile, forever and ever and ever, I try hard now, but the fear that my camphor has aged, that I have failed, haunts me.

The last letter I received was not written by Auntie Badeea, my mother sent one to both of us, I was thirteen. She had journeyed to Mecca for hajj, she wanted her sins forgiven, her errors absolved, she was so happy, Auntie Badeea was terrifically proud, my mother hired a local scribe, who signed her name in the lower right corner, to regale us with her joys, she circled the Kaaba counterclockwise, seven circumambulations, she kissed the black stone, ran between the two hills, she sent us a picture standing all alone under a blood hot sky among the women's tents, all in white, no veil, though the camera was too far from the subject, her face was no more than a smile and a squint against the sun, she smiled as if God had just approved of her and had delivered the news a few moments earlier.

That was it. No one had heard from her since. When she did not return to Cairo, Auntie Badeea inquired for her whereabouts with the travel agency, with the Saudi embassy, with the Egyptian government, the Yemeni government, nothing. There was no record of her leaving Saudi Arabia, dying, or anything, she simply vanished. My father tried to help, he called a couple of Lebanese politicians, even asked a minister to intervene, nothing. Auntie Badeea wrote me letter after letter trying to explain, but there was nothing to explain. My mother might have met a man who charmed her into being his wife, and she could do so only by starting afresh, releasing all dues and obligations of her life before, she would have had to, he was a hajj, she a hajji, it could have happened, it could. At the hajj of the year before my mother's disappearance, two hundred and seventeen pilgrims died during the stoning of Satan ritual, I would not be able to find out how many died while my mother was there and whether she could have been one of them, Auntie Badeea was told all deaths were accounted for.

I did not kill her, Satan said, I was not even there, these people stone a few walls and think they're hurting me, I, who withstood a storm of sulfurous hail, you can't blame her death on me. The Devil appeared to Abraham the Prophet wishing to tempt him, the Angel Gabriel said to him, Pelt him, and Abraham threw seven stones at Satan so that he disappeared, then he appeared once more, and Gabriel said, Pelt him, so Abraham pelted him with seven stones and Satan vanished, but returned for a third time, and Gabriel said, Pelt the deceiver, so Abraham shot seven stones using an old-fashioned sling, and Satan withdrew. Satan's roaring laughter hurt my ears, I love that story, he said.

I could hear my mother in my head, her voice had never faded, but her face sometimes eluded me, like crickets at night in Cairo, I heard them every night, but my imagination had to construct what a cricket looked like, Auntie Badeea told me they were small, not much bigger than a bee, my mother said their color was pale green, Auntie Badeea disagreed, she thought it was light brown, the color of earth, male crickets chirped by rubbing the top of one wing along the teeth at the bottom of the other and lifting both like sails to disperse the sound into the night air, the song restless and unending, females had their ears on their forelegs and they sought the males whose longing sounded the most beautiful, only when they joined would there be quiet, my mother told me they looked like grasshoppers, I could paint the image of a cricket in my head long before I saw one. Why didn't you look it up on Wikipedia, Satan asked, YouTube must have hundreds of videos with crickets, the number of chirps in thirteen seconds plus forty gives a reliable estimate of the outside temperature in degrees Fahrenheit.

I e-mailed my father last week for the first time in years and years, grandfather to five now, he had married a Finn by the name of Tuula, which excited his parents since they wished for nothing more than to purify their bloodline, to rid it of Arabness, I wanted to know if he had a picture of my mother, I thought he might, it took him a whole week to reply, something about two of his European grandtots staying over, he apologized for he could find only one photograph, and it wasn't a good one, from the same hajj, he shouldn't send it because it was silly, but he scanned it, it showed my mother posing for the camera with about thirty other women, she was veiled, only her eyes showed. This morning I spent more than an hour looking at the just-received photo on the screen, with a felt-tip, my mother had drawn a curving red arrow that descended from stringy cloudlets within a blue sky and pointed to one woman covered head to toe in white, her, I presume.

Stridulation, that was the word, I rubbed my wings in longing.

Satan's Interviews

Death

"I can't be sure what happened to his mother," Death said, his voice phlegmy and burlapy after so many cigarettes. A hoary cloud of smoke had settled above his head, making him appear even grimmer and gloomier than usual. "I too drink from Lethe every now and then. I am unable to keep track of everyone."

"It would help Jacob if you could bring yourself to remember," Satan said. "This remains an open wound."

"I don't do wounds," Death said, "or windows, for that matter. Ask one of your saints." The flick of his hand caused his cape to drop from his shoulder. It remained wedged between his back and the chair. "Why do you care? When did his mother disappear, forty years ago? So he forgets about her for decades, then you prod him with your spade-fork? You stress him out, and now you need help relieving him of said stress. And people think I'm the one who's uncaring. Listen, do you know how many of those working ladies he grew up with in Cairo disappeared? A woman would go to the store one day and never return, another would visit home, and whoopsie, we no longer know where she is. The aunties were interchangeable, and most of them had more time for the boy than his mother did. But no, a million times he should ask *her* pardon, five million ways the cats meow about how much he missed *her*. How poetic! How pathetic! Spare me, please. Do you know how many Arabs vanish every day? Every prison in the region is filled with breathing corpses who were once human, with full lives or semi-full, since they are Arabs, you know. Syrian jails, Moroccan, Israeli, Saudi, Iraqi, all overflowing with the they-were-once-human. But no, he wants his mommy. How ridiculous! Remember Joseph, the boy's tormentor in school? You must remember him, the one who always ran pencil lead under his fingernails hoping to appear less bourgeois, a reverse French manicure. He disappeared after the war. He tried to pass for a civilian, the idiot, and the Syrians simply snatched him and left the taxicab he drove on the side of the road. He has been rotting in Mezzeh for over twenty years, but who pays attention to someone like him? No, your boy makes sure to paint *her* face in his memory. Why? Because he's not sure he remembers her as she was, all he has is an impression, as if anyone's remembrances are anything more than fuzzy impressions. He suffers because it's his mother, the same one who sent him away to the lands of oblivion."

Margaret

"You mock me," Satan said.

"All in good fun," Margaret said, ever immaculate and self-possessed.

She jiggled the string in her hand, and above her the baby dragon balloon flapped its wings, changed colors from red to iridescent green depending on the angle. The cross at the end of her staff lay upon her lap, within the folds of her skirt. The helium dragon's flight called their attention to the window and its sky: cold blue and grays, ordinary, the sun on its deathbed, indifferent and lukewarm, bankrupt.

"This interview would be better if it were raining, don't you think?" Margaret said. "I would prefer a day more remarkable, for the boy's sake, if nothing else, more memorable." Her gaze left the window and fixed on her interviewer. "I must say I did not quite like the way cruel Death went on and on about Jacob's mother, and moreover, he was quite wrong. Jacob's remembrances of his mother shaped him the way the outline of a shore is crafted by its ocean. They resurfaced often. You can ask me. I know. I was there. Maybe the lord of heartlessness meant that the boy did not spend enough time with his remembrances, did not contemplate them much or wallow in them, but isn't that Death's work? He rarely takes souls in full bloom. People give him pieces of their souls gladly, and continue doing so until the end, when they no longer have much of their life to keep, so little to fight him with. Here, take this part of me, I don't like it, take this memory, you can have that trait."

"Whenever someone mentions him," Satan said, "a little piece of me dies."

"Clever," Margaret said. "I like that. When the boy's mother disappeared, he thought about her every day, every moment. His memories were still fresh, and then too, a year or so after, Badeea sent him a parcel filled with memorabilia. So on top of the sophomoric Stockholm snow globe, he had photographs, few as they were, anklets, the besequined veil, the sleep mask. Those items were easily able to prompt recollections, to revivify his sense organs: the touch of her lace, the scent of her veil, the feel of her lush lipstick on his lips."

"His mother's blood flooded his eyes," Satan said.

"Exactly," she said. "But then those things were taken from him. The shoe box with the black-and-white snapshots was the first to vanish. Those lost items transformed into little more than impressions, their effects on his senses much diminished. Some items were misplaced, some mispacked, others taken, but it was not his fault. It wasn't. After those horrid classmates assaulted him at graduation, he was flown out of Beirut in the middle of a civil war, flown to Stockholm never to return. His belongings were packed for him, the poor boy. Death cannot blame him for this."

"And yet he does," Satan said. "May I ask why you are defending the boy so earnestly?"

"I loved his mother," Margaret said. "I thought you knew that. She could have been one of mine had she called on me while pregnant. She should have been mine. I failed her. The poet was born on the day he discovered her disappearance."

"Oh, yes," Satan said. "Remember this:

Bolt your doors, my heart.
Snuff the candles,
Break the cups.
Roll up the carpet, dear heart,
And bury your grace.
No one returns.

One of my favorites."

"I miss that boy terribly." Margaret gazed out the window once more, the wrench of tears could be seen in her eyes, but none dropped. "Yes, I would have preferred a rainy day to this, thick irrational rain as in the days of Noah."

"How many rains must fall before the stains are washed clean once more?" Satan asked.

Atop her bosom, the antique medal depicting her and a majestic conquered dragon lifted up and down with each long breath.

"Bring him back," she said.

"He gave up on poetry," Satan said.

"What poet hasn't?"

"He is writing prose now," he said.

"Just ramblings," she said.

"The flights of a mind on its last wings."

"No," Margaret said, "not last. Tired wings—the flights of a mind with exhausted wings. A poet is tormented by the horrors of this world, as well as its beauty, but he can be refreshed, reborn even; he can take to the sky once more. Think phoenix, not Icarus."

Jacob's Journals

That Boy

That dark-haired boy with the censer in the church, his name was Yusuf, but of course that was not what he went by, Joseph was what he wished to be called. I felt the change to Joseph was a shame, for Yusuf of the Quran was the most beautiful. He was the only boy I recognized, so I gravitated to him, a mistake, of course, like a stray meteor, I always sought the wrong planet to crash into. But the first day or two were fine, he talked to me, he too needed an ear, before he found out mine was too foreign, I listened.

On the second evening, I accompanied him to the secret smoking area behind the old rectory, which had been turned into the school library, and he surgically extracted a single cigarette from a plastic pen case, It's a Kent, he told me proudly, the match both lit and shadowed his beautiful face, he did not offer me one. He had a mother who loved him, he made sure to tell me between shallow puffs, but his father had died and the family needed help so he was boarding for only a while, not that he needed to, but, you know, the education was better than anything in his village, he chose to be at the school, and once he soaked up all the great influences he was heading back to his real home, where he would be welcomed with open arms and the most astounding meals this side of the celadon Mediterranean.

He was thirteen, an adult in my eyes, but not physically, for he had yet to mature, and before he stopped talking to me, before he joined the pack of ardent imbeciles who peed on me in the common shower room, he told me that he was born blond and his hair darkened to black, but he made sure to inform me that he was anxiously awaiting the majestic arrival of his pubic hair since it was guaranteed to sprout quite blond, just like the virgin hair he was blessed with at birth. I believed him, but he insisted that I examine the location for myself, I was not averse to that, as you can well imagine, Doc. There was some light, the moon was a weak silver, plump as a carp, presaging autumn, and he unbuttoned his pants and bade me kneel before him, before the smooth wedge of doughy flesh, Look, he said, look, and even though I could see his cock, I knew that was not what he wished me to notice, I told him I could not see any hair, which made him inexplicably happy, smug even, You would be able to see the hair if it was black, he explained, but not if it is light.

I wanted to explore further but I did not know how then, did not understand what I wanted, what I needed, but I felt the longing, the stirring of that elusive enigma we demystify by naming it desire, one whiff and the tectonic plates of that mystery shifted, delicately, subtly, they rearranged themselves. I was frightened, Doc. He above, me below, my natural place, we looked at each other and we both knew. I was frightened by what I saw in me, he repulsed. I was not a boy like him, I was not like any other boy. He buckled up and strutted away, left me there bound to the earth, my stained knees on browning pine needles that had gone soft from being crumpled, the night and my body darkened.

The psycho shower incident occurred at the end of that school year, when the boys who ignored me all the time discovered that their assumption that I was a simpleton was erroneous, egregiously so, if you ask me, that my schooling, whoreschooling if you will, was not so ludicrous, I was taught by Auntie Badeea and her pathetically broken French was easily correctable, her English better than most of the nuns', and her Arabic, forget about it, I was Sœur Salwa's favorite as soon as I set foot in that French colonial parody, and the converted old rectory that was the library with its lively spiders and broken beams, its torn ribs and dangling struts, I may have been unwelcome anywhere else on those grounds, but I lived and loved in that hive of words, the only one there I was, the earnest reader. Placed in the class for the weakest students when I arrived, *la classe des cons*, as it was called, I was moved up twice in two terms, and I aced the end-of-year exams, which was the signal for the guardians of the social order to remind me of my place in this world. I was part of the group that showered on Monday, Wednesday, and Friday nights, no showers on Sundays, five showerheads, five boys at a time, I knew I was in trouble as soon as it was my turn because the four who joined me were the standard-bearers of popularity, the deciders of right and wrong, as soon as we were within the dank, peeling gray walls, while a number of hooligans watched from the entrance, their shadows conjoining into a grotesque silhouette, the naked pack pushed me to the floor, four-cornered me, to the north, south, east, and west of me, yelling all kinds of insults and unimaginative curses, mostly variations on the whoredom of my mother and her blackness, and the gargoyles proceeded to spout pee on me as I hedgehog-huddled atop the swale of the drain.

When they were done, cheerful and laughing, they began to shower. I shrugged, got up, showered, and went to bed. I was mildly traumatized, but I had been expecting the attack forever, and when it finally arrived it was minor, they peed on me in the showers, for crying out loud, how witless was that? In some of the bars I frequented in later years, I found men who would pay good money for that privilege, they knelt, sat, or lay in tubs or on the floor and begged to be showered by the patrons' recycled beers. I was afraid, on edge for my entire time at l'orphelinat de la Nativité, a condition that seemed to satisfy both the boys and the nuns, no further abuse was needed, or at least not much more.

Remember the time I slept at Lou's when a Kaposi lesion made its first appearance on his inner left thigh, remember? Well, we spent the entire night talking instead of resting, he could not sleep and nursed a mild buzz, sipping anodyne wine, finally regaled me with his hellish anecdotes of high school. What a night, death a glimmer not yet mature, Bach measured stirring counterpoints and cool intervals, Lou looked so lovely in yellow pajamas with an Elmer Fudd print, his brown hair still lush, incarnadine cheeks under soft

light, Yusuf of the Quran, the most beautiful of all, yes, like
Satan before his fall. Thou wast perfect in thy ways from the
day that thou wast created, till femininity was found in thee.
On Lou's lips a trace of pinot and out of them poured tales
of acts of viciousness worthy of the great Lucifer himself,
stories told through the night, the tortures, the beatings,
the broken bones, every school has its Tigellinus, but his
had more than one and each with followers, all-American
boys who delighted in discovering how much pain a soul
could withstand, two suicide attempts and all his parents and
school could do was try to make Lou change his behavior,
his behavior, his behavior, *his*, *his*, *his*, to modify his being
just a bit. It gets better, Doc, fucking gets better, no one
dared suggest that maybe the family and the school should
change, or heaven forbid, that it was the all-Americans who
should be modifying their beings, no, the homo should grin
and bear it dumbly, punch me harder now because when I
grow up I'll be working for Google.

My time in school was pleasant in comparison, I was
shunned and shunted to the periphery, not one boy wished
to spend time with me, no student could think of a worse
calamity than being assigned as my bunkmate, I was kryp-
tonite, I was the plague, I ate my miserable lunches and
dinners in Cain-marked isolation while the boys mocked me
and guffawed, but no violence, at least not till graduation
day, and that beating turned out to be a blessing more than
anything else since I ended up in a hospital in Stockholm.

When I was with the whores in Cairo, if I needed to
be admonished, Satan entered the conversation, if I ran
too fast, I'd risk tumbling into Satan's domain, Iblis would
enter the room if I left its door open, when I was with the

nuns in Beirut, if I needed to be admonished, it was forever my mother, if I spoke out of turn, I would grow up to be impetuous like her, if I was tardy, unreliable like my mother, if I did not confess my sins. I could grow up to be evil like Satan or my mother, why not both, I ask you.

I ate alone for years, always alone, boys came and went, new boys, graduating boys, no one sat next to me during breakfast, lunch, or dinner. Joseph and his brothers graduated, they passed the Lebanese baccalaureate, not the French, don't ask me how because their combined intelligence could not outwit an ass, he returned to the orphanage a few years after, while the Lebanese civil war was in full glorious swing about us, to proudly exhibit his plumes, his militia outfit and phallic weapons, Joseph even allowed the young boys to play with his loaded revolver and its six-chambered cylinder, much to the consternation of the nuns, who, like me, watched the armed criminal from the sidelines, the man they used to cane on a biweekly basis, he in full gloat, his eyes excited and hashish-dull, he asked loudly how my mother was, and not thinking I answered rashly, I wish I knew.

The Ass

Pinto died peacefully during a violent night of storms, a garnet-colored sack above his hospital bed. As per his request, the doctors had turned the machines off, his mind was morphined, his pain alleviated. Strangely carved features adorned the thinnest face he had ever had, badged with the purplish lesions of martyrdom. Pinto's emotional-support volunteer wept alone in one corner, younger than all of us, he was new to all this dying stuff, Pinto used to tease him by suggesting that his dying was deflowering the virgin. Such a boy he was, stooped upon himself, his hands covering his face, crying silently, it was true, he was no longer inexperienced, my memory of him is foggy, tender hands, freckles, brown eyes, and long lashes, I can't recall his name.

I rubbed lotion onto Pinto's dry feet, the streetlamp lit the rain from below as in a Romero horror movie, I watched through the picture window until forked lightning distorted the effect, a flood, a deluge to commemorate the passing. I felt a little guilty because I had sent Jim home, offered him the choice of not being there and he grabbed it. He had walked fifteen blocks to the hospital, arrived soggy and haggard, his mind a bit drifty, not morphined like Pinto's, doped up on Jah's blessing. Go home, I told him, go home, please, I'm here, Greg's here, you don't have to be, he would understand, and by he I meant either dying Pinto or his lover who had died not ten days earlier.

As soon as Pinto's heart halted, his face turned green and uninhabited, not even a ghost of him remained, just his remains, I kissed the top of his head, smelled a whiff of sour sweat, tasted a hint of peat moss and earth, the Dormition of Pinto. Water collected in clear sumps on the lower lids of Greg's eyes, his left dropped a tear before his right.

After Pinto had his first bout with pneumocystis carinii pneumonia, the death sentence, he began to joke about wanting to be buried ass up, offering the world the choice part of his anatomy, he wanted an open-casket funeral so the men who had spent weeks and days and hours and hours worshipping his ass could pay it final tribute. He was joking, of course, but I believe he also meant it. In some ways, the fact that he had what most men consider an impeccable asset was what defined him, his pride, so of course that was one of the first things the disease deprived him of. After that first bout of PCP he descended a spiral of weight loss, and his butt shrank, melted, the seats of the designer jeans that used to hug and highlight began to flap when he walked, not long after he lost so much fat that his derriere floated in the denim as if it were in a bathtub. He loathed inchoate hip-hop and its sagging pants, it made him furious.

He made me promise not to bury him in Colma, Anywhere but Colma, he said, I'm a San Francisco boy, I can't end up in the suburbs, God, the indignity. We cremated him. Poor Pinto.

Cobra

On the walk back home
the moon hidden but full
an electric bus stalled
the long hook on its roof
discharged bright sparks
fiery into the night air
detached from the power line
it hissed like a vicious cobra
and fell flat death rattle

— — —

Your poison coursed
through my blood

my nervous system
wouldn't trade it for anything
you flung my doors open
Every day
every moment
I miss you terribly

Poetry

I couldn't write, I couldn't write, stop all the clocks, poetry has gone and left me and the days are all alike.

I was left alive so I could be lonely, bereft of any company but that of ghosts and automatons in this vapid city where I walked until the early dark deepened and a light sheen of mist formed on the leaves of trees, a little crepuscular promenade, my mind filled, to the exclusion of all else, with Satan's voice saying, Pick up the pieces, numbnuts, pick up the pieces, you need a spring cleaning if not a colon scouring, you need an upheaval, a revolution.

The first revolution was Egyptian, of course, the Seth Rebellion of 2740 BC. That's stupid, Satan said, the first rebellion was mine, I, the angel of light, I, all pulchritude and glory and blazing fire, I rejected blindness, I broke the chains of conformism, and you're still paying for that one, all else fails and pales in comparison. I shrug you off, Satan. Shrug me off as much as you want, Satan said, but until you remember that the first sin is oblivion, your poetry will remain shit.

I decided to give up, poetry, that is, I should have a long time ago, I gave up on life, why not poetry, I ask you.

A man who does not engage life should not engage poetry, Satan said, accept Lucifer as your muse, when Adam, still unstained by guile, first bit into his luscious apple of gold and wax red and licked its juice dribbling down his chin, poetry came to life, through a dilating crack he and his buxom consort were hurled into this sunlit world of contrast, when they were tossed out of banal Paradise like yesterday's used condoms, the serpent of old offered life and verse and art.

I hear you not, Satan, I hear you not.

I miss Eve, Satan said, she's my homegirl.

I pelt you with stones, Lucifer, father of lies.

Listen to me, Satan said, his eyes infused with flames, get thee out of Eden, poetry can never be unstained.

Satan's Interviews

Denis

The fur on Behemoth's back bristled as soon as he saw Denis holding his mitered head on his lap. Behemoth hissed, unleashed a rending meow, and jumped right back into the closet.

"Funny cat," Denis said.

"Bothered by the head," Satan said.

Had Satan doubted for a moment that the cephalophore was the most vain of the fourteen, the cloak would have ensured that he would never do so again: it was of the most luscious silk, a radiant Yves Klein blue with a needlepoint illustration of the city of Paris in gold thread. His crosier was emblazoned with golden luster and more inlaid gems than a magpie's nest.

"Are you?" Denis raised a recently waxed eyebrow.

"Of course," Satan said. "Standard rule: if cats dislike something, I usually do as well. I feel uncomfortable talking to you and you know that. Instead of looking at where your head is supposed to be, I'm staring at your crotch. I can't concentrate on much else than the autoerotic possibilities. I know that's the point, but can you at least hold your head in the crook of your arm?"

"If I hold my head higher while I'm seated, my two halos clash."

"Put it on, then."

"I usually wear my head only when I need to think," Denis said.

Satan enunciated his command slowly. "Put. It. On."

"Oh, all right." Denis returned his head to his shoulders; it fell into place with the subtlest of clicks.

"Why did you abandon him?" asked Satan.

"I did not," Denis said. "He abandoned me, he abandoned us. I was with him from the start, not because of him, but because of his mother. She needed me and I was there. Now, she—she was devoted to me and my arts. But the boy was different, slow in some ways. Surrounded by desire, he knew not how to partake. He was a virgin for I don't know how long. He was Catherine's boy long before he became mine. And then he unleashed his desires and I thought there would be no stopping him, but he stopped. He stopped, not me. Can I have some tea, please?"

"No."

Every time Satan met the dandified bishop, he felt a wrench of urges: he wanted to slap Denis, to knock the idiotic miter off his head—he wanted to behead him.

"Go back to the beginning," Satan said. "When did you first meet Jacob?"

"Catherine came first. The rest appeared to him when he began to recognize us, but we were there long before. He simply never saw us. I remember things Jacob doesn't."

"Tell me," Satan said. "This is what we're here for. What do you think he has forgotten?"

"Well, for me, I think the important erasures are the whorehouse years. He has skipped over much, his remembrances are a surreal game of hopscotch. He remembers the Cairo house in detail, but he erased most of the city. It's not just what he remembers, it's how he does. He remembers in his head. If I were to remind him about Cairo—if, mind you—I would ask him how the light felt falling on his face during winter afternoons. How gooey was the riparian mud he stuck his hand in the first time he walked along the Nile south of the city? A haptic memory perhaps?"

"An expedition into the depth of his tactile memories," Satan said. "The brush of the coarse bricks on his calves as he dangled his legs over the midget wall across the street from the house."

"Yes, yes. Does he recall feeling nervous during a visit with Badeea to Khan el-Khalili when he was five? He held her hand as she shopped, how his hand felt in hers, how small he felt next to her, the scent of fresh eggplant and green squash, the pots cooking Egyptian mallow, the smell of fresh rabbit turd under the cages. Does he remember? And the crowd thickened as if a ton of roux had been dropped into the human soup, everyone so much larger than him. Fear, anxiety, he was terrified of being trampled. Badeea lifted him up with her left arm, that woman had the strength of ten men. Does he remember touching her cheek, laying his head on her shoulder like a drooping tulip on the rim of its vase, looking back at the gathering crowd, safely tucked atop her bosom, the feel of her forearm on his behind? You see, he thinks he doesn't remember, but of course he does. It's just that our memories are rarely where we think they are."

"So you think you can help him remember Cairo?"

"Yes, I do," Denis said. "There was a small mosque but two streets away from the house. The boy used to love hearing the muezzin's melodious call, and that teenager had a glorious voice by any standard, and he was blind as he was supposed to be. The child Jacob was so enamored by the sound that he wondered aloud why the household didn't attend the mosque. Badeea took him that one time. Does he remember the ablutions, the warm water on his skin, it was summer, the rug beneath his bare feet in the women's section of the mosque? He might recall why he never went back, how unwelcome he was made to feel because of Badeea, how the other women shunned her, did not look her way. Even as little more than a toddler, he knew what that was; he was as sensitive to ostracism as any budding homosexual."

"He thinks he has never been inside a mosque," Satan said, "but too many times inside a church."

"Well, he's wrong, isn't he?" said Denis. "Not that he received better treatment in the church."

Denis tilted his head back and sniffed the air twice. A scowl began at his brow below the miter, eyebrows scrunched, nostrils dilated, lips turned downward, chin rising up, a rictus. The red scar of his beheading made a theatrical appearance from behind the robe's neckline.

"Who's been smoking in here?" he asked.

"You know who," Satan replied.

"That son of a night. He knows I'm allergic to tobacco."
From one of his robe's pockets, Denis brought out a hand-
sized gold thurible, from another, an antique gold lighter
with an engraved crest of the city of Paris. Without moving
from his seat, he shook the smoky apparatus all around him.
"The standards," he said. "Frankincense and myrrh."

In the closet, Behemoth hissed loudly.

"Are we done?" Satan asked.

"Yes, sorry." Denis placed the censer on the hardwood
floor between his feet. "As I was saying, I remember more
than Jacob does." He did not return the lighter to his pocket,
flicked it on distractedly a couple of times.

"I need to clarify something," Satan said. "Now, do you
truly believe that he remembered the Cairo house in detail,
but not the city?"

"Yes," Denis said. "Well, no, not exactly. He remembers the specifics of the house in detail, but not what happened in it. He writes that the men who visited the brothel
ignored him, but you know that's not accurate, not always.
When he was old enough he had to help with a number of
chores. His first incarnation was as a brazier boy." He lifted
the thurible off the floor and swung it gently a few times.
"When the room was full, the boy had to rush around re-
plenishing charcoal in every dying hookah. If he was slow, a
man noticed him. His second was foot massager, of course.
For some men, especially the Russians, this was part of a
sensuous evening. A customer would lounge on the couch,
call the boy, who had to run over, get on his knees before
the man, take the shoes and socks off, and work the feet."

"On his knees before the man," Satan said.

Denis flipped the top of the lighter and struck it seven times in a row. "Why does he choose not to remember these details?"

"He will now," Satan said.

"What about the henna incident? How could he forget that? He wrote that the prepubescent Joseph's hairless crotch was the first he'd seen."

"Tell me."

"He learned to henna his mother's hands and feet at an early age. She used to decorate herself, whenever she knew a client wanted something different or less familiar. Then the boy turned out to have a talent for it. Once every ten days or so, his mother let her son draw on her skin. He did so for about six months before a soused East German noticed the designs from across the room. He demanded to know what was on her hands and feet even though the poor woman was entertaining another man. She explained, pointing to her son as the designer. The loud East German demanded his own henna design, a strange request obviously, but the brothel was known for being accommodating. The boy rushed over with the gourd and reed, and knelt before the seated man, golden blond he was, big and sturdy. He looked at the boy, who was gazing up at him, waiting for instructions. The East German snickered, stood up before the kneeling boy, undid his pants while the whole room, European men and subaltern women, watched. Out jumped his fully erect blutwurst, almost slapped the poor boy's face. The boy didn't move, but even had he wanted to, he wasn't quick enough because Badeea jumped up from her divan, lifted the boy by his shirt collar, and pulled him behind her. She berated the man, but he grew belligerent, demanding that his penis be drawn upon or the house would suffer unspecified consequences. The men were amused, the women horrified, no one budged. Badeea was about to call on the lazy oaf who was supposed to be the bouncer when the intervention occurred."

"Halimeh," Satan said.

"You remember her too," Denis said, resting his chin on the palm of his hand. "The girl with the pigtails—love her now, worshipped her then. She was thirteen, still a virgin but not for very long. While Badeea was telling off the ugly rascal, who refused to pack his insistent penis, Halimeh, seemingly out of nowhere, knelt before him, shocking everyone, including the uncouth European himself. While all gasped, she dipped the reed in the gourd, held the penis in her left hand, and began to draw with her right. No one but the girl moved, the only sounds were the tap of the reed on the gourd and the East German's heavy breathing. He almost erupted at least twice. For the entire time the girl went about her chore, everyone including our boy remained still, observing the unfurling image, the tiny dark girl on her knees before the giant with overgrown blond pubic hair. The penile design was nothing exceptional of course, and it was ruined because he couldn't maintain his erection long enough for the henna to take root, so ogees, swoops, and arabesques were nothing but blotches at deflation. But what Halimeh did was exceptional. She became the most desired Arab whore ever. The East German pleaded to take her back to one of the rooms, but even he knew that he could not afford her virginity. They brought in a West German for that. He paid a considerable fortune for her Arab hymen."

"And the poet recalls only her pigtails," Satan said.

At the Clinic

Gluteal Poems

Ferrigno the Iraqi, who was to lead me back to the waiting room, failed to keep a straight face, quickly glanced
around the examining room, grinned, No poetry, he said,
not questioning, just matter-of-fact, he knew I wouldn't,
and Satan said, The staff probably had a pool on whether
you'd break, I wonder whether this inflatable Iraqi bet for
or against, let's graffiti the walls, no, no, ask him if you can
write on his badass booty, I wonder what he'd say to that,
I bet he'd let you, ass for art's sake, ask him, you can write
Ass You Like It.

I told Satan, Do not go gentle into that good butt.

Ha, screeched Satan, he's the emperor of ass cream,
now compose an ode to a gluteus turn. I told Satan,
My heart aches, and a drowsy numbness pains
My sense, as though off your ass I had drunk

Some dull opiate that emptied all my brains
     And all my senses Lethe-wards had sunk.

No, no, said Satan, we're not to mention that damned
river.

I followed Ferrigno's callipygian semaphores, up and
down with each step my eyes kept track. His pen dropped,
I began to lunge for it, but it swung from a string that connected it to the clipboard he held against his sizable forearm that had a barbed-wire tattoo, I flashed on an image
of Auntie Badeea pulling thick thread through vegetables,
making rosaries of peppers, sights and sounds of my early
years reconfigured for my modern world, with each step now
my head would shift from the pendulum pen to Ferrigno's
sliding butt muscles as if I were at a Wimbledon final. My
cell phone vibrated, Ferrigno heard the buzz, didn't glance
back, I knew it was another text from Odette but I did not
want to look, I did not want to be connected to anything,
I wanted the wet wool of my mind sheared, I desperately
needed to pee.

Ferrigno waited outside the bathroom, he was grin-
ning when I came out, he leaned his head through the door,
I guess a black ink pen would have been better, he said. I
like this guy, Satan said, he's mocking you, as all should.
Nah, I told Ferrigno, brown is just fine, I'm limbering up,
once I get going, your ass will be wiping poems all night.
His ass is a kneaded eraser, Satan said, we need to get him
to drop his pants.

At the entrance to the waiting room, Ferrigno told me
he would be back for me when the doctor was ready. See,
Satan said, he's playing with you, even he knows you're
not insane, let's go home. The waiting room was empty and

quiet, no one, the bespectacled lady was probably getting counseled. I looked at Odette's texts: the first was, Please don't shut me out, you fucker, and the second was, I'm your best friend and I'll mess you up if you don't tell me what's going on, and the third was, Now, bitch. So I did, I asked her to please not interfere, said I was a bit depressed, that I was having hallucinations, not dangerous, but disturbing enough that I needed to get rid of them, that I was waiting to see a doctor, and that I would not pick up if she called because of where I was, and no, I wasn't going to tell her where that was. As soon as I pressed the last send, I felt lighter, even Satan's snickering couldn't weigh me down.

You look tired, Satan said, I told him I was, that I did not think I would have trouble sleeping in this uncomfortable chair even though I was without my two primary sleep aids, Behemoth and a YouTube recording of a vacuum cleaner, the Hoover WindTunnel. I don't know why I find the sound comforting, Doc, when I was a child in Cairo, my afternoon naps coincided with the rhythmic beating of carpets outside the bedroom, I was used to sleeping to that sound, but no one beat carpets anymore, a shame, though lo and behold, I found that not only did a vacuum cleaner remove dirt more effectively, it summoned Hypnos just as well as a beating, and there were twelve-hour-long recordings of all kinds of household machines online, welcome to America, now go to sleep.

Maybe I should have told Ferrigno that a black ink pen would be better, I had a fountain pen once, beautifully lacquered, with a silver nib, belonged to my father, a Christmas present he deigned to offer me from afar when I was twelve, I filled it with real, honest-to-goodness ink from an inkwell, encaustic the color of night sky, deliberate, slow to dry, so very patient. Disloyal I was, my infidelity marked me, I do not even remember when I abandoned the pen, ink, black like the inside of my head, the precise color of sorrow. Not only do we drink from the black river, we drop bodies into it as well, objects we once loved, tools we once used, rusted treasure litters the bottom of Lethe. I took the brown Sharpie out of my pocket, Praise be, Satan said, and I pulled back the left sleeve of my shirt, upon the hairless skin of my inner forearm I wrote:

When Death came to visit me
I had nothing to offer
My cupboard was bare.

Jacob's Journals

Veil

I have become invisible, Doc, it was not always this bad. When I first arrived in this country, I was ignored but not necessarily by all, you saw me, Greg saw me, as did a few others, I was young and fulfilled some erotic fantasy for a small number, pedophilic, if you ask me, but I'm not complaining, dark, small, and exotic, let's fuck him, yes, please. For most though, I might as well have been wearing a veil, to all patrons of trendy bars I was invisible, and it became much worse. I walked the roads, in cheerful daylight or at night, none paid attention. Have you ever noticed that in the English language we use attention as if it is currency, and it is, is it not? Buy me some. Heloise begged Abelard to pay the debt of attention he owed her, and you owe me. The other day, though, a woman saw me, she was coming out of the supermarket, I was going in on my way home from work, she glanced at me before holding out her green reusable shopping bags for me to carry, I ignored her, kept walking through the electric door, didn't look back.

Auntie Badeea would not wear a veil, every Cairene of her time understood that forward was the only way forward. My mother covered her face when she was in Yemen, but once in Cairo, she wore a veil only if an American or a European wanted to dally with a stereotype. I saw a veil only rarely in the Cairo of the sixties, and never in Beirut—well, not a real one.

In the summer of my first year at l'orphelinat de la Nativité, when half the kids and most of the nuns went on vacation, I was doing homework—even that first summer, I grew to hate what we called *les devoirs de vacances*, they were unbearably unfair. Evening, I was tired, the old rectory's windows were quite decorative but would not open, constrained heat made even the books sweat, I slumped over my notebook and fell asleep. I knew not to do that because when I napped on a book or an open binder I usually woke up with reverse text inked on my face, which I actually loved, loved deciphering my face in the mirror, but I would be mocked by anyone who saw me, and truly I could not afford to be noticeable in any way, I lived in the safety of not being seen. I woke up suddenly, did not have time to check if my face had added a written patina, a flicker of light out the window caught my attention, it was a flicker of a woman in silver between two pine trees that raised a protective cupola above her, I considered that she might be one of the remaining nuns, but as I walked up to the window, the glass smudged and dusty, I knew it was not so, not just because I didn't recognize her, she wore a habit like our nuns but hers included a veil that covered all but eyes that seemed to be contemplating the moon, which unveiled its peerless light and threw its silver mantle over her.

The woman frightened me. I watched her through the window before I gathered enough courage to leave the rectory, I remained a safe distance away, and she remained motionless gazing at the sky, between the pines that wept odorous gum and balm, I was behind her, she could not see me. Yet in a resonant clear voice she said, I did not think we would come out of our hiding place, I told her it was the library, not my hiding place, and she said that she knew what it was, she had been there many times. It was then that she turned around and faced me. We can approach, she said, but I refused to uproot myself from where I stood, so she left her spot under the pine nebulae and walked over, glided, and when before me in all her glory, she reached out and caressed my cheek, and I was no longer scared, I would follow her to Hell and back, do whatever she asked of me, I would love her, a seraphic love, of course. I felt seen for the first time, by expressive eyes that no painter of portraits could ever capture, intelligent eyes, sparkling, penetrating, and the oddest color, the yellowish green of an unripe guava. We have grown up, my little Ya'qub, she said, and I told her I was still short, and she said, And we shall remain so. She was beautiful, I did not need her to lift her veil for me to know that, but then she did, she lifted it and kissed me on my forehead before she returned to her place between the pines to gaze at the constellations, those dark creatures outlined by stars.

She wished to be alone, so I left her, but upon entering the main house, I encountered the French mother superior roadblock, where I was intercepted and cross-examined. Where have you been, little man, she asked me, and I told her I was studying in the library but then I saw a woman under the pines who I thought might be the Virgin Mary, since everyone at the school knew that she appeared quite often in Lebanon, but of course, the ever-baleful French mother superior, her skin as white as stream stone, looked doubtful, there was no reason that the Mother of God would grace an Arab speck like me with her presence, so she said, Did you ask her if she is our Blessed Mother, and when I admitted that I had not, she sent me back out to do so. The veiled woman was no longer under the pines, which seemed to irk the French mother superior no end, she sent me to bed with a dismissive command, The next time you see the Mother of Hope, ask her what kind of penance she demands from you for being a liar.

The woman visited a number of times that August, mostly in the rectory while I was reading or studying, I did not ask if she was the Virgin, did not have to, I knew she was not, I knew she was one of us. I had to wait for the following semester before Sœur Salwa explained who Saint Catherine of Alexandria was and why the Roman Catholic Church no longer believed in her existence while it kept the inconsequential Italian Catherines, Sœur Salwa spat every time she mentioned a Catherine from Siena or Bologna or Genoa, the Church took away Barbara and Margaret, Cyriac and Agathius, they removed our Christopher's sainthood but kept that of the idiot from Milan, the Church slew the fourteen, martyred them once more and again. The Mother of Hope might have been born one of us but she no longer deigned to spend time in the colonies, she preferred to get her pedicures on Via Veneto. But Catherine, my Catherine visited me, and at first, our conversation was minimal, I would read while she perused the books, she confessed that she had read them all, and when she did speak during those early months, she sounded like my father's postcards that used to arrive in Cairo, or my mother's letters, Study hard, my son, pay attention in class, be diligent, studious, and earnest, always do what you're told.

On the first day that Sœur Salwa secretly taught us about our saints, Saint Catherine came to the rectory, as soon as she opened the door and saw me, she recognized that I knew her, I asked her, I said, Are you Saint Catherine, our sacred martyr, and she smiled, and an inchoate halo formed before my very eyes, she did not even have to nod, to acknowledge, to respond, she no longer needed a veil in my presence, she was known to me.

Betrayal

I don't think you know how Greg and I met, Doc, I never told you and I can't imagine he ever would have, he was so decent. Why did you keep me for all those years? I hated you that night, loathed you, I knew you were screwing other boys, you insisted on an open relationship, even I began to fool around with others when you no longer cared to make love to me, but it was just kissing and making out, I mean, I knew you were doing a lot more than that, but I was not ready yet, but then you brought that boy home, I was making you dinner for crying out loud, okay, it was spaghetti but still, I was boiling water with salt and a touch of olive oil in the kitchen. Sorry, you said, we had nowhere else to go, which was patently untrue, you liar, you could have gone to a bathhouse, but no, you had to make me see, make me understand, and I did, he was so deliciously cute, I hated you, you had your arm around his shoulder like a boy holding his favorite Christmas toy, sight hateful, sight tormenting, you two imparadised in each other's arms. You took him into your bedroom, yours, no longer ours, you closed the door, I was holding the colander in the kitchen, staring out the small rectangular window above the plastic dish drain, unable to move, as if I had just woken up with sleep paralysis, temporary though that might be, I was shuffling frantically within minutes, I grabbed my keys, my wallet, and walked out of our home.

I did not know where I wanted to go, had no plan, wished only to be away from you and that inconsiderate whore you brought back with you, I walked and walked, my steps moving more quickly than me, from one neighborhood to another, from salutary to sleazy in less than five city blocks, found myself in the seedy and needy neighborhood south of Market Street, I refuse to call it SoMa. You should see what it looks like now, Doc, a dandified eunuch, that's what they turned it into, everything seems new, the city's memories have been cordoned off, there's a Whole Foods store, our history elided by the fashionable, there are dainty boutiques and designer bistros, Folsom Street Fair has become a fetish mall sponsored by Wells Fargo, Wholesome Street Fair. But it was not so then, I was in front of the Eagle, not sure what pulled me in that night, I never cared to before, always thought that leather men looked like a parody of masculinity, why would anyone want to wear so much cow, it went deeper than that, I believe the Nazi aesthetic offended me, but no matter, I went in.

What can I say, right time right place, or wrong time, or whatever, I was there, I was like a jumpy child alone at an intersection for the first time, look left, look right, look left again, step onto the pavement. Men, men, men in that nest of iniquity, bikers, truckers, those pretending to be, all with facial hair, shaggy beards and trimmed, all white men, made whiter by the black leather ensembles, and by me. The bartender looked me up and down, a short distance, but then welcomed me a bit too effusively, fresh meat and all that, I wished to order a gin and tonic with a lime twist, but I knew not to, just as I knew not to ask my mother for that lace embroidered face mask when I was a child, American beer it was, and a shot of Jäger.

I had no intention of doing much, I swear, I had never considered that I might enjoy a place like that, let alone its patrons, but I was not going to let these men think of me as an innocent lamb, I was no Agnus Dei, I would be the sophisticated observer of this tribe of aboriginals, an ethnographer of its rites and rituals, I would record their behavior for later examination under better lighting, fool that I was, Shakespearean fool. Stars, hide your fires; Let not light see my black and deep desires. I sat on a shelf beside the pinball machine, nursing the insipid beer, watched men in couples and in groups, arms encircling each other, kissing and touching while they talked, groping butt and crotch, I watched. So many handkerchiefs in back pockets, different color codes that I could not crack, the leather men were less loud, none of the frenetic exhibitionism and braggadocio of other gay bars, yet they preened in uniform, sporting the handkerchiefs like peacock tails, an invitation to debauchery in your ass pocket.

A group of five to my right passed a joint around, they all turned my way at the same time, someone must have mentioned the ethnographer, one extended his hand, I inhaled a couple of drags of the joint and returned it. A man led another in full rubber body suit and an ominous-looking head mask across the room by a chain, the master sat on a bar stool and his chained partner knelt on the grimy floor beside him, a ritual of the primitives being played, under the fluttering dim light the master seemed to grow taller in his chair. The air was thick, resinous with tobacco smoke, marijuana, and a miasma of carnal pheromones that I absorbed with all my senses, my being, my mind murky, my erection unrelenting. And I saw him. At first glance, he did not seem different from the rest, the requisite leather jacket and chaps, Levi's, motorcycle cap, but on his side was a coiled black knout, I paid that no mind, an accessory, I thought, an egregious error of judgment. The manner in which he devoured me with his minatory eyes, the slanting leer of his lips, the flickering of his black mustache, I knew not how to resist had I wanted to, the Budweiser sign above my head must have changed to one screaming Use me, abuse me, fuck me, dump me back in my home country. He flicked his head, a signal saying, Come here, but I did not understand or I would have crawled over, not until he sneered in frustration did I figure out what he wanted, and I was about to slide off the shelf when he ambled over, angry, the room watched his approach, my eyes were forced to track him, up, down, his eyes, his highlighted crotch slightly bleached, he took the bottle of beer from my hand, downed the contents in one chug, grabbed my arm, and pulled me off my seat.

I would have followed him, but it was not to be, there was an interruption, catlike, Greg jumped from the group of five on my right and grabbed my other arm, knout man felt the tug, turned around, saw Greg holding me, and literally growled, while Greg with a stoner smile simply said, Fuck off, but it sounded more like Fockoff. There I was, two handsome, manly men tugging me, one on each arm, about to fight over me, my mind so muddled all I could do was grin at Greg and ask, Are we Irish? Greg shook his head in puzzlement, I had this effect on men when I was young. Knout man squeezed my arm harder, it hurt, he hissed at Greg, Let go of what's mine or I'll kill you, Greg seemed unperturbed, he repeated, Fockoff, which only increased my certainty that he was Irish, at which point the four in his group jumped into the passion play insisting that knout man leave me be, one shoved him but he still hung on to me, it seemed all the patrons of the bar including the once-welcoming bartender surrounded us and as a Greek chorus chanted, Leave the boy alone, asshole, You're not welcome here, You're a sick weirdo, Get the hell out, and knout man's hand released its grip but not Greg, who pushed me behind his back until the evil man left the building, threatening and cursing, his walk toward the exit much less masculine.

The bartender told Greg's group, You guys take care of this one, and then to me, And you had better get smart real quick. Greg and his cohort explained that knout man's last trick ended up in the hospital for four days with both internal and external injuries, worse, according to a man in the group, knout man did not even visit once, much worse, according to another, knout man was a cop, a hat trick of offenses, eighty-sixed from the Eagle after that night.

I hung on to my knight in shining armor, my hand held his arm for the entire time we stood in the circle at that bar, I did not consider whether he found me attractive that evening, or whether he cared to take care of me, I was going home with him, he had no choice that first night: he saved me, ergo he owed me. I followed him through the dark night, oblivious to anything but him, his red hair, his mustache, wondering what color his pubic hair would be, was he uncircumcised, I stepped around winos and druggies, stepped over smelly lumps covered in filthy blankets, breathed in the stench of souls, walked and walked.

He lived one block away from us, convenient, bigger house, bigger bed, giant abstract paintings, and an in-house dungeon. Come ye and let us go down to Greg's underworld and he will teach us the ways of our lord and master. He checked the answering machine for messages, turned on the reel-to-reel machine that was wired to the downstairs playroom, three-hour tape of the Brandenburg Concertos mixed in with Tangerine Dream, Jean-Michel Jarre, and Vangelis. He had to take it slow with me, he said once he undressed me, and he did, he kissed me before he whipped me, I tasted his tongue before I felt the exquisite flick from the tongue of his lash. The dungeon's cold concrete floor iced the soles of my feet and I was happy to be lifted off it, Men are less sensitive to pain at night, he told me as he anchored my restraints to the rings on the Saint Andrew's cross, you're a creature of the dark, and the black walls made the myriad of hooks and eye rings fixed on them look like refulgent night stars. He introduced me to my gregarious nipples, Hello there, meet Mr. and Mrs. Clamp, did you know Roman soldiers used tit clamps to fasten cloaks around their shoulders? My ass met the paddle, my mouth its gag, my back the cat-o'-nine-tails, my skin its sustenance, that night, all night, Greg disinterred me, polished the dust off my well-trampled soul, he took it slow, at least that first time. I did not scream once, I couldn't, he had me bite a leather strap with teeth marks of novitiates, I bit and bit, he'd brought it back from a trip to Peru, llama leather, and it was black, black llama, what becomes a virgin most. I didn't scream, but I wept throughout, I bawled as he released me and carried me back up to his bed, hugged me, spooned me, loved me, poured guidance and affection into my ears, and like all saints before me, I relished the ecstasy of martyrdom.

While the morning sun was in mid-sky, my soul afire, my mind still drifty from its ecstasy, my body returned home like a horse with slack reins. Walk of shame, my ass, I was sizzling. Self-tempted, self-depraved, that was me. I walked into our apartment thinking I would have to explain to you what happened, where I was, but you were asleep and your boy was getting dressed quietly and haphazardly, he seemed less sober than I, he noticed me only when he left your room, almost ran into me, and you know what he said? Not hello, not sorry, he asked if I could make him some coffee. I looked into your room, the sheets were half off the bed, you spread-eagled, floating atop the extra-soft mattress surrounded by an archipelago of stains, sleep drool dried on your lower cheek, your chest hair needed untangling, unconscious you were, and happy, and the window's sunbeams illuminated your wallet on the dresser. I took it, I wanted to teach you to be wary of bringing strangers into our home, I would return it once you discovered your folly, but when you wore that inerasable grin at the kitchen table, drinking the coffee I made you, and told me that fucking that boy whore was worth two of your wallets, nay, three, well, I didn't give it back, did I? I tore up your wallet, you died thinking the boy stole it, but it was me, Doc, it was me, do you still think it was worth it?

The Mask

As a six-year-old I considered my mother's lace-embroidered sleep mask the most beautiful object in the entire world, the material a baby-rose satin, the lace black, a fake pearl sewn onto the bridge. I did not have to be told that asking for it would have been horrifying, tantamount to matricide, but I longed. I developed debilitating migraines, maelstroms of pain behind my eyes, any light was fatal. In the whorehouse, I was offered what I wanted as an anodyne. Here, darling, this will make you feel better. For years, probably until I left for Beirut, all I had to do was think of that lace-embroidered sleep mask and I would feel profoundly sleepy.

About a year after my mother disappeared, Auntie Badeea sent a parcel filled with keepsakes, she knew to include the sleep mask. On graduation day, when I was supposed to leave l'orphelinat de la Nativité and begin to unlock the secrets of the real world without being given a key, the other boys in the graduating class decided to offer me something more effective: a beating. Even by the high standards of the civil war in Lebanon at the time, that was no ordinary attack. I ended up needing surgery that the Hôtel-Dieu Hospital in Beirut could not perform because of the shortages during those years. I was flown to Stockholm as part of a mercy mission, swapped pine trees for cold birch and larch. I was not conscious for much of those seventy-two hours. The nuns, knowing that I would never return,

packed one suitcase. They did not include much, definitely
not my mother's mask. The French mother superior would
never have considered that I would want such a thing.

Drought

Was it a coincidence that we began to drop dead while
we had a severe drought? Who wilted first? Who? Lou—
Lou wilted first, his first lesion appeared on his inner left
thigh, verily the mark of Cain. A mere purple dot it was, an
innocuous-seeming barnacle that tore us out of life like a
page and collaged us into the book of the dead. I wanted to
run as far away as possible, take me back to Cairo, to Beirut
even, where bullets and mortars killed more efficiently, I
wanted out, I could not bear the idea of his death sentence,
and yours and Greg's, which I was sure would follow, and
mine, of course, but the maker of marks had planned a
different torture for me, hurled headlong flaming from th'
ethereal sky.

Lou called me at work, no one ever did, I was startled
when the office manager deigned to enter our windowless
word-processing room and announce that I had a telephone
call, she emphasized the word *telephone* as if it were a Martian
apparatus, Lou had called Greg to get the number that even
I did not know, but he did not tell Greg, not then, he told
me first, and I did not know why. It had started, he said on
the other end between sobs, and it certainly had, no longer
on the horizon, what we were all terrified of had begun,
all our delights would vanish, we were to be delivered to
woe, he had a lesion. What could I say? I hung up and left

work, I could not go to him at first, I could not, I walked
and walked, for hours, Castro was a street of ghosts, dead
and alive, all lost in loss itself, only the impaired appeared
on the street, only wisps remained of their once carefully
tended mustaches, their faces the color of parched lichen,
they stood accused, our comrades, exiled and stateless in
our native city, they could not run away, everyone else did,
turned into strangers. I walked among the canes and the
walkers, immortal age beside immortal youth, inhabiting
the same body, coterminous, coexisting, co-dying.

Only the day before you had pointed out the laurel next
to our house, Look, you said, Daphne is dying, we had no
water, her leaves were a jaundiced green, like all the trees in
the neighborhood that day, but Daphne was made of sterner
stuff, she withstood and did not crumble.

I could not go to Lou, I could not be there for him, I
walked until the soft saffron sun disappeared in the Pacific,
long is the way and hard that out of Hell leads up to light,
or better yet, leads to a boutique wineshop, four bottles of
pinot, and then I walked to Lou's apartment, where he was
by himself, we were all so afraid in those early days, under
dim lights we drank good wine and listened to the languid
hum of the four-petaled ceiling fan stirring the same stale
air that every now and then reached us as if it were fresh,
and he told me all about his story and all that he once longed
for. He loved life, he said in a whisper that barely scratched
the silence, barely heard above the fan's hum, but the feeling
wasn't mutual. Remember me, he said, and I do, thou wast
perfect in thy ways from the day that thou wast created,
always and forever, I remember you, Lou, I do.

Jacob's Stories

A Cage in the Penthouse

My wife bought a new wardrobe for the party: a five-row pearl necklace choker, matching earrings and bracelet, black pumps with heels that should have been declared a dangerous weapon, and two black dresses that I wouldn't have been able to tell apart for a million dollars, which was almost what they cost; two because "But, darling, if I gained a pound by next week, or even felt a little bloated, then this one would just not do, I'd have to wear this one." She considered tonight the most important social event of her life, hence our life. If we did not make a wonderful impression, we could forget about unpacking and return to Muncie with our tails covering our privates.

I loved my wife dearly, and if I sometimes sounded as though I wanted to slit her throat from one carotid to the other and watch blood spurt all over her outfits, it was because I sometimes did.

Her preparation for this evening included practicing stances before our new apartment's only mirror, rehearsing questions that were engaging but not challenging or off-putting, and making sure to mention over and over that I should not ruin her big moment by saying the wrong thing, as was my wont when I was nervous. She assumed I would be a little off-kilter, not just because it was my boss's party, but because it was sure to include quite a few of "the gays and the liberals." This was the big city, with all kinds of different people living here. She insisted I did not know how to put on a happy face, which was not true. I could, my face might be slightly less joyous than hers, but only just.

"Remember your breathing exercises," she said, forcing a smile as she knotted my tie. "Before you say anything, breathe in deep all the way to your pelvic floor, at least three times, and then speak. Not only will it relax you, breathing makes you look serious and contemplative."

In the cab on the way to the penthouse her whole being shone with exuberance. Even the driver, one of those Indians or Pakistanis with a turban the size of a bald eagle's nest, seemed impressed. He kept staring at her in the rearview mirror and shaking his head like the bobblehead doll on his dashboard.

My wife crossed her legs to stop them from quivering. "I know he's your boss, darling," she said, "but don't let that get to you. He loves you—well, not that way, but he does. He brought you to New York, so relax." She looked stunning; if sophistication relied entirely on looks, she would pass with the highest of grades. "Do you think he's the most famous homosexual in the city? After Elton John, Ian McKellen, and Brian Boitano if they lived in New York?"

The oppressive city heat was doing a number on my mood. I had slathered an inch of deodorant under my arms, yet I still felt sweat beginning to percolate in my pits. She looked unaffected, her pores would not dare perspire tonight. "You forgot Ricky Martin," I said.

"Don't be snarky," she said. "Not tonight. You're going to love the gays tonight." She sighed, a long foghorn note. "I wish I could have left you at home."

I tried to interject that I was just making a joke, that I wasn't being snarky, but she had already unpacked her compact and begun interviewing her face. "Their apartment is sure to be fabulous," she pronounced in a garbled voice as she reapplied lipstick.

Fabulous was exactly how I would describe my boss's home. A delightfully mild breeze replaced the relentless outdoor heat. Someone must have thought it was a grand idea to transport an entire Victorian mansion into a New York penthouse. There were three vintage gilded mirrors in the foyer alone, and enough marble busts for a few quorums and a plenum.

The hosts, dapper in their dark trim suits and matching designer beards, were effusive in their welcome. They kissed my wife's cheek, twice each, and my boss patted my back in what passed for a hug. His much younger partner took my wife by the arm and led her out of the foyer, saying, "Now, what was a divine creature like you doing in a place like Muncie?"

For my wife, it couldn't have been a more propitious entrance. I somehow expected a herald to shout, "The

Marquise of Muncie and her accompanying dork," as they entered the living room and I slunk in a step behind. The room was filled with people posing under strategically placed lights and black waiters serving hors d'oeuvres. No one sat on the furniture. I wanted to find a seat, but the liberals apparently did not appreciate the comforts.

My wife held court in the middle of the room, just as she did wherever she went. "Our apartment is still empty," she announced. "I didn't want to buy anything until I saw how things were done here. Any decorating tips would be much appreciated. I have so much to learn from you people."

All attention was on her, and none on the most striking thing in the room: no, not the purple velvet drapes that covered the floor-to-ceiling windows, but a giant gold cage that contained a dark man in an unfamiliar costume sitting on a cheap wicker chair and reading. I approached the cage as discreetly as possible, wondering if the man was the evening's entertainment. I stood before him, my nose almost scraping the golden bars, but he did not look up, kept reading his book intently. He was wearing some long white dress, probably a Victorian male nightgown in keeping with the penthouse theme, but why the tattered headdress and the plastic flip-flops? He was dark, if not as dark as the turbaned taxi driver or the fluttering waiters. A long, unkempt black beard covered most of his face around a nose that would make Pinocchio blush. There were two sandboxes on either side of the cage, each a couple of feet square, looked like litter boxes, though the sand within was so pure that I wondered if my boss had had it delivered directly from some desert, and at that moment I realized that the man was an Arab and the book he was reading

was the Quran. I was so startled that I involuntarily took
a step back.

"Don't worry." My boss had sneaked up behind me.
"He's perfectly tame."

"But he's reading the Quran," I said, sounding less
frightened than I was. My wife would be proud of my apparent equanimity. I breathed in deep all the way to my
solar plexus and then spoke. "Isn't that a bit dangerous?"

"Oh, no," my boss said. He was now surrounded by
most of his guests. "We took all the naughty bits out. It keeps
him distracted and less lonely. This one is a safe book."

"Not completely benign, more PG-13," his partner said.
"We didn't want the book to be totally harmless, after all,
or it would be utterly boring."

"Less Disney Quran," my boss said, "than Pixar."

My wife laughed, and the rest of the congregation
joined her. The Arab, however, continued to read his de-
fanged Quran, oblivious to his surroundings, his eyes never
leaving the page, his lips voicelessly reciting suras.

"How simply fascinating!" My wife then used the in-
flection she had practiced all day to ask, "Why do you have
an Arab in your living room?"

"I'm allergic to cats." My boss's partner seemed to be
an excitable fellow, and likable. The more he talked, the
grander his gestures became, and the higher his voice. "It's a
terrible affliction. Whenever I'm anywhere near a feline, my
nose turns into Niagara. You wouldn't want to be near me."

"And dogs are too much work." My boss flicked his
hand dismissively.

I wondered what the gays had against man's best friend,
but I didn't ask, didn't want to embarrass my wife again.

"It's not like we could get a python."

I saw how the lad looked adoringly at my boss, almost pleading, the look of Love with a capital L.

"Can you imagine what the co-op board would have said about that, a python?"

"So we got an Arab," my boss's partner said. "There are two others in the building, and 5C are thinking of getting one."

"We have one," said a woman with a high chignon and a humongous pendant diamond in her ample cleavage, "but her cage isn't as fancy as this one. We've had her for a while, so the children are quite fond of her."

My boss's partner rolled his eyes in a much too exaggerated way, I thought, and as if that were not disapproving enough, he let out a loud sigh.

"Of course," the chastised woman said hurriedly, "ours doesn't have this one's pedigree. It's by no means special, just your run-of-the-mill Arab, you know, just the regular garden variety."

"Yours is a poet from Albuquerque, Marge," my boss's partner said. His perfect blond eyebrows almost reached his hairline. "All she does is recite mediocre verse about her grandfather's olive grove in Haifa, in Southwest-twanged English, no less. Please, darling, I appreciate camp, but really, how many words can one rhyme with olive before it gets tired?"

"Well, she also has poems about the orange orchards that burned during a heart-wrenching incident in 1948," the woman said, looking around for some support. "And the children love her, I swear."

My boss's partner was about to say something, but my wife, her arm still entwined with his, gave him a smile

I knew too well, one that said, "Take a deep breath, relax," except he received a gentler one.

"Our Arab was caught in the wild," my boss said. "He had to be tamed before being brought to us, and then we had to train him. That makes all the difference."

I had to admit that I agreed with my boss. I don't know much about Arab poets from Albuquerque, but this thing in front of us looked like the real deal; he had the "I once was savage" appearance down pat. He didn't seem to be aware that we were occupying the same space, let alone that we were talking about him. I doubted any Arab poet from New Mexico or New York or California could be that earnest and dedicated a reader.

"Can he do tricks?" my wife asked.

She was turning up the charm volume, and the hosts were eating it up. My boss smiled at his partner, giving him permission. "Watch this," the young man told my wife, though I was sure he was including all of us as audience.

My boss's partner took out his smartphone, pressed an app button, and the purr of an expensive car engine emanated from hidden speakers. Upon hearing it, the Arab seemed to wake up as if from a daydream. He kissed the front page of the Quran, put it aside, and stood up. He looked in our direction toward a point beyond, not seeming to notice us, as if we were translucence incarnate.

"Driver," he yelled in highly accented English, "bring out the Benz. I want to buy some real estate."

"Wow!" My wife clapped her hands in joy. "That sounds like such an authentic accent."

The Arab sat back down, and my boss's partner pressed the same app again. The Arab stood up once more. "Driver, bring out the Rolls. I want to buy some girls."

"We call those the Rich Arab Tricks." My boss nodded toward his partner to carry on. "We should all move back a bit for the next one."

The new app produced the sound of a machine gun, and this time when the Arab stood up, his face turned crimson, his eyes grew wide, and spittle spewed out of his mouth as he shouted, "Kill all infidels, slaughter the unbelievers, exterminate all the brutes, down with the Great Satan!"

"My, my," my wife said, her hand went over her heart. "That's certainly impressive. He looks so fiercely beautiful. He's like outsider art, you know, art brut."

"That was the al-Qaeda trick," my boss's partner said.

"Don't worry," my boss said. "This will calm him down."

From the speaker came the adhan, soft, then building volume. The Arab seemed shocked at first, perplexed. I thought I saw him tearing up, but I doubted it because the call to prayer set him in motion. The muezzin's voice sounded exotically beautiful, for a moment at least. The speakers were obviously of the highest quality. The Arab moved toward the sandbox on the right, bent down, and pushed his hands into the sand delicately. "In the name of God," he whispered.

"What's he doing?" my wife asked.

"Cleaning himself," my boss replied. "They must approach prayer in a pure condition. They use sand if they can't use water. I thought about putting a faucet in there, but it would clash with the decor."

The Arab rubbed the sand onto both hands, then scrubbed up to each elbow, up and down three times.

"They're supposed to brush their teeth or gargle with water," my boss's partner said. "Luckily, this one is smart enough not to try that with sand."

The Arab lifted sand in both palms, bent his head, rubbed his face.

"The second sandbox is his litter box," my boss's partner said. "There was an accident once. He used the dirty one to wash up. The poor thing was so distressed he almost killed himself. We had to intervene."

The Arab took a small rug from behind the chair, laid it on the floor facing east, and began his prayers.

"They're supposed to do this five times a day," my boss said. "Can you believe that? Now he doesn't have to do so many. We actually let him do this trick only when we have guests."

We watched, all of us, entranced. I thought about making a minor joke but was unable to. The room remained silent as he knelt, genuflected, and stood up, knelt, genuflected, and stood up. My wife was right as always: we were watching something similar to art. When done, he put the rug away, sat down in his chair, and returned to reading his Quran.

"That was magnificent," my wife said. "You must have worked terrifically hard to train him, but it was so worth it. Thank you—thank you for this."

My boss and his partner beamed, the cheeks above their matching beards flushed, making them look much younger, like overdressed cherubs.

"He's tired now," my boss said. "Let's let him sleep."

A large velvet cloth slowly descended from the ceiling, the same purple as the window curtains, with gold tassels at the bottom. It draped over the cage, hiding the Arab behind it.

"Mistah Kurtz—he dead," I said, but no one seemed to get my joke.

"This is amazing textile," my wife said, quickly changing the subject. "So luxurious. Where did you get it?"

"It's original Victorian, the last batch was manufactured in 1852. We couldn't risk using it to cover the cage until we were sure he'd been totally tamed. He loves it now because it's so thick, yet soft."

The party turned out to be lovely, the canapés sumptuous. After engaging with different people, I came to realize that there was no discernible difference between the liberals and my people back in Muncie, we were the same, we could be happy in their lands.

As we were about to leave, my wife turned to me. "We must get one," she said. "Now I can't imagine living the rest of my life without my own Arab."

"I'm not sure we can afford one," I said.

"We don't have to get a wild one," she said. "An acclimatized lighter-skinned Arab would be less expensive, I'm sure." Then she addressed our hosts. "Though obviously, he won't be as divinely authentic as yours."

"The cheap ones can still be fun," my boss said, quite graciously, in my opinion.

The woman with the large diamond pendant that contained the wealth of the world said, "Mine once rhymed orange blossom with playing possum, which was quite clever, if you ask me."

"Please don't get a poet," my boss's partner said. "They're a dime a dozen. Though by far the worst Arabs are Lebanese novelists. They're the cheapest because all they do is whine. Maybe a sturdy Yemeni, they can be good and are undervalued. We'll go shopping, you and I. We'll find you an Arab that's just right for you."

As hard as she tried to keep her composure, my wife could not stop herself from blushing. She had arrived. We would most certainly not return to Muncie.

It had been a few hours since the cage was covered. Its Arab was supposed to be asleep, but when I passed by on my way out, I heard him whispering in a winsome singsong voice, "And such are the parables We put forth for humankind, but only those who have knowledge will understand them."

Satan's Interviews

Blaise

Tiredness became Satan, his features softened, his cheeks sagged, his posture relaxed, less stark and threatening, and the insanity residing in his eyes departed for a short vacation. He wondered which of the fourteen was best at healing inanition, who the rejuvenator was. Not Blaise.

"Forgive me for bringing this up," Blaise said, a quiver in his voice, "and please inform me if I am being inappropriate, please. I wish to say that I admire your commitment, and, of course, his. I can see many connections between you and Jacob, but I am trying to understand what—or maybe which one of them—keeps you two inseparable."

"Inseparable?" Satan said. "You mean like your Armenian saying, Two butts in the same pants?"

"No, I would never speak that phrase." Blaise blushed streaks of crimson, coralline floating atop a sea of green ascetic robes. "I could not. It's not Armenian. I'm sure it's Lebanese, delightful people, but methinks a bit uncouth."

He looked to be in his late forties, with a riotous white beard, sharp nose, anxious eyes, and a wisp of hair hanging down on his forehead. No rings graced his fingers, no jewelry adorned his person, no cross, no crosier, he held only his two plain white candles, which he laid on his lap. His halo was barely perceptible, a mere shimmer in the air, an old threadbare nimbus. Like Pantaleon, Blaise was a physician, and like Denis, a bishop, but unlike the flamboyant flamer and the pompous dandy, he was pathologically shy, finding the company of others painful, if not the company of beasts. A Eurasian lynx lounged before the sylvan saint, her belly warming his bare feet. Her presence suggested that poor Behemoth might not come out of the closet for a while. On Blaise's right lay a sizable hound with a wide Cerberean mouth, and on his left sat a wild boar on its hind legs.

Satan's stomach rumbled. He worshipped pancetta.

"I meant only that you have been with the poet longer than any of us," Blaise said. "We all care for him, but your devotion is exemplary, as well as inspiring. I wish to discover why you have remained with him, why you returned after so long. If the question is too personal, please feel free to ignore it, for I do not place a higher value on my curiosity than on your peace of mind."

Satan decided to tell the truth.

"I find him thoroughly entertaining, perhaps my chief delight," he said. "He is most certainly difficult at times, dull even, but for the most part, our relationship survives because he amuses me. In spite of his vinegary outlook these days, or maybe because of it, he rejuvenates my jaded heart."

"And I am sure he values your commitment," Blaise said.

"I doubt it."

"He must," Blaise said, sounding muffled as he bent to scratch between his lynx's ears. "It may not seem so to you, but I'm sure he finds you as amusing as you find him." Blaise's white hair was shaved in a Roman tonsure, and when sunbeams struck his bowed head, it looked like a sunny-side-up egg. "I'm envious, for I miss him. I wish he would call me back."

"Why do you like him?" Satan asked.

"That's easy," Blaise said. "Because he's likable. He loves his beasts and they love him right back. Who else could have fallen in love with Behemoth? Such a delightful troublemaker, Satan's spawn." The palm of his hand quickly covered his mouth; his cheeks turned a deeper coral. "Oh my, I apologize. I meant it endearingly."

"And I took it as such. I am proud to claim Behemoth."

Blaise looked toward the closet, shut his eyes for a moment. "It's time to come out, my dear boy."

Behemoth jumped out, landing on the hardwood floor delicately. He looked around, sauntered past the wild boar, hesitated momentarily in front of the lynx, then leaped into the saint's lap. He circled twice, shoved both candles off with his paw. One fell on the floor, the other on the lynx, who seemed perplexed. Behemoth settled in and began to chew on a rear toenail.

"Such a beautiful boy," Blaise said to the purring cat.

"So you love Jacob because he loves animals?"

"No, but that was how it started," Blaise said, "the first impression, so to speak. There are a number of monsters who loved beasts, and I don't return that love, I couldn't."

"Adolf loved animals," Satan said.

"Worse," Blaise said, "the pope's pet from Assisi does as well. Francis surrounds himself with cute animals."

"Don't mention him, please. Francis needs a fisting."

Blaise grinned. "No, it wasn't only about Jacob's love for beasts. You remember what Catherine Deneuve said about that fascist Brigitte Bardot, that it was easy to love animals, much harder to love people. Well, Jacob loved both, in spite of what he thinks. He was the one that held that group of friends together."

"You think so?" Satan said. "That's comical because he believes the opposite. He thinks that they only tolerated him, that he was the seventh wheel!"

"But he was the one Greg loved best. He'd have had nothing to do with the rest of them if not for Jacob. Pinto considered him his doppelgänger. Does he think any of the others would have befriended Lou if not for him?"

"Enlighten him," Satan said.

"Lou was the pretty one, definitely not the smart one. He once told the poet that he had never read a single book in his life, not one, *People* magazine was where it was at for him. Where was he from? I can't remember. Maybe Omaha or Lubbock or Midland. He wasn't the masculine one either. The others could camp it up, but if need be, they could all pass for normal, or almost normal, as was the case with Jacob, who learned to put on the mask at an early age. Not Lou, he was a hairdresser after all, dedicated to his profession. He made all of them uncomfortable except for Jacob, and Lou loved him for that, adored him. I remember one evening when none of the seven were remotely sober, every conversation ending up lost in a maze as they lay about the room, draped over the couches, splayed on the rug. They decided to play the What Superpower Would You Want game. Doc wanted to be irresistible so he could seduce anybody. Greg wanted flight, Jim, mind control. Of all things, Jacob wanted speed-reading, the ability to read every book ever written within his lifetime. His was not the strangest, though. Lou wanted to be able to stop time like Professor X, not to become famous, rich, or powerful, but because he saw so many horrible hairdos while riding the bus and he always fantasized that he could stop time, give the offending party a quick trim or *coup de peigne*, and return to his seat without anyone being the wiser. The other five groaned loudly, what a boring superpower, and wondered aloud whether that was his life's ambition. It was. Jacob, on the other hand, considered Lou's desire both wonderful and laudable. He loved the idea of someone using superpowers to help others look better."

"You know," Satan said, "he hasn't had a good haircut since Lou died."

"That hair, my lord!"

At the Clinic

Satan Therapy

Alone in the waiting room. Alone I used to walk the grounds next to l'orphelinat de la Nativité, through the Catholic cemetery with its headstones of moribund marble, so many alabaster Jesuses on crucifixes, where I once saw a cortege of mourners quietly walk between two juniper bushes and away from a crypt within which they had surely discarded the recently deceased and bade their farewells, and I thought that was the one place given to us to be completely alone, but then I had you cremated, Doc, just as you wanted, but you didn't get a place, I dispersed you all over, where are you now?

The fractious wind picked up in the alley, but the bleared windows, rickety though they were, refused to rattle, it was my time to be rattled, saddled with spooks and Iblis, the angel of the bottomless pit.

I prefer angel of light, thank you very much, Satan said, the most perfect of us all, and by the way, why do you call those fatuous statues with exposed hearts and barbed-wire crowns Jesuses and not Jesi? I am aware of his tongue and its dangers, Doc, his words lead me astray. Satan said, You're trying to deceive these mental ill-health amateurs to check you into an institution and you think I'm the one who's leading you off the path, I swear, I've worked with thick protégés before but you take the cake and the rainbow sprinkles.

The Lord God always said, It is not good that man should be alone, and the American Psychiatric Association agreed, which is why it gave the world group therapy, and a couple of men came through the clinic's doors heading directly to the frizzy redhead receptionist behind the triple windows, I could hear their commotion but not see them, psychotics should be seen and not heard, Well, now you won't be alone for long, Satan said.

I was always alone, Doc, solitary whether I wished to be or not, ever since I could remember I wished to be lost in another, thought that somehow I could disappear into that heart of yours, take walks within your veins, wander through the bones of you. You had friends, Satan said, you loved and were loved, you must not forget that, at least not that. But did I allow anyone in, I asked Satan, and he said, Did you, does anyone?

A man with a snippet of a mustache came into the waiting room, sat in the farthest corner, lowered himself carefully into the chair as if gauging whether someone was already sitting there, refused to raise his eyes from his untied shoelaces and the frayed hems of his khakis, looked as if he had been subsisting on meals that would leave a housefly famished.

Ask him, Satan said, ask him if he'd let you in, and I snickered. Out of his coat pocket, the man fished an orange and began to assiduously defrock it with his thick fingers, concentrating as if he were defusing a ticking bomb, and when he bit into it, a tear of juice slid languorously along the spiral peel still clinging to the white rind of the fruit and dropped onto the floor. Charming, Satan said, and I said, Only the best of us come here, the man was a cleaner facsimile of Deke, asymmetrically gelled flop of blond hair, mismatched shirt and T-shirt, and if that were not enough to signal his heterosexuality, the way he claimed all space within his vicinity by spreading his legs would have tipped the straight scale. I should make wedding arrangements, Satan said, winking at me, but I was not interested at all, whatever pheromones Blondie secreted, my receptors were not impressed.

Hey, Pantaleon, Satan said, bring back the Iraqi, this one is a no-go, and he frowned at Blondie's outstretched legs, They just don't teach manners the way they used to, come to think of it, who do you think instilled more decorum in you, the nuns or the whores? I told him to shut up for the umpteenth time, wished I could afford a private shrink instead of the free clinic, but I was desperate, even though I had been working for the same law firm for decades, I had no health insurance, I was hired as a temp and never made permanent, and Satan said, You are a temp in life.

Jacob's Journals

The Black Bear

The winter had lasted years and years, but the bees in their blissful hive were mostly awake now, the workers made heat by whirling their butter-color wings, the queens lounged about demanding to be serviced, the cold in the air eased, almost disappeared, in floated the fragrance of leaves, of early flowers and fruits. Some bees went to work, filling their bodies with sweetness, some of the small creatures danced and danced, how could we not moan in happiness? Then the black bear woke, much too hungry after hibernating for so long, not a delicate thing that bear, how large a body it carried, hunger demanded destruction. *Smack*, the hive was torn apart, *crack*. What could we do? Our stings were as nothing, our resistance flicked away with a mere gesture. We disappeared in his fur, we dissolved under his breath, vanished into the curl of his tongue.

Some survived, befuddled we flew away and flew, we no longer noticed how warm the still-rising sun was, how lovely the shape of clouds, how white the daisies, how unsteady blossoms broke into flames, how swaths of fierce lilacs released bewildering sirens of scent, that stupefying smell of spring. How could we?

Sorrow makes for lousy honey.

Tears do not make good ink.

Let winter return.

Revolution

About a year before the latest Egyptian revolution, Auntie Badeea wrote me a long letter describing many of the changes in the city. She had been keeping me abreast of the goings and comings of her world, about one letter a month for as long as I could remember, and even though I had been e-mailing my replies for years, she preferred old-fashioned epistolary pen and paper, not because she was a Luddite, far from it, but because like most Egyptians, she was a romantic. Naguib Mahfouz once wrote that it was a most distressing affliction to have a sentimental heart and a skeptical mind. What was different about that letter was the exasperated tone in which she chronicled what was happening in Cairo and, more important, at the house with its new clientele of upscale Egyptians. She had always paid protection money to the double mafia, police and army, she'd bribed politicians, but it seemed a new breed of ill-bred idiots were coming to power and coming to her whorehouse, entitled bastards she called them to their face. Apart from protection and bribes, these new boys demanded a cut and an ownership stake, and as part owners, they no longer felt the need to pay for what they fucked. One of the boys was the president's grandson.

When he and his sycophantic entourage first appeared at the house, the workingwomen were all atwitter, how wonderful, how fabulous, they would climb one or two rungs up the ladder of desirability, if not respectability. Auntie Badeea, however, was not impressed by the boy, like his grandfather, she wrote, that boy doesn't have enough blood coursing in his veins to sate a mosquito, which alarmed me, since no Egyptian who valued her skin should insult the president, and the aunties were quickly disabused of their infatuation, the president's grandson was no Uday or Qusay Hussein, he did not torture any of the girls for pleasure, he was just a brat, and worse, a bore, and worst, a tightwad. Once the boys even brought an Israeli in young and trendy civilian garb with a not-so-subtle military demeanor, they preened more than usual, look at how modern we are, the boys declaimed, grandstanding, showboating, and flaunting, the Israeli humored them, seemed amused, and he certainly tipped his girl more than any of them, and they all departed into the late night laughing.

Auntie Badeea had had enough, but what could she do, she asked, not much, she wished to kill them with her bare hands, risking her manicure. The ubiquitous Arab shame, she called it, having to endure eternal humiliation in your own home. When the boys appeared next, she prophesied the end of their empire, Fools, she told them, your time is nigh, and they laughed. They shouldn't have.

Not too long after I received that letter, a bereft young fruit peddler in Tunisia doused himself in paint thinner and set himself on fire. On that day, Auntie Badeea sent me an e-mail, it was time, she wrote. It took a while for a demonstration to get organized but it did, I was late getting to work the day it started, I swear, Doc, it was the first time I was late in years, but I couldn't tear myself away from the wavering transmissions on the television, I switched from CNN to BBC to ABC, I had Al Jazeera blaring on my computer screen, that first day, Doc, that first day was miraculous, pride pricked every morose cell in my body, dignity filled my soul, I knelt by the chair in the living room and wept until I laughed and laughed until I wept.

In yet another letter, Auntie Badeea told me she was doused with a water hose, not paint thinner, but aflame she was, in her seventies and no longer wishing to bow or kowtow, The police wanted to stop this body with a measly water cannon, she wrote, this body had endured Suleymah's massages at the hammam, believe me, the water barely made my fat jiggle, let them come with bullets. They did the next day, they shot at the crowd and the crowd grew bigger, from thousands to millions, we had ourselves an honest-to-goodness revolution.

An Arab is an Arab is an Arab, Satan said, such a sucker, you fooled yourself once more, didn't you? O Satan, take pity on my long misery.

Within a few weeks of the beginning of the Egyptian revolution, Auntie Badeea began to tweet, every demonstration, every arrest, every shot, every beating she shared with the entire universe and its foreign constellations, the revolution got rid of one president, then another, but the arrests kept on, the tortures never abated, A permanent revolution is what we need, tweeted Auntie Badeea, quoting Trotsky. She still had not given up hope, but I did. Revolutions are a Lernaean Hydra, Satan said, why do you think Death likes them so much, you cut off one head and two take its place, when you're getting fucked over, it matters little if it's the president or the general, you can throw as much tea as you want into the harbor, you'll still have to bend over, baby, eternal justice for the rebellious.

I gave up hope, I gave up, when Mubarak was pardoned by the military government, with each bomb that Assad dropped on his people, with each suicide bomb in Baghdad or Benghazi, in Barca or Cyrene, a razor blade cut through another vein. I bled whatever pride the revolution had engendered. Hope might be the thing with feathers but in the Middle East we hunt those birds for sport.

I could have saved you so much trouble, Satan said, but you never listen to me.

I know thee, stranger, who thou art, how great my grief, my joys how few, since first it was my fate to know thee.

Procrustes

I dream of him, Doc, I do, Procrustes, do you remember what I told you about him? The Greek who waylaid travelers — well, he offered his hospitality to passing strangers, come in, come in, join me in a meal and rest your weary legs, I have a special mattress, no, an iron bed, one that fits the exact measurements of every man, magical, yes. Once the guest was in the bed, if he was too short, Procrustes took out his smith's hammer and stretched him to fit, if too tall, he chopped off the excess length. He had the bed for the perfect man, searched for such a one to fit, why bother with a glass slipper, I ask you, Doc, he was an anthropometrist, just like you. We, your boys, had to be a certain height and weight, never varied, one size fits all, you were a specialist.

In this morning's dream I'm back at l'orphelinat de la
Nativité in the infirmary iron bed surrounded by white,
including the hood and wimple of the nun nurse except
she was an unshaven man under the garb, obviously Procrustes himself since he carried a silver smith's hammer,
bang, bang, he'd make sure I was dead, except his thick
Greek lips were trembling, just like my mother's when she
had a decision to make, should she put on the red dress or
the green dress for this evening's entertainment. Around his
neck, the only color in the room, hung a long coral necklace
that reached below his belt and swung like a pendulum.
When I woke up, I wondered why the school's infirmary,
I fit that bed, the one that was unlike the others at school,
I felt comfortable there.

We slept in school beds that were all the same and I
used to look forward to being ill in the infirmary because no
one troubled me much, except for the nun nurse with the
slightly ducklike nose who checked on me twice a day at
most, but I could not remain there for long, as I was always
sent back to my hard bed with everyone else. The nuns,
those learned torturers with shrill instruments, had rules
and laws and regulations that all us boys had to follow in
order to make perfect men out of us, they taught us to add
and subtract and sing French, to read French history and
literature, and à la Yeats, to be neat in everything in the
best modern way. Ye sons of France, awake to glory — well,
enfants de la Patrie manqués we were, all of us, bottomless cru-
cibles of sin, they would bleach our tawdry hearts, blanch
our sooty souls, they would scour away the lees and dregs
of barbarism, lest we thought we could someday return to
our aboriginal ways. The collars almost choked us as we

matured, but it was for the best, all agreed, because truly, who would not want to be civilized, we dressed alike, walked alike, studied alike, and when the civil war started most of us joined fascist militias in order to keep Lebanon pure and not Arab. The French still sing about spilling impure blood in the "Marseillaise." Most of the other boys joined militias, but not me, the militias would not have accepted me, you know, Doc, every now and then I may have been able to pretend that I fit the bed, but I was never able to sustain the deceit.

It was summer, through the infirmary window I saw the Mediterranean, the blue in the west unraveled the luminous threads of saffron signaling the descending night, but I wished to stifle the beauty of the world since my head throbbed with delicious pain, hark, hark, the lark at heaven's gates shrieked, hark, hark, my soul, and the saints appeared before me at the end of the bed, all haloed and incandescent. I believe it is time you met us, Saint Catherine said, all of us in glory, she sat next to me, held my hand, and began the introductions, one by one, as if they were the von Trapp children saying good night at the Nazi party. This is Saint George, born in Lod, Palestine, the city of Zeus, he defeated the dragon of the lake in Libya, at first my idiot heart was terrified and I remained as still as a lizard, and this is Saint Blaise, the Armenian bishop with his crossed candles, he was tortured, scourged, and beheaded, he had the face of a generous accountant, Saint Erasmus loved Lebanon because that was where he hid from Diocletian for a while, except he made my stomach cramp since his intestines were wound around a windlass, Saint Pantaleon in a checkered doctor's coat who survived burning, a

molten-lead bath, forced drowning, and stretching on the
wheel, until he was finally beheaded, and then the Sicilian
Saint Vitus with his palm leaf, and the giant Saint Christopher who looked even taller because of the child with the
coral necklace on his shoulder, and Saint Denis carrying his
own head, and Saint Cyriac who had conjunctivitis in both
eyes, Saint Agathius the Greek wearing his soldier's vest,
Saint Eustace who saw a shining cross nestled in a stag's
antlers, Saint Giles of Athens who suckled on the milk of a
hind, Saint Margaret of Antioch who conquered Satan in
the form of a dragon, and last, though by no means least,
we have the beautiful maiden Saint Barbara, beheaded by
her own father, Dioscorus, who was immediately struck by
lightning, fire from Heaven.

My migraine, soft sift in an hourglass, dissipated. The
saints and I chatted, shreds of conversation, scraps of poetry,
fourteen saints they were, twenty-eight healing hands that
touched me when I needed solace, help me, Doc. But no
traveler fit the bed of Procrustes, he adjusted them all to
death, and the secret as to why not a single man had the
right measurement was that he had two iron beds, not one,
he placed each traveler in the bed that did not belong to
him, and do you think the nuns had just one bed? Of course
not, they slept on different beds from ours, but we must
pray to the same God. *Liberté, egalité, fraternité, ce n'est pas
sérieux*, we're only kidding, *allez-y*, you boys must pursue
civilization, not that you could ever attain it, bitch, please,
the endless pursuit is where thou shalt remain, look up to
us, lift up your eyes and look to the heavens for it is there
that you will find us. And then the gargoyle nuns gave me
my own ill-fitting bed.

Unpitied

Querulous skylarks settled their squabbles in the bamboo grove right outside my window, in my neighbor's yard, Behemoth on his haunches on the duvet watched with unrestrained longing, desire full of endless distances, tremors of his mouth, spasms of his jaw, whispery wistful meows. I ached for him, damn you, feathered things, frolic elsewhere, end his torture. On the screen of my laptop, I read the last words of a three-year-old Syrian girl, mortally wounded, besmeared with immortal blood, I'm going to tell God everything, she said. Wonderful, I said to the Facebook newsfeed, just wonderful, make sure to tell that son of a bitch his firmament of Hell still stands, still spouts cataracts of fire upon his unchosen people while his privileged practice yoga asana, the forgotten suffer their drones and missiles, unrespited, unpitied, unreprieved.

As it was in the beginning, said Satan, lying on my bed, so shall it be in the end, so shall it be first, last, midst, and without end, basically you're screwed, Jacob, you know, the supremacy of Western civilization is based entirely on the ability to kill people from a distance.

I could not bear it anymore and jumped Satan, wanted to pummel him, but who was I kidding, I had never thrown a punch and never would, he laughed as I struggled to hold the angel of light. Next to us Behemoth watched us instead of the birds, imperturbable, refusing to budge. In one swift motion, Satan turned me over, sat on my midriff, held my arms down next to my head on the pillow, brought his face down next to mine, You can never win, Jacob, he said, and kissed me. Call me Ya'qub, I told the Devil Iblis.

Satan's Interviews

Death

"Father," Death said, "I am peace incarnate."

"Do tell," Satan said.

"Bloviating Virgil wanted souls to be tormented for one thousand years before they suffered enough, were purified enough, to be permitted to drink from Lethe and find peace. Your ancient Roman poet considered a thousand years' sad exclusion from the doors of bliss quite acceptable, if not outright glorious. Now, he was a reed-and-papyrus kind of guy, grandiloquent and verbose, whereas I am modern, one hundred and forty characters and quadruple microprocessors, that's me. I offer peace on demand, instant gratification. Step into the future, leave memories behind, welcome to the land of latest. Want a sip? Go ahead, please. Democratic and ecumenical I am. New and improved, I am Lethe brownies. Eat me."

Barbara

"If one can't kill the savage or castrate him," Barbara said, "what is to be done? How does one convert a Muslim?" While she spoke ambrosial fragrance filled the room, sweetness of the Lebanese mountains, jasmine and lavender, pine and a hint of cedar, scents that belied her irritation. "Mary, Mary, quite contrary, Mary, Mary, Mary, how does your garden grow when your chastity belt stops any kind of flow?"

The seat of all saints looked most like a throne with Barbara in it. Her back remained regally straight, her demeanor rigid, a modest crown upon her head. The peerless academic with fishwife tongue held a miniature tower in her lap, no more than a foot in length, yet impeccably detailed, down to the three tiny windows of the top room, the Trinity.

"Those fucking nuns kept trying to shove Mary down those poor boys' throats," Barbara said, "and those were the Christian lads. Our Jacob arrived a Muslim, allegedly; he needed a megadosage, a supersized Mary with fries. Why cut off a boy's balls when you can freeze them right off with an icy virgin?"

The smell of orange blossom and lemon trees wafted from her; one could practically lick the sour sumac in the delicious air. Satan did not need to goad Barbara, who commenced her sumptuous diatribe as soon as she appeared—no tea required, no apple, just venom.

"And it wasn't Jewish Mary from Bethlehem that these nuns worshipped. Theirs had nothing to do with ours. Once the West appropriated our religion they turned our poor mother into a frigid altarpiece, no trace of humanity

allowed. Their Bethlehem sounded more like Stockholm.
Mary became their arctic suppository. They came to our
lands with their corrupt religion, the nuns, the missionaries,
and the popemobile. Worshipping Catherine or Margaret
was uncivilized. The mountain saints? Heretical! You're
no Christians, the nuns told our boys, bend over so we can
shove our higher catechism up your ass."

Perfume of sweet gardenias and tuberoses fanned out
from her pure form like gentle breaths. Her halo shone
brighter than the brightest star. Her hair was a dark black,
her cheeks a sparkling strawberry red.

"Sleep on, blessed brown people," Satan said. "O, yet
happiest if ye seek no happier state, and know to know no
more than what we tell ye."

"Belief should develop organically, and it did in our
mountains, but all these new religions, Christianity, Islam,
Judaism, all of them were forced upon us from far away. Generations of boys and girls were raised broken and unwhole."

"Why do you think the nuns did their worst damage
through Mary?" Satan asked. "I'm not sure I follow that."

"Original sin," Barbara said. "Ave Maria and all that,
Ave derived from *Eva*, inverted because Mary restored what
Eve lost. To the nuns, to those disciples of a sanctimonious
god, Mary was the antithesis of sin, the boys its embodi-
ment. The Mother of God was supposed to wash clean all
the brown races. You know, the French mother superior
walked around with a rolled-up map of the Levant in her
pocket that she continuously stroked while speaking to the
boys, it comforted her, provided her with solace, it pleased
her to caress the world she was about to release from darkness. I loathed that soulless bitch. On my feast day, Lebanese

children wore masks and went door-to-door in the villages asking for coins or sweets, a ritual that had gone on for hundreds of years. Within one generation, these stupid Europeans erased it. Only the old people remember now—old people and our poet. He remembers now."

Death

"Barbara is still raging," Death said. "All her fire has gone into her temper. That indignant virago has been angry since she lost her head."

"Can you blame her?" Satan said.

"Of course I can."

"Effulgence in my glory, son beloved. You have always been so unforgiving."

"I am naught if not forgiving, Father," Death said. "Barbara is the one who isn't. Should she have held a grudge when her father decapitated her? Of course. Should she still grasp it tight to her bosom more than a thousand years later? Of course not, but she's a Semite through and through, Levantine to the core. They lip-synch the same tired songs every day. The same mitered man who removed her from the liturgical calendar had made Mary the mother of the Church. Should she still be hating him some fifty years later? Please."

"Which one was he?"

"Paul VI, John XXI, Rocky IV, who cares? They're all the same to me. I forgive them all. Even that French mother superior. She gulped her Lethean cup with the relish of those who desperately cling to their assumed innocence."

At the Clinic

Poems in Sharpie

We sat in silence, four in the waiting room, five if you count
Iblis but let's not, but then he said, For idle hearts and hands
and minds the Devil finds a work to do, tell a joke or something. Blondie was peeling another orange, the slight shadow
of stubble on his jaw reminded me of someone, not Deke, I
couldn't think who at first, but now I realized it was Jim he
took after. I missed Jim, I missed you and Jim and Pinto and
Chris and Greg and Lou and how I was with you in my life,
who I was. My phone buzzed, a text from Odette that said,
I'm waiting for you, fucker, accompanied by a picture of all
five feet of her smiling, a loud new streak of red in her hair
that matched her pants, arms akimbo, looking like a perfervid
mini Superman, I couldn't help myself, I began to laugh.

Many years ago we spent an evening at home trying
to decide which superhero we were, she always wanted

to be Superman, and I could never decide between Robin and Wonder Woman, I mean, Robin is ideal because he was always being captured by baddies and then rescued by Holy Rusted Metal Batman, Holy Buttfuck, Don't untie me yet, we have a few minutes, but then who wouldn't want the lasso of truth and Steve Trevor, Wonder Woman's fiancé, who was willing to postpone the wedding ceremony until she made sure evil and injustice vanished from the earth, but how could two mini brown people like Odette and me be Superman and Wonder Woman? We drank, we dressed up, struck poses, drank, took pictures with digital cameras because that was before camera phones, we vogued, drank some more, until the Ecuadoran with arms akimbo and red panties was Superman, and the Arab with the ratty wig and tit-socks stuffed with basmati rice was Wonder Woman, and as soon as we convinced ourselves that we could pass, we passed out. Satan said, You never wanted to be Storm or Static Shock, no, you always wanted to be a white superhero, didn't you, and moreover, you couldn't be Robin because he was a pushy bottom and you were more pussy bottom, so no, it wouldn't have worked, but nice try.

How do you explain Satan in a text? I wanted to, I wanted to tell Odette all that had happened, was happening. Patience, I texted, pressed the send button,

I will tell you all
I always do
You have been with me
Though this long and protean night
Will sing you my song
When I'm able to write a stanza again.

Her response was instantaneous, Which clinic you at, mariposa?

How could you forget the poem you carved into the wall, Satan said, you are the lord of weak remembrance, can I borrow your Sharpie?

No one else in the waiting room saw Satan walk to the distressed sign on the wall promising that the clinic would provide quality psychological services with compassion, dignity, and respect to its clients in a collaborative environment, and begin collaborating by writing Auden's lines on the sign in smaller lettering,

> *For the Devil has broken parole and arisen,*
> *He has dynamited his way out of prison,*
> *Out of the well where his Papa throws*
> *The rebel angel, outcast rose.*

Remember, Satan said, how I made you memorize my verses, every line, word for word, by the light of the kerosene lamp in the old rectory, do you remember, I made you write down poems in dark ink, Baudelaire, Goethe, Milton, and Auden, I the Prince, I the chief of many throned powers that led the embattled seraphim to war. You're wrong, I said, I didn't learn that Auden poem by the light of the kerosene lamp, not that poem.

True, he said, it was not the kerosene lamp, which ran out on us the night we copied *Danse Macabre*, we had to borrow Sœur Marie-Claire's cobalt blue oil lamp, you had only one matchstick left and if you blew it we would have been blind for the rest of the night, but you didn't and the room bloomed around us with the shadows of all the books in the library, you wrote and wrote, and as you did I allowed to be audible in the rectory only the scratches of pen on paper, a sound just like Shemshem used to make while nosing around in the dark interiors of the kitchen wall, making a nest of shreds, first Auden, then Baudelaire's litanies, *Ô toi, le plus savant et le plus beau des Anges*, me, the fairest of angels, you do remember, Satan said in my head, *de profundis, clamavi ad te, fili mi.*

I examined what he'd written, four lines jam-packed within the sign itself, not one word outside, easy for Ferrigno to wipe off, a new kind of poetry: Papa throws psychological services with compassion and the outcast rose in a collaborative environment. Odette sent another text and I replied right away, This mariposa will be all right, I thumb-typed, and I took back the Sharpie and wrote on the wall beneath the sign,

> *To become a butterfly*
> *you must forget*
> *that once upon a time*
> *you were a caterpillar*

>> *But the life span*
>> *of a butterfly is short*
>> *a month a week*
>> *a day with no memories.*

And Satan said, Not one of your best but not completely horrible, let's work on it.

Jacob's Journals

The Suit

Misery is what you get for not dying—misery but some good stuff too. If your harpy mother hadn't cleaned me out, I would have ended up with different beautiful inheritances from all of you, Lou's prized mahoganettes bookshelf, Greg's china, the money from selling Pinto's Honda, not a bad haul, and another good thing about not dying is you get to see everybody go before you and you know what to expect. Greg saw what happened with Chris's family, how they purloined the body and forbade Jim or any of us to attend his funeral. Because Greg was the oldest of us, thirty-nine when he died, and he was an estate attorney anyway, he was the most prepared, but then was he, can anyone be prepared, I know you were not, Doc, I know, I'm sorry. A man who lives fully is prepared to die anytime, but has anyone ever lived fully?

Greg had a will already drawn up, no detail of his medical or post-death care left to arbitrariness, he was meticulous, and toward the end all he had left to decide was whether he wanted to be viewed before cremation in a suit or in his leathers, not an easy choice because if he went with the suit, he would betray his clan, and if he chose his chaps, he would shock his lawyer friends. You weren't part of the decision, Greg and I talked about it for hours, even before he was diagnosed, he knew, he knew where the road he had taken was to end. Oh lord, the day he was diagnosed was overwhelming, commotion for me, not so for him, he had a floater in his eye, nothing scary, he told me, just an annoyance, like a hair in a camera lens, the big things were sure to come, he said, but this wasn't it yet, but of course it was. Cytomegalovirus, his doctor pronounced the verdict, in those days CMV was rarely found without the presence of another opportunistic infection, tests were needed, what cruel and unusual death sentence would it be: lymphoma, pneumocystis carinii pneumonia, toxoplasmosis, Kaposi's sarcoma, mycobacterium tuberculosis, cryptosporidiosis, Hodgkin's disease, multifocal leukoencephalopathy, encephalitis, cryptococcal meningitis, and many many many more, including of course crucifixion by CMV itself, would you like a little dementia with that?

Upon hearing himself declared one of the many walking dead faggots, Greg did not return to work, but went home and began cleaning his glorious home, a spring cleaning to end all spring cleanings, and when I let myself in, he was polishing the brass pinecones at the bottom of the banister, he did not wish to speak, together we waxed wood, relined shelves with contact paper, we took blinds from the windows

THE ANGEL OF HISTORY

and soaked them in the bathtub, we removed every damn book from the bookshelves, wiped the dust off and reshelved alphabetically, sent all the New Age and self-help ones to Goodwill, bleached every corner of all the bathrooms in the house, for five days we worked until the apartment smelled like a hospital corridor. You know, Doc, for years after, every time I smelled powdered cleansers I would get a debilitating migraine, I'd have to hide under the covers in my darkened room avoiding light and Judy Garland, and I couldn't remember why, I thought I was allergic to heavy antiseptics, I forgot, Doc, I forgot.

Greg wasn't satisfied with tidying up surfaces, he emptied out closets, threw out clothes he no longer wore, designer shoes meant for galas he would not attend, impulse purchases, T-shirts, T-shirts, and more T-shirts, jockstraps, bikini underwear he should never have bought, floral silk shorts that had never touched his skin. He threw out record albums, who listened to those anymore, tossed his law degree from Hastings, his Leaving Certificate from Ireland, who was going to ask for those, jettisoned school yearbooks, debate ribbons, class papers, notebooks from lectures he couldn't remember attending, and his porn stash, his dildos, his sex toys, who needed those anymore? He wanted to control the afterimage. Did the scouring and scrubbing help him, getting rid of so much stuff? Yes, I think it did, during the process he was most his body and least his mind.

I don't have to tell you what that time with him meant to me, I loved him, always had, but he did not want me, well, didn't want anyone, couldn't commit, he told us, he was not a we man, he said, but I loved him, and only when he was diagnosed did he let me into his heart, my Irish Greg.

What good is love when all you do together is weep? Weep and make decisions, we did that, in bed atop the cotton sheets among scattered pillows and handcuffs, he told me he wanted his ashes dispersed in his hometown of Limerick, there once was an emerald city in Ireland, I hadn't known where he hailed from before, we had all assumed Dublin, but no, he wanted to be returned home. Could I possibly separate his ashes, would it be too much trouble to take some to the University Maternity Hospital where he was born, some to St. Mary's Cathedral where he was baptized, dump some in the dark, mutinous Shannon waves, some in the estuary, and leave some next to his parents' graves, could I do that? And he decided to be cremated wearing a suit with a black leather vest over a shirt and under a jacket, with a black handkerchief in his breast pocket instead of the pocket next to the left cheek of his ass, when Death came, he would be both Gregs, and it was to be not just any suit but his favorite one, which hadn't fit him in at least a few months, like Pinto, he had been wasting away, and none of his clothes fit anymore, none, even those we didn't throw out. Greg did not want to go through what Pinto had undergone.

The first tailor we visited almost had a psychotic melt-down as soon as Greg walked through the door, he refused to have anything to do with us, when I asked him why, he asked if I was crazy, he worked with pins, didn't I know that, he was visibly trembling as he screamed at us to leave his shop, as if we were going to pinprick his smarmy soul all the way to Hell. We ended up going where we should have gone in the first place, to Benjie, the fairy Filipino tailor, who not only welcomed us but guaranteed his work, he didn't want us to worry, You lose more weight, he said, I will adjust again, lose more and I adjust again, and again, and again, no problem. You remember him, Doc, don't you? He used to tailor his own jeans so tight he could take only small steps, heaven forbid if he ever needed to run, that angel, he died too, about a year after you did. Twice I had to take Greg to Benjie for suit adjustments, Jim drove us the second time because Greg had begun to dance with Saint Vitus, even with a walker he shook so much it was difficult for him to move, and when we helped him out of the car, passersby walked a wide circle around us untouchables as if even the air about us was a vesicant. The more Greg trembled, the steadier Benjie's hands, the pins penetrating exactly where they were supposed to, on his knees, Benjie would tell Greg, Save me a place when you get up there, tell the angels I'm coming, tell them to be ready for me, I want big big wings, swan feathers, fitted, of course, tight at the waist, don't you forget now, golden threads for everybody. Greg got his suit, he got what he wanted.

Thank you for helping me with the dishes the day he died, ill as you were, Doc, it was a lovely gift, standing with you, shoulder to shoulder at the sink, weeping together and washing the dishes, there were so many of them.

Clouds

Do you remember Hibernia Beach, Doc, men parading shirtless in front of the bank on Castro Street under a blanket of flaxen sunlight, promising acts that should be performed only under cover of darkness? It's gone, disappeared, erased from our collective memory. Feeling benighted one sunny day when not a single breath of fresh air came through the open windows, I decided it was time to lie under the sun, its light turning me darker. I would seek in one of the parks a patch of grass the length of a coffin to lie in, not read, not think, become part of the landscape, not fauna but sessile flora. Backpacked nothing but towel and sunglasses, descended the stairs only to find Behemoth sprawled along the door's threshold, which he never did on weekends, never, he did that only early before the sun came out, only at five in the morning when I wanted to leave for work, he would rush down the stairs, I almost stumbled trying to avoid stepping on him or because I'd forget about the slight swell on the fifth step, he would spread himself, weather-stripping the bottom of the door, two black feet pointing toward either side, and pretend to ignore me. I would pet his tummy and scratch it, and he wouldn't budge, it took me a few tries while he was still a kitten to figure out how to move him back to the stairs, block him from blocking the door again. I found myself talking to him every morning, I must go work, I'd say, I can't just quit, how am I going to feed you, why can't you be like those cute cats on the Internet? I must be crazy for talking to a cat, Doc, mustn't I?

Remember the day we were all together in Dolores Park, I was trying to get Lou to venture out six weeks after the dreaded lesion appeared, but he refused to take his shirt off as we all did, Pinto was down to his bikini swimsuit in less time than you can say Phoebus, Lou remained covered in long pants and long sleeves, dispensing weak smiles. Do you remember Chris's wild paisley board shorts? I can't remember whether that was the last time all seven of us were together, do you? Whisper in my heart, tell me you are there. I lay with my head in your lap, my knees straddling Greg's thighs. Little did we know that we should have been happy because everything was going to get worse, even worse than we expected. Your thumb caressed my cheek while a long shelf of clouds hung above us, the sun ignited their pipings, pink flame, orange flame, red and vermilion, and I said to all of you that these clouds had so many colors but not silver and I asked where the phrase Every cloud has a silver lining came from. You understood me, your hair transparent before the insistent sun rays, and you said, To see the silver, you must cut a cloud. How the clouds moved on, how they thickened.

I did not go to the park, I allowed Behemoth to remain a doorstop and went back up the stairs. Baudelaire once wrote that the poet was like the monarch of the clouds, familiar of storms and stars, and God said that Iblis wished to place his throne in the clouds above the earth, becoming equal to Him. Cut a cloud open and you find Satan, you find the poet, cut me.

Innocence

You balanced my thighs on your chest
my back arched to meet your thrust
our sacral rhythm.
I remember, I remember now.
You looked into me,
looked into my eye —
the left eye, Auntie Badeea used to say,
through the left eye one could see the soul.

You hung my calves on your shoulders
like laundry I draped.
Framed by my knees your face was marble white.
Where is he that is black like me?
I kissed you and felt on my tongue
the fleeting taste of mint and the moon.
I felt the ribbed arch of your chest,
you bit my ear, you licked my lips,
left a trail of saliva to mix with mine.
My body has its memories too.
You found my armpit with your tongue,
 tickled me irreverently.
I laughed so hard with you inside me.
You loved me while in me
but you couldn't keep it up, could you?
Loving me was hard, Doc, I know.
I was young enough to not understand
that falling in love is just a metaphor.
I was innocent then, knew so little.
I know less now, but I'm no longer so innocent,
no, not so.
Do your fingers still remember me?

Satan's Interviews

George

Satan saw it coming.

George slouched in the chair, younger-looking than the other knight protectors, Eustace and Agathius, his dark Palestinian hair severely parted as if with a razor. His grand reputation did not match him, he looked like an adolescent overfond of self-abuse. Short, petit of frame, dainty even, he barely left an impression on the chair. His cross-tipped lance stood thrice his size.

Behemoth adored him on sight, taken by the golden halo. The cat crouched on the television table behind the saint, stalked the halo, threw a glance at Satan momentarily asking for permission, shook his butt right and left a few times, and flew for the kill. In the air, he expanded and dug his claws into the dazzling halo, which was nothing but light, of course, so Behemoth smashed into George's hair.

The saint sprang up, his lance clanked as it struck the floor, he squealed as if his voice was yet to break, raised his arms up toward the ceiling. The tumbling Behemoth managed to hang on by sinking his claws into the chain mail on George's back. Satan roared in joy as George pranced around the room with arms flailing at his own back trying to dislodge the great beast.

It was only when George realized he was being laughed at that he stopped flopping about and stood still. Behemoth did not release his hold but slowly climbed the back and sat on the saint's shoulder. The cat licked the drops of blood from the tiny puncture wounds in the saint's scalp. George purred.

Back in the seat, George and Behemoth nuzzled noses and whispered sweet endearments.

"This is some fiend," George said. "Such a healthy little monster."

"The great emasculating cat," Satan said. "Did you know that Jacob has been unable to pee standing up since Behemoth commandeered his life? Whenever Jacob tried, Behemoth attacked the stream, and the poet is too soft-hearted to shut the door. Ever since he has had to sit on the toilet like a good little girl."

Behemoth returned to eyeing the halo. Atop George's shoulder, he extended his arm languidly to bat at it.

"I doubt that was much of a sacrifice," George said. "Masculinity was never Jacob's forte. May I have something to drink? I'm parched."

"Tea?"

"With a finger of cognac."

From the kitchen Satan asked, "Would you like anything else in the tea, milk, sugar?"

"Another finger of cognac would be great," the saint said. "Why am I here, my dear fellow? I would like to help as I do like Jacob, but he has rarely if ever called on me. You know that. He avoided conflicts, let alone battles. I had little to offer."

Satan returned with a large-bottomed bottle covered in dust.

"How about we forget the tea?" He swigged the cognac in a noisy gulp and handed the bottle to his interviewee. "Jacob bears the wounds of all the battles he avoided. He no longer eschews conflicts, can't afford to now that he's aging. Hell, he fights me all the time. Thankfully, he has become curmudgeonly."

"Oh, good," George said in between sips. "Nice people bore me. I have tried to kill Agathius many a time, to no avail."

"Jacob doesn't think he can handle this battle," Satan said. "He wishes to withdraw."

"We can't have that," George said. "Cowardice is the worst of human vices. Why it is not considered one of the seven deadly sins is beyond me." Blood rushed to his face, he banged his fist upon his chain-mailed chest, and with no little animation declaimed, "We must anneal his heart for battle, toughen it and fill it with courage. The Cross is victorious. *Deus vult!*"

Satan shut his eyes. He reclaimed the bottle and downed the rest of its contents in one gulp.

"No," he said, with a long sigh. "Not quite. *Non Deus vult*, thank you very much. Jacob has been away for too long and forgotten what few fighting skills he had."

"Like the hero exiled to the island while the army went off to war."

"Which hero?" asked Satan. "What island?"

"The master archer who was bitten on his foot by a vile snake. Do you not know the story? His army left him on a desert island because his left foot exuded a noxious odor. The soldiers went off to war for ten years, only to discover they could not win any war without the hero and his bow."

"Philoctetes," Satan said.

"Yes, him," George said. "So Jacob has exiled himself for quite a bit more than ten years, and we need him to win this war. We must sail to the island and bring him with us to fight. We must heal his foot."

Satan moaned, shook his head, and walked to the kitchen. "Let me see if I can find another bottle of cognac."

Catherine

Catherine covered her mouth as she giggled, a modesty that surprised Satan. She arched her eyebrows, gently mocking him, then dropped her hand. A trace of grin remained.

"*Deus vult!*" Satan said, and this time both laughed.

"What did you expect?" she said. "Soldiers have their uses, but once used, we should send them to a stud farm."

"Glue factory."

"Or that," she said. "So you and the toy soldier are supposed to bring Jacob and the bow of Heracles back to Troy? Which one of you would be Odysseus?"

"Not me," Satan said. "I prefer to be the bow."

"May your aim be true," Catherine said. "We must succeed."

"We must."

"Are you not afraid that Jacob might not be able to handle that which is at hand?"

"Of course I am," Satan said. "It's a risk, but allowing him to live and die duped as a productive member of a comatose society is a neglect of my duties. We must wake him and hazard the consequence. We must offer the apple."

Catherine positioned her elbow on the arm of the chair and leaned her forehead on her hand. "I wish you had told George that sometimes cowardice is our only choice. Jacob was young, his heart too small to handle such grief. He did what he had to do during the time of sunder, he girded against the dirge."

"He is no longer young," Satan said. "A child no more."

"Only children get scared," Catherine said. "Men might feel afraid, might even feel terror, but men don't get scared."

"We must expand his strictured heart," Satan said, "a flood of blood."

"Let it grow," Catherine said, "and grow, big enough to withstand an arrow's piercing."

"You and I together?"

"All of us."

At the Clinic

Hey, Doc

As he spoke, he frequently grimaced as if he were softening a jawbreaker in his mouth before crushing it, which was not a good tic for a psychiatrist, if you asked me, but there he was, I had successfully moved up the system. I took a deep breath to pacify my mind, I wanted to be calm, or at least appear to be. You're not serene, Satan said, you're depressed. What little could be seen of the doctor's brow was bright red and his nose a purplish potato shade, he had big black eyeglasses and big white hair that he raked away at least three times between introduction and interrogation. He asked how he could help.

    I'm unable to cope, I said, I can't bear life right now, I don't know what to do. He asked me if I lived alone, what my day-to-day routine was like, I wake up early on weekdays, I said, I go to work, I come home and go to bed, I read, I write prose and non-poems, do yoga, watch bad television, obsess about government surveillance, count the number of drone killings, get upset with Obama and curse Bush, watch my dreams wither on the vine, things like that, dull this life of mine. Oh, and I told him about you, about Greg, Pinto, about Saint Catherine and Satan, who clung to my ear like a limpet, but I was weary of explaining the unexplainable. I walked through the world like a dead man who cared not at all about the petty miseries of the living, I was tired of scars and stains, of bleared pains and panes.

He seemed particularly interested in Satan, probably because the beast talked so much. What does he sound like, the doc asked. Tell him, Satan said, tell him I sound sophisticated and erudite, I, the star of day, the son of morning, the angel of worship, and the heart of Heaven, I sound like a Miles Davis trumpet, like a Bach partita, no, wait, a Bendel bonnet, a Shakespeare sonnet, whereas you're a worthless check, a total wreck, a flop, but baby, if you're the bottom, I'm the top. He sounds weird, I said, says the oddest things, he has a deep voice, as you'd expect, slightly nasal, as if he hasn't completely recovered from a mild cold, doesn't sniffle though, he speaks English, his mother tongue, but with a slight angle to his pronunciation, which makes it difficult to pinpoint his origins, upper-class Jamaican would be my first impression. Kiss my ass, Satan said, can't believe you said Jamaican, such an ingrate, why are you diddling, all this psychiatrist wants to know is whether you're suicidal, he's obviously going to prescribe antipsychotics, but if you want three days of rest and recreation, tell him you're thinking of suicide, contemplating, that's even better.

I'm not suicidal, I said. That's good to note, the psychiatrist wrote in his leather-bound booklet. I could not lie, Doc, I have never thought of suicide, during dark night or deep abyss, it never occurred to me. And every morning, Satan said, you blunder along this slushy path like everyone, look at him frantically writing, wearing that translucent shroud of composure, but you're not suicidal enough, he's not going to commit you, you're failing, I'm winning, no insane asylum for you today.

Seventy-two hours, Doc, that's all I wanted, at St. Francis Psychiatric. I loathe Francis, Satan said, the tree-hugging, animal-loving, organic-eating, leftist pretender, he's the saint of all things banal, whereas I, Iblis, I am the angel of light, the lord of this temporal world of yours, listen to me. The doctor kept writing and writing, wouldn't look my way, into his copious notes he spoke, something about a mild antipsychotic and selective serotonin reuptake inhibitors and I should come back and see him sometime. I felt my heart sink, no restful seventy-two hours for me, and I heard Satan hiss Yesssssssssss.

Jacob's Journals

Possession

I lie on my side, head sunk in the pillow, waiting for first light, for the lift of the curtain, waiting for you, how your right hand used to entwine with my left in slow dance, how our bodies fit in bed, yet you didn't show up, Behemoth cuddled beside my chest soaking up warmth, I scratched below his left ear, which twitched at the sound of the starlings waking up outside our window, and I adjusted the pillow, my cheek felt its new coolness. I knew I was not psychotic, surely not insane, though at times I had to consider that I might have been possessed, Satan had made a bed in my ear and slept in it, and Satan said, This is not possession, if it were, you would do what I tell you and not refuse my counsel, for I am no creature of mere light, I am of fire born, fire of fire, the blood in the veins of the world is lit up by my flame, I am life's primal force, you are the child at the

end of the diving board afraid to jump into the pool, a mere
poet you are, a stiff and common poet who does not know
the meaning of words.

But I do, Doc, I do know what possession means, I
know Iblis stories too, Auntie Badeea told me a few when
I belonged to her, in the evenings, while tucking me in bed,
I would dream of the evil one while asleep so I could be
wary when awake. Has the story of Iblis come to you, she
began, and I held on to the turquoise charm pinned to the
shabby sleeping gown I wore every night, for he might lead
me astray if my fingers did not grip the apotropaic amulet
while the story was being told, and she would tell me the
tales of the Garden, of the Fall, of Iblis refusing to bow down
before Adam, so the angels genuflected, all of them together,
except Iblis, he refused to be with those who bowed down.

Bow no more, Satan said, you know, I was hissed at,
never spoken to, of course no one asked me nicely, would
you mind bowing down to this piece of stinky clay, it was
always bow down, kiss my ring, kiss my ass, by the way, I
prefer to be called the Cast-Out Angel, Fallen Angel is just
wrong, I didn't fall out of Heaven, it's not as if I tripped or
something, that would have been a big oopsie.

A Sufi story went like this, one day while Adam was
at work Iblis came to visit Eve and with him was his son
al-Khannas. He told Eve to watch his son and went on his
way, when Adam returned from his job at the office, he
recognized the son of Iblis, flew into a rage and killed the
boy, chopped him into little pieces and hung each from a
branch in a tree like fruit. Iblis returned and asked about his
son, Eve explained what had happened, and Iblis called his
son, who put himself back together and followed his father

home. The next week, Iblis asked Eve to care for his son again, while he went off on errands. At first Eve refused but Iblis insisted and like a buzzing fly in her ear he went on and on until she relented. Adam berated Eve and yelled and burned al-Khannas and threw his ashes into the wind and into the river and spilled them into the estuary and into the loden-green sea. Iblis resurrected his son from the scattered ashes. The week after that, Iblis returned and this time Eve said no, no, no, but like a serpent, Iblis whispered into her ear and beguiled her with words of a poet and left his son with her. Adam killed al-Khannas and fried him with beer batter, and he ate half of the child and Eve ate the other half, and Iblis laughed because a part of him now resided in Adam and Eve. Within man's breast was his eternal abode.

Were you already a vegetarian when Badeea told this story, Satan said. I was five, maybe six, when I stopped eating any kind of meat, a young boy at l'orphelinat de la Nativité, mealtime was more troublesome than Mass, the monitoring nuns arched their eyebrows every time they passed me, tsk-tsking as they noted how I ate around the meat. A plump, shortsighted, asthmatic boy always asked, Are you eating that, before fork-stabbing the chicken and transferring it to his plate, his face suffused with joy, happy to mock the only boy with lower status. After dinner, while some boys ran wild and others rushed to the secret smoking area, I hid behind the pines, under sky the color of wet ink, talked to its stars. You talked to me, Satan said, I was always there, the antidote to loneliness, you have always discounted what I meant to you, always pretended that I was a mere inconvenience, a nuisance. You have been the bane of my existence, I told Satan. That's what I mean,

Satan said, such an ingrate, without me you're an insipid cog in an indifferent machine, that's what you are, what I don't understand is why you don't unleash an unpunctuated scream, not just you, but all humans, howl at the moon and mourn your losses, those nights behind the pines you desperately wished to cry out to the sky, but no, you didn't want to attract attention, and I told you then, All right, I said, you don't want to disturb the peace, you're too afraid of upsetting the system, go write some poems, and you did, I am your muse, always have been, no one but me.

He wasn't the only one who considered himself my muse, Doc, a couple of months ago, during my monthly call to Auntie Badeea, she insisted that I tell her why I sounded so unhappy, and I did, a little bit at least, told her I was talking to Iblis in my head, her response shouldn't have surprised me, for even though she raised me to believe that he was the great evil, she was ever the pragmatist. All poets have jinn as their muses, she said, it was always so, the greatest of them, Imru' al-Qais, had a muse who went by the name of Lafiz bin Lahiz, the poet was seen walking the desert paths talking to his jinni and what glorious words poured out of his mouth, all muses were considered jinn once upon a time, and she couldn't imagine me settling for anyone but Iblis, the lord of all the jinn. And Satan said, I wish you had explained to her that I'm not a jinni or a demon, that technically I'm an angel.

Behemoth stirred himself awake, I stroked his tummy, the air in the room felt thick and syrupy.

Well, I am the prince of air, Satan said, Badeea has changed her mind about me, you know that, she doesn't consider me so evil anymore, I'm just someone who finally said no to an unreasonable demand, conform or be cast out, those were our options, sure, I've done a few naughty things here and there, who hasn't, and unlike you, she can empathize, she finally said no too, her whole country did, she understands me, Badeea is poetic, not like you.

The light would not come, I could not turn around to note the time on the clock on the nightstand because I didn't want to disturb Behemoth, my nights grew longer and darker, I wondered at times whether I would wake up and this would be just a bad dream, a nightmare that I could wish away, I had the same fantasy when you were sick, Doc, that I would one day wake up and you all would be healthy and alive. Do you understand me now, Satan said, when things go wrong I seem to be bad, I'm just a soul whose intentions are good, oh lord, please don't let me be misunderstood.

My cat turned over, craned his head and licked my lips good morning, and Satan said, All those who say no follow me.

So Many Ashes

How would I describe my life before Iblis made his latest uninvited appearance? I would say it was pleasant, which in and of itself is a wonderful thing, I mean, people worked awfully hard to arrive at pleasant, paid a lot of money to live in nice, a lovely meadow of spring flowers, of daisies and daffodils and pansies and pussy willows, okay, so maybe my career in the windowless room was not forsythia, and maybe my sexless life would not remind anyone of jasmine and roses, maybe it was a bit lonely, but it was calm, and

I needed calm, Doc, I needed it so much. I blame Iblis for the mud and slush.

After you died, after Jim, the last of the apostles, died, I was dropped into a sea of turbulence without a boat, a dinghy, or a paddle, what was I to do, I was left with so many ashes. Greg wished me to disperse him all the way in Limerick, across the Atlantic, Lou wanted me to leave him somewhere pretty but far away from Oklahoma or Nebraska or wherever he was from, Jim had wanted his ashes mixed with Chris's but then that became impossible after Chris's family stole him, and you, you couldn't care less, you said, you wished me to cast you into the wind. I did not do anything, lived among the ashes for a while, but Odette, who later moved into your room, convinced me that having so many ashes around was morbid, it was, and that I should execute my friends' wishes. She helped me book a grisly vacation to the Emerald Isle, and to ease my panic, she decided to accompany me. But how do you pack ashes, would they show up in an X-ray, would I have a million American guns pointed at me as I attempted to board, how many people did you kill, murderer? Would the Irish customs agent try to open one of the cans and would Greg's remains pop-goes-the-weasel onto his countryman's face because the can might have shifted during the flight and expanded and he could no longer be contained?

Three nights before we flew to Dublin, where we had to connect to Shannon and then rent a car and drive to Limerick, I experienced an apposite panic attack, full quailing and shivering and everything, sleepless at two in the morning, I got dressed and walked to the twenty-four-hour drugstore and bought large containers of vitamin C, ibuprofen,

coenzyme Q10, and echinacea, all of them capsules. Instead
of mapping out my vacation or packing, I spent hours and
hours and hours stuffing all your ashes into the capsules.
First I uncapped every single one and dumped the contents
into the toilet, only five capsules at a time before flushing
because I was paranoid—I thought that someone, anyone,
might be checking the color of my flushed toilet water, I was
tormented by an image of a man with a weak chin and a tan
windbreaker holding ampules of my toilet water, yelling, Eu-
reka, we got him, the villainous weasel is hiding his friends'
remains in echinacea. The granules in five vitamin C capsules,
flush, five ibuprofen, flush, coenzyme Q10, flush, and then
putting you all in the capsules was by no means an easy task,
and worse was deciding whether I should separate each of
you into a different drug, should Greg be ibuprofen, should
Pinto be vitamin C, but then, without Chris, there were five
cremations of you, and I had bought only four humongous
bottles, so I had to mix and match, and I decided that you were
all going to share eternity together. Holding the two sides of
each capsule, I would dip both sets of fingers into one can of
you at a time, and twist it closed. All of your ashes had little
bits of bones remaining, like tiny seashells in the sand. My
hands were covered in a pallid film of my loves. I couldn't fit
all the ashes in, but I felt all right with that, I scattered what
remained under Daphne the laurel and watered the ground
so all of you would seep into her widespread roots that creep
secretly underground and underfoot, seeking sustenance in
shadows. I flew you guys in pill form to Ireland.

A pleasant vacation it was not. It rained nonstop for the
entire week, Odette hardly left our room in the inn despite
the beige shantung wallpaper, she visited used bookstores in

Limerick, bought books of Irish poetry, Derek Mahon and Paul Durcan mostly, and ensconced herself on the divan, whereas I took long walks in the rain under a rickety umbrella that flipped inside out with each malicious gust of wind. I walked and walked and saw little of anything, if you asked me to describe Ireland, I'd say griseous and verdurous. Before each walk I'd fill my pockets with pills, but I found it difficult to dispose of them at first, did Greg want to be inside St. Mary's Cathedral or on the grounds outside, I did both, sneakily, like a cat burglar who left things instead of taking them, I'd hold a number of capsules, make sure no one was watching, and relax my fingers a little, allow one or two to drop near a pew, on the grass. Even as I stood by the river pouring its tumbling songs toward the sea, I could not throw the capsules overhand or underhand, just in case someone unseen was spying on me and I would have to explain why I was tossing my friends into the Shannon, I went to the edge of the alluvial bank, pretended to gaze at a hawk or some bird in the far distance, like a sunflower, my hand bloomed, drooped and died and dropped its seeds, and I allowed you to tumble into the halcyon surface of the river.

At the Clinic

Failure

Alone once again, I'm going home now, my fingers texted Odette, no need to take care of Behemoth, come over tomorrow, please. I felt my heart ready to explode into a thousand pieces, I could see shards and blood in my future, I was about to weep but couldn't do so in the waiting room. Let's leave this shitty place then, Iblis said, let's go home. I don't think I want to be with you, I said.

Come, come, Iblis said, I am your shadow, brighten up, remember, you were made from clay and I from fire, together we are fine porcelain, one day life gives you fine china, another day paper plates, but never ever accept plastic, let's leave this place, it is God who's sick, He who's taken leave of his senses, not you, you don't really want those pills. I told him I wanted the option, I couldn't be sure he wouldn't lead me astray. To the good I act as guide, Satan said, the dry branches I rip off, and a calamitous drought has settled upon this world of ours, rip, rip, rip I must, but you, my boy, have always been good.

Iblis sat to my right, looking better than I've ever seen him, his handsome face invigorated, didn't seem a day over thirty, so happy. I'm lost, I said, just as Ferrigno returned with an Ativan, one pill for tonight because I was allegedly anxious and it might help me sleep, he called in my full prescription, a daily Lexapro and five days of the calming Ativan until the antidepressant kicked in. He held the door for me, and as I was stepping out, he said sotto voice, Ya'qub, ya Ya'qub, don't worry so much, you'll be fine, and if not, come back and we'll figure out something else.

I was able to take only four steps outside before I had to sit down on the curb, the smell of human soup seemed more noxious than when I first arrived. Satan said, Do we have to sit here, the ground is still a bit wet, which will ruin my suit, it's a Versace, I'm no low-rent Lucifer. His suit was the color of sunlight. I told him, I can ignore you, you know? I know, he said, still in high spirits. I threw my gaze at the Ativan in my hand. Don't be silly, he said, we both know you're not going to, why don't you call them, they're waiting for you and they're much better than a stultifying Ativan, whatever happened to quaaludes? The night was chilly, I buttoned my windbreaker, the sky clear and moonless, and the goddamn streetlamp was buzzing nonstop, seemed to shine with added light, nothing works in this inane city. Call them, Satan said.

I knew how to call, it had been years, but I recalled my prayer from when I was the darkest boy at l'orphelinat de la Nativité, in order of their saint days I called them, as I was supposed to, as Sœur Salwa trained me to, Great princes of Heaven, Holy Helpers, I, helpless, beseech thee to hear me, deliver me, come to my aid, and one by one, in the urine-redolent alley, they appeared before me in all their halos: George, dragon slayer; Blaise, benefactor of the poor; Erasmus, protector of the oppressed; Pantaleon, exemplar of charity; Vitus, protector of chastity; Christopher, intercessor in dangers; Denis, shining mirror of faith and confidence; Cyriac, terror of Hell; Agathius, advocate in death; Eustace, exemplar of patience; Giles, despiser of the world; Margaret, champion of the Faith; Catherine, defender of the Faith; Barbara, patroness of the dying.

Shit, shit, shit, I said out loud, I opened my hand, contemplated the Ativan once more. Margaret approached first, I could see her face even though it was covered with seventy diaphanous veils of the most exquisite black silk, each as thin, as insubstantial as mist, she had His face, and she lifted her veils and kissed my forehead. Barbara approached next and with a snort and a harrumph she slapped the Ativan out of my hand and it plopped into the puddle, breaking the thin film of oil floating atop the water. Agathius sat on one side, hugged me, Pantaleon on the other side said, We're going to have such fun, darling. But Catherine, my mother Catherine came forward, she tried to muss my hair but pulled her hand back instantly, Still the worst hair ever, she said, and I said, Nothing changes, and she replied, True, and everything does. I told her I was not sure I could bear living with memories, she said, Look up at the stars, look, they are not there, what you see is the memory of what once was, once upon a time. She knelt on the filthy tarmac, eye to eye, she placed her right hand upon my heart, through my chest, through my ribs, her arm penetrated for a moment and then withdrew, and Agathius held my hand, had me open it, and Catherine placed my heart where the Ativan was a moment ago, some magic trick since I could still feel the steady ticking in my chest, anxiously beating a tad faster but still there.

Allow me, said a saturnine voice I didn't recognize, and Death, all in black cashmere giving off a whiff of naphthalene, delicately picked up my heart, held it up to the light from the streetlamp, out of his wide sleeve he took out an archaeologist's hand brush of the softest bristles, dusted the rust off my heart. Allow me, said Blaise, and he showed my heart to his Eurasian lynx, who licked it clean. I will polish it, said Giles, Let me warm it up, said Eustace, and he cupped my heart in his hands and blew into them, and Satan took my heart, kissed it lovingly, before handing it back to Catherine, who put it back in me.

Time to go home, I said, and stood up, we walked north, my posse and I, but before leaving the alley, Pantaleon halted, Look, look, he said, you shouldn't miss this, and in the gloomy space between two short buildings, under a ladder that rose from the ground up toward the black sky, a man in full leather gear leaned against a dark wall, his eyes shut, his cock out of his pants, and another man, a chain around his neck, knelt before him offering a worshipful blow job. Wow, I said, a bit too loudly, the man opened his eyes and looked at me, the kneeler tried to pull away but the man held his head where it belonged. The man smiled. Thank you, I said, and the man gave me a thumbs-up, and I kept on walking. For some reason, George said, I expected a wrestling match between you and Satan tonight. Ignore him, Catherine said. I should ignore all of you, I said, but I don't know if I can, Doc, I don't know.

I walked home. I took my brown Sharpie out of my pocket and on the thick glass of an overly lit bus stop I wrote

> *Tempt me, Satan, I beseech thee*
> *Beguile and dazzle me*
> *Hidebound brute*
> *Hunger for fruit*
> *Feed me*

I walked and walked, the night nippy, my arms wrapped around myself. On a No Parking sign, I wrote

> *You all dead*
> *I still walk*
> *Therefore I am*
> *I know it is so*
> *For I long*
> *I long for solace*
> *How does one find such*
> *Among so many ashes?*

I walked and walked and walked until I found myself in our neighborhood, Doc, ours, and there next to me was our bookstore, where we met, though now it was another trendy clothing store with T-shirts celebrating diversity for a hundred dollars. I'm not proud, I never was, and it didn't get better, not for me. On the shopwindow, on the glass, I wrote, This is where I met you. Come night, environ me with darkness whilst I write. Two stores up, on the glass of what used to be the burrito place, I wrote, This is where you first kissed me.

On a store window around a corner I wrote, This is where we bought identical pairs of jeans. Above a building's lineup of mailboxes I wrote, Chris lived here, he used to be the best Saint Agatha with vanilla frosted birthday-cake breasts on a tray, the nipples were marzipan. In the entryway to the building next to Chris's I wrote, I sucked a guy's dick in here, didn't even take my clothes off, in an apartment with swagged velvet drapes and damasked wallpaper, if you can believe that. I wrote notes, jotted identifiers along my walk home. This is where Jim worked, this is where Lou was baton-beaten during the Bad Cop No Donut demonstrations, this alley is where Jim was introduced to water sports, this is where we used to buy ice cream. I walked past self-confident plum blossoms preening on branches, past discarded fronds of palm trees, past piss-scented flowerpots and newly painted benches stippled with newer grime. This is where a bumblebee stung me, this place under the stairs with its intoxicating smell of must and wilt and blight is where a stranger fucked me.

You looked inhuman when you were dying, Doc, your eyes glistened like dimming stars, you were wasting away and life was leaving you piecemeal, your soul no longer fit your body, you hated it and I hated it and I couldn't recognize you and I couldn't see you and I was so frightened and I never knew what to do, I looked for the man I love in you and I searched for who I used to be around you and I couldn't find either. I was hurled headlong flaming from th' ethereal sky. I reached for your once strong and supple face at the end and you whispered, *Noli me tangere.* On the door to my home I wrote, This is where I loved you, this is where I once composed my good poems, this is where I betrayed you, shadow that hell unto me, and I went in.

Acknowledgments

Many thanks to Nicole Aragi, Duvall Osteen, Joy Johan-nessen, Elisabeth Schmitz, Katie Raissian, and everyone at Grove. And to readers who suffered through early drafts of this book: William Zimmerman, Ashraf Othman, Raja Haddad, Pam Wilson, Reese Kwon.

I'm indebted to Amila Butorovic for help with all the Satan/Iblis research, to Barbara Dimmick for introducing me to the coterie of saints, to Theresa McGinley for taking me to all the psych clinics around town, to Karin Winslow for lending me the S/M books, to Helen Oyeyemi for reminding me of Lethe, and to the staff of the Bancroft Library at the University of California, Berkeley, for help sifting through the papers of poet/performance artist Wayne Corbitt (1952–1997), whose life and work were a big part of this book.

The cage story is informed by the great Slawomir Mrożek's "Birthday."

As ever, I probably would never have been able to write a word without the support of my none-too-sane family.